Praise for the *The*

"Weird, bold, intimate, and devastating, *The Ragpicker* is shatteringly lovely. Easily the best thing I've read this year."
—Kerstin Hall, author of *The Border Keeper* and *Asunder*

"If humanity is information, what happens when that information degrades? This astonishing book takes us into a future that feels utterly real, and introduces us to characters we can't help but love as painfully as they learn to love each other. Gorgeous, strange and unforgettable."
—Kate Heartfield, author of *The Embroidered Book*

"Surreal, lyrical, and boundlessly inventive, *The Ragpicker* is unlike any novel I've ever read. An apocalyptic tale with a bloody beating heart at its center."
—Keith Rosson, award-winning author of *Fever House*

"An engulfing, absorbing trek through a unique post-apocalyptic Earth where the titular character is haunted by the remnants of a former age and yet discovers what is lost is not necessarily gone forever."
—Eeleen Lee, author of *Liquid Crystal Nightingale*

"Equal parts cozy and horror . . . explores our human need for love, for forgiveness— and for meaning, illuminated in flashes via ancient texts and even a lightning-strike of a one-act play. A gem of a post-apocalyptic novel about kindness and hope."
—Genoveva Dimova, author of *Foul Days*

"An action-laden quest story of a girl and a wanderer and a baby. It's a mesmeric post-apocalyptic narrative . . . full of heart and angst, courage and belief."
—Eugen Bacon, *Aurealis Magazine*

"*The Ragpicker* is a genre-defying mashup of post-apocalyptic greatness . . . comprised of one-part post-apocalyptic doomsday with an undertone of darkness for the average everyday horror fan; one-part science fiction with enough emotional edge that hardcore fans of Ursula K. LeGuin will love and adore—as well as a modern touch of traditional cyberpunk that tech-junkies will recognize and appreciate."
—Jon R. Meyers, *The Horror Zine*

THE RAGPICKER

JOEL DANE

Meerkat Press
Asheville

ISBN-13 978-1-946154-59-0 (Paperback)
ISBN-13 978-1-946154-60-6 (eBook)

Book cover and interior design by Tricia Reeks

Published in the United States of America by
Meerkat Press, LLC, Asheville, NC
www.meerkatpress.com

For Lee. Everything.

"Knit another sock and wait for the spring."
–Scarlett Thomas, *Our Tragic Universe*

Ysmany

In my town, we named ourselves in the winter of our ninth year. That's when I became Ysmany.

Before that, everyone called me Alice Ann. My father and mother, Server, the other kids in the children's tent, everyone.

The morning after I took my new name I wished I hadn't.

I missed Alice Ann.

×××

Even when I was knotting alone in the silence of the frame houses, I felt them—my family and friends and neighbors—linked to me with invisible chains, with what Server called strings or ligaments.

"That's what love is," my father told me. "Connection."

"So is hatred," I didn't say.

My father was a good, ordinary man, and easy to hurt. Also, he was right: I loved him.

I loved his ordinary goodness.

×××

"Is love your greatest weakness?" Server asked me. "Or your greatest strength?"

"How the shit should I know?" I said, to prove I wasn't scared of her.

×××

During town meals, I squeezed between Luz and Dmitri on our

bench in the dining tent, where black-blistered acorn flatbread was served steaming from the clay oven. We tore off pieces to smear in sauces and syrups.

On celebration days, everyone got a little drunk. I liked the swimmy, floaty, bodiless feeling. Luz glowed and spun while Dmitri fell quieter and more beautiful.

Despite my gift for knotting the lampstack ligaments, I never felt more connected than during a sing-along. That rare moment when my voice stumbled into a harmony.

One time, Dmitri noticed my voice ringing true.

He smiled at me and I lost the note.

Kindness was important to him. Sometimes I thought he worked too hard at it, but even a strained kindness was still a true kindness. Maybe the truest of all. Plus, he was beautiful, with black freckles on brown skin, like Server's lessons of braille and morsecode.

She'd started taking me aside for special instruction long before I became Ysmany. For years and years, even though I'd begged her to stop. Her attention pulled me apart from the others. Her attention loosened the weave.

Also, my father once cried after he caught us alone.

×××

The grownups were afraid of Server. I was afraid of other things, like abandonment and pregnancy and the scentless billows of information that engulfed us, even after all this time, every moment of every day. A million million yottabytes of data humming with static in our atoms and cells and breath.

"We're living inside a corpse," I told Luz, as she plunked acorns into a basket. "The cloud is a corpse."

"It's not a corpse," she said. "It's just history."

Actually she said, "Don't be stupid, Minnie."

So a few nights later, I stood up during a meeting and said, "What if history is the corpse of the god we used to worship?"

I talked like Server sometimes, to make the others afraid.

xxx

My mother thought there was something missing in me.

"Some essential lack," she said.

xxx

Server told me that causation operates identically in both directions, and that she obeyed the laws of physics but not of chronology. Something like that. She was sick in the head. All twitches were sick in the head. The secondskins that had kept them alive through the end of the world, for a hundred years or whatever, the technology that preserved their bodies also poisoned their minds.

Server had served—*hah*—the community for a long time. She'd built this town over generations, but now she was missing something essential.

She always treated me gently, though.

Like a kindred spirit, or a coconspirator.

xxx

The twitches were finally dying, after a long decay. Like a lingering illness, my father told me, that had lasted his entire lifetime.

Server isn't dying, I said.

Not yet, he said. But she's slowing down.

He lowered his voice and said: Losing her grip.

xxx

As the twitches dwindled, travel between settlements increased. We started seeing one or two people every few years, one or two groups. They usually shied away from our town, though they always left offerings behind.

"To help us build the lampstack," Dmitri said.

"To appease Server," I said.

Early that spring, a wagon stopped a day's journey away and waited for us to make contact. When we did, they shared food and gifts. They called themselves "pioneers" in a slowly, syrupy accent that took everyone else a few days to understand.

Not me. Accents were just another kind of pattern.

The pioneers were three mothers, two fathers, a handful of

grandparents, a mess of kids and a baby named VK. Their wagon was drawn by water buffalo that looked like myths. Luz fell in love with their curved horrible horns and booming chests and placid eyes. She said they reminded her of Dmitri.

We invited them into our tents and they told us about a town called Isabella where a thousand librarians recreated the enklopedia pages that flickered onto a screen scavenged from a smartfridge which technicians powered with generators remagnetized or respooled from alternators.

I didn't understand any of that, but I thrilled to the thought of peeking through spyholes at lightning strikes of history.

×××

The pioneers talked about a land bridge.

They talked about a mass wedding.

One grandfather carved pictures into flatplanel displays. He carved the twins, Tracy and Liam, on opposite sides of a single surface, so when you looked through you saw them both at once.

Except it wasn't Tracy and Liam, it was Server and me.

×××

The pioneers wanted to trade a buffalo calf and aluminum foil for safe passage and sweet orange preserves for the children.

"What about VK?" I asked. "He's too young for preserves."

A mother stroked the baby's back. "What do you think he'd like?"

"A toy," I said. "For when he's old enough."

She looked at the tokens I'd prepared. "One of those?"

"No," I said, and Server drifted into place behind me.

The pioneers fell silent at the chilling proximity of a twitch, then listened attentively as she explained the lampstack. They already knew what it looked like: a thousand cords dangling from the rafters, joists, and beams of empty house frames, each cord knotted with dozens or hundreds of objects.

But they didn't know why.

Server usually called the cords "strings" and the objects

"nodes" so I usually called them anything else: knots, tokens, ligaments, lines, circuits, charms, trinkets, strands.

"Is it like an abacus?" one brave pioneer mother asked. "Or an oracle?"

"The lampstack is not reducible to metaphor or simile," Server told her, with a fatal rasp in her voice.

Nobody else noticed. Not then.

×××

Server bristled at the concept of Isabella, where librarians investigated the past.

"That is dangerously unwise," she told me. "Retreating into history."

"Oh, bullshit," I said.

She spun toward me, her secondskin exhaling tension.

"The past is roots," I said. "How's a tree supposed to grow without them?"

"It's dangerous," she said, clasping her hands behind her back. "This 'enklopedia' they consult is a cave wall and the past is shadows cast."

"What's that supposed to mean? You're afraid they'll (just) learn the same lessons that killed everyone the last time?"

"Fragmentation," she said. "Is a prerequisite of survival."

Then she started ranting about hyperconnectivity, so I walked away.

×××

"Don't test her," my father warned me.

"I won't," I promised, but he knew I was lying.

Server scared everyone else, so I liked to badger her. To push the limits. Maybe I wondered what would happen if I pushed her too far.

She didn't need me but she thought she did.

I told myself that amounted to the same thing.

×××

I collected a basket of lamb hooves from the kitchen then sat cross-legged on the lowest step with them warming my lap. They smelled of myrtle and nettle and fat, but when I licked one it didn't taste like much.

Some I put aside for the lampstack, others I returned to the basket for the cooks and farmers. For bonemeal and broth and stuff.

"They're all the same," Dmitri said, squatting beside me.

"They're miles apart," I told him, and one by one I showed him the angles and slopes and cracks that made each hoof unique and beautiful.

He said, "Everything's different from up close."

I said, "Then come closer."

No, I didn't.

I said, "Yeah," and ducked my head.

×××

One of the pioneer fathers told me and Dmitri that hundreds of "towers" still stood, scattered across the land. He said, "Each tower, she broadcast her signal to the nearest towers, and attracts their signal in return. Forming paths between them."

"Like ligaments," I said.

"Or paths," another father said.

"Her signal, she keeps twitches away, yes?" the first one said. "She says, 'No entry for twitches.' So for us, towers are safe harbors or, or oasis in the desert. You know oasis?"

"We stick to the paths for safety," the second one told us. "But there are stretches of land you cannot cross fast enough before you are caught."

"They live thirty-five, forty miles apart," the first father said.

"The towers do?" I asked.

"La-sha," the first father said. "And between them? If a twitch catches your scent, they come, yes? Crack you open like a nut."

"Now the twitches are dying," the second one said. "Running out of the juice."

Except the towers were running out of the juice, too.

The towers were failing, one by one by one.

×××

The grandfather swore me to secrecy and opened a safe that contained four envelopes. Each envelope contained a slip of paper that contained a broken paragraph from a long-ago source.

The grandfather said, "This is our entry into Isabella."

"That's what you'll give them so they'll let you in?"

"Yes."

"What is it?"

"Perhaps the reason," he told me. "Perhaps part of the reason."

I flipped through the packet twice.

We are marching backwards, this tangle of thorns.

The grandfather wouldn't let me copy the words into my folder so I memorized them.

×××

I woke to find Server beside my bed, whispering a string of words: ". . . gravediggers, explanations, exhumations, infections, addictions, documentations . . ."

My heart turned to water. "Are you talking about the pioneers?"

"Plagues and wonders," she whispered. "Validation, verification, annotation."

"What are you saying?" I asked. "Just tell me."

"Annotation," she repeated, and the machine bulk of her drifted noiselessly toward the tent flap. "Marginalization, vivisection, selection, election . . ."

I didn't know what to do, so I didn't do anything. I watched her leave, then I went back to sleep, that's what I did. I went back to sleep, and that was the night she—

That was the night.

×××

A week later, I stretched out on the floor in the house frame numbered 307.

The concrete slab was cool on my back through my shirt.

Cascades of knotted cords dangled from the beams and fell around me like a downpour. Colors shifted in and out of focus. My eyeballs itched on the inside: something felt out of place, like bats on a branch in daylight.

The ligaments connected me to fence lizards and concrete slabs and boargrass, but mostly to people. I counted two hundred and twenty-four souls in town. Everyone else counted two hundred and twenty-three.

That was not close, that was a chasm.

I was going to betray them: my friends, my town, my father. Server. Maybe even myself.

I needed to, though I didn't know why. Why now? Why for *this*?

I didn't care why. "Why" didn't mean anything. We didn't ask "why" when we wanted an explanation, we asked when we wanted a myth.

×××

The two hundred and twenty-fourth soul in town was the baby.

Server murdered his mothers and fathers, his siblings and grandparents. She killed them and left the corpses for me to weave into the lampstack.

She'd kill the baby next, if I didn't take him away, and I couldn't take him away.

Not without help.

×××

Days passed. Weeks. Server watched the lampstack, I watched her.

Then Liam and Rucky reported an intruder camping past the reservoir: a wanderer, a twitch, moving across our land like an eagle's shadow.

Liam's twin sister Tracy frowned. She hated that Server sent Liam on sentry duty but not her.

"Boys are less important," Suzena told her. "That is biology."

"He's so unimportant he gets to do whatever he wants," Tracy said.

"The wanderer could be a scout," Liam told Server. "Or could be an outcast."

"He looks like a twitch," Rucky repeated.

He looks like an opportunity, I didn't say. He looks like my only chance to save the baby.

"Take a team," Server told Rucky. "And retrieve a datum for the lampstack.

The Ragpicker

I am a scholar of abandonment, I am wise in the ways of things left behind. What I am is, is a curator of decay, and at the moment I'm lying on a hillside in foothills that smell of manzanita and sagebrush.

I'm on my belly pretending to watch the house looming above me, a monument of polished stone, rectangles set into rectangles, with three high decks and a dry swimming pool that is littered with seedpods and cellophane and a topsoil scum of windblown dust from which sprouts catalina lilac or peppermint acacia. Taxonomy is not my strength, but in any case, the pool is clogged with spine-edged leaves, leaving no room for more timid seedlings to root among the cracks and buries.

I mean root like saplings not root like pigs. Pigs are feral, monstrous now, eighty generations distant from the slaughterhouse.

The point, if you are attending me, the point you'll recall is that I'm not watching the house, the house is not the object of my scrutiny. My gaze is on the curved mirror leaning against a snail-studded stalk to my left; I am watching a blurred reflective crescent of hillside behind myself.

I appear alone but I am not.

They've been following me for two days.

At least two days.

Two of them, or four. Just out of sight, never drawing nearer, never falling behind. They stalked me from the reservoir through the stretched shadow of that tilted bridge and across the cloverleaf gap. The prickle of strangers' eyes raises welts on my neck. I smell a human scent when the wind shifts, and I haltingly, experimentally record these words onto internal media for an audience that may never exist—

Wait.

Pardon me.

I'm new to this, coltish and uncertain.

Well, here's something you didn't expect: massive cockroach die-off in the cities after the blissful end. Though perhaps they've rebounded, I don't know. I stay away from cities now. Cities are dangerous for twitches like myself, we unfortunate souls who survived the final days while trapped in terminally-compromised secondskin bodysuits that we can neither remove nor ignore.

The air in cities is full of unwanted approvals.

The air here, however, snakes through the undergrowth, and in the mottled glass of the mirror I track each individual gust of wind.

My mind fires fast.

I am optimized for irrelevancy.

I am also weary of being pursued, fretful and agitated. Unease tightens the scars on my neck into a rope. My pursuers won't face me; they know what I am. They will retreat if I turn upon them, only to later return, so I must engineer a confrontation, an ambush of sorts, after which I'll continue on my way.

I am heading home.

There. That is something you should know. We are heading home. This is the story of my journey home, like a classic tale of, of

At long last, we're heading home.

I am lashed onward by the desperate hope that I'll recover intact fragments of my husband in a hidden homestead cache. It's not likely, mind you. It's a remote and attenuated chance, a squeamish squirming and underfed chance but a chance—and odds are funny things.

That's why they're called odds.

Three years and three thousand miles away, plus or minus, I put my hand on a syncable in a gutted maintenance van. I'd been stealing eggs from the doves that roosted in the vehicle—plump graypink birds, at least—and I found there amid the weeds and guano a rugged case containing a syncable—an Arielco MT-MT Forensic Bias Syncable—of precisely the correct compatibility.

The syncable is not a cable but a squid-shaped device that transfers data—memories—across platforms, and this one boasts a self-contained power source which, even after all this lost time, positively hums with hope. So I am heading home to recover whatever fragments of Nufar still exist.

Except I cannot proceed without resolving this pursuit.

So after many idle hours I approach the polished stone house. In the colorless moment before dawn I rise with evaporative sluggishness to a flagstone path. A thicket of rosemary is rotting from the inside, dense with mildew or—no.

A human corpse is strapped to a networked lawnchair entombed inside the thicket. I don't eat people, despite the fact that of all the animals I might consume, a human is the least strange. The meat is my meat, the flesh is my flesh, and what stronger claim do I possess than to my own species?

Still Nufar disapproves, so I hesitate to—

Wait. Perhaps I should linger a moment to explain that my husband Nufar and the other "obits"—programmed personifications of the beloved dead—exist in partial suspension in my personal digital network as does Default, a virtual assistant that stiches together information from tattered databases and wiki patches. She lost contact with the satellites decades ago and now relies upon locally-stored data, the water-damaged footnotes of a once-global network contained in the lumps on my shoulders and spine under my secondskin, the implanted grandchildren of the smartsets and retinserts that once fused humanity into a single global nervous system.

I unstrap my pack: my heart, my hearth, my husband, my hope . . . my simpleminded stratagem for confronting the pursuers, for giving them such an ambush fright that violence becomes unnecessary.

I cross upheavals of concrete and botany and prop my pack against a boulder.

When I turn toward the house, I feel my pursuers watching me. I feel their stares lifting and rotating me, examining my flayed cross-sections, straining toward me, urgent with appetite and algorithm.

The exterior glass walls collapsed long ago, to earthquake and mudslide, to roof-rat and carpenter bee and indifference. When I step inside, shards shatter beneath my boots, which reminds me of music.

Playlist, I tell Default.

Playlist not found, she tells me.

I unwrap one of the rags from my wrist and fashion a hilt for a thick wedge of glass. Knife at my belt and crowbar at my hip, yet I fashion a crude glass blade because I like the shape of the wedge and because I prefer using tools in the location from which they sprung because I, I, I don't, in truth, trust becauses anymore; I'm only backfilling them now on account of recording this story.

There is an open space with a kitchen and a kitchen island and a dining room with a table that is constructed from some thousand-year material, though the chairs are stumps, and to my left there's a stone wall with a fireplace.

I ignore the kitchen.

Here's a fact about the end of the world: there is plenty to eat.

There is plenty to drink.

There is plenty.

The Earth is an endless cornucopia garden. There are fish in the streams, mushrooms in the forest, there are roots and stalks and leaves, not to mention powders in unbreached containers, game animals on every highway and meadow, and three fruit trees within two minutes of where I stand, or four if avocado is a fruit.

Avocado is a fruit, Default tells me.

Maggots add fat to our diet when avocados aren't available but intact fabric isn't as easy to find so I slip across the mudcaked tiles, past rotting wallboards half-concealing sheafs of copper wires, more copper wiring than makes sense, and I slink into the bedroom then shiver with fear.

I am no longer within eyeshot of the front of the house. I am no longer within eyeshot of my pack and using my pack as bait is using my life as bait. Still, what am I, what are any of us, if not lures cast into murky currents for the purpose of—

Also, my pack is too cumbersome for undetectable theft.

I will notice them making the attempt.

So I'll make a show of discovering the liquor cabinet—liquor does not degrade—and wait for them to conclude that I pose no threat. I'll bait my trap with the pretense of drunkenness, though first I enter a bedroom that looks like eight or seven decades of squirrels and damp and owl pellets and two corpses lazing together in a once-padded social industry settee. They're largely gristle now, impregnated with insect eggs and elevated into ecosystems, but they died happy, that much I know, they died engaged with distant truths, which even after all this time I find a comfort.

I also find a sealed box in the closet, and inside the box there is a Daisy P sheet used to cushion the more-delicate contents, a sheet which depicts an elegant woman in a yellow dress sitting on a pink chair surrounded by flowers that make Nufar smile in my mind, so I wrap the sheet around myself and request that the obits admire me.

Opinions are divided, as always, so we talk instead about

what the corpses left behind—the pool, the view, the synaptic links to society—and then I look for the liquor cabinet but when I turn a corner what I find is a bear.

Ysmany

Sometimes I found more meaning in the spaces between things than in the things themselves.

×××

Tracy snuck after Stoney and Veracruz to help track the wanderer, because she was fast and fierce in the scrublands.

I snuck after her, because I was going to betray the town.

Tracy discovered me at dusk and cuffed my head every four steps for the whole mile to the men's camp. Then she made me wait sniffling in the darkness while she crept up on them unawares.

The wanderer vanished that night.

The others spread out to find him and left me hiding in the bushes. Then Liam came to the camp and I told him to fetch Server and he left again.

People listened when I talked about Server.

When Veracruz tracked the wanderer to the house on the hillside, there was no time to send me back alone.

×××

The wanderer didn't move like anyone human. He barely moved at all. He spread like mildew across a damp wallboard, slower than the hillside dawn.

He dropped his pack and disappeared into the house.

×××

Silence, heartbeats. Sweat on my face.

The shade of a passing cloud.

Inhuman growls spilled from the house. Crashing, barking. A howl of pain and surprise and confusion.

Then another silence crept from the house. A new silence that cut itself on jagged frames of the windows.

The wanderer shuffled into sight, unsteady and wounded—

No. Not the wanderer: a bear.

Shaking blood from her face, her matted pelt twitching.

×××

After the bear dragged away, Stoney snatched the wanderer's backpack. And despite my tears I left a string of tokens to point him in our direction.

I didn't need the wanderer to distract Server.

I needed him to distract everyone else.

The Ragpicker

Although the bear is brown, Default tells me it is a black bear. Default tells me that I should not run, which I already know, and that I should remain calm and speak in a low, steady voice. She tells me that if the bear attacks I should direct any reciprocal violence at its eyes and nose.

Some bears tend to perform a "bluff charge," Default tells me, but she does not know if black bears exhibit this particular behavior, so I shift my grip on my glass knife and attempt to speak in a low, steady voice.

I am not good at speaking. After a handful of syllables, my voice loses coherence.

I believe this is due to damage to my throat but Nufar claims the damage is psychological. He believes I am cognitively compromised. I believe that what I am is, is characterologically adapted, though this is not why I am alive and he is dead. I am alive and he is dead because of luck.

Luck is the ultimate because.

Default informs me that black bears are typically timid and conflict-avoidant. This specimen is of average size, she says, and the bear charges me in an onrush of mass and musk and pressure, then heat and moisture release me snarling into the

stone wall and the glass shard splinters in my fist and I strike
with my knee

and

and

and

and when I awaken, the sun shining through my eyelids paints
the world a lovely coral pink.

Playlist, I tell Default.

Playlist not found, she tells me.

There is blood in my sinuses but my tatters and secondskin
absorbed most of the impact and pain doesn't bother me much.
Pain is just another kind of attention and I am a machine that
metabolizes awareness. I am a scholar of dependence, an archivist
in the library of psychopharmacopeia.

That's what we died of: addiction. Not meteors or wars or
drought or plague. We died of rapturous immersion in our reciprocal connectivity. An easy departure for most but not so gentle
for those who lingered beyond the early days.

Some of us linger still.

Nufar once told me that attachment is suffering, but another
obit—Iris M or my mother—reminded him that the reverse is
also true.

When I open my eyes, liverish flecks speckle one wall of the
corridor in which I am sprawled. I hope the bear is not badly
injured. I killed a bear once. Not for meat, not for fur, not in
obeisance to any ritual. A grizzly. He died too slowly. I am still
ashamed, but you cannot beg forgiveness of the dead.

That's what religion is for, Nufar tells me.

My memory of Nufar appears above me. He is looking down,
the sunlight turning his brown curly hair into a glowing crown.
He is a fat, hairy, powerful man. He looks gentle but is not. Or
was not: this truncated, idealized obituary of him replaces his
incision and ruthlessness with banal warmth.

I miss his brutality. It granted me the permission to enjoy my own. Maybe that's what I'll discover when I return home with my syncable; the unforgiving core of him that loved me despite everything.

I'd settle for the roughness of his hands on my wrists.

Nufar is my most prioritized obit and the integrity of his data is failing. I forgot his scent years ago. I mourned when I realized, I wept and fasted. Now I remember only that I once loved the smell of him.

As I stand in the hallway, Nufar vanishes. I wipe the bear's blood from my face with my wrapped glove and slip between wall-studs tumored with paperwasp nests. Outside, I move through a ginko tree toward the decorative boulder and

My pack is gone.

I repeat: my pack is gone.

The pursuers stole my pack. My heirloom seeds, my postcard collection, my sugar and my spare boots, two pairs of hexfabric boots that match the ones I'm wearing. I found four pairs six years ago and they are my most prized possessions after the Arielco MT-MT Forensic Bias Syncable.

Syncable,

sinkable,

sin-cable.

I plunge behind a terracotta planter before a flight of arrows impales me, but there is no flight of arrows. There is a flock of gray-green birds, small and round, teacup tits that swoop among the bushes and branches, and there is an overheated insect chirping from the hillside below and the smell of crushed saffron as the sun oozes from behind the roof-edge.

Despite wearing eight or twelve or eleven layers, my six-inch pelt, my shambling ragamound, I rarely sweat. My secondskin is temperature adaptive and fused to my flesh like a wire fence swallowed by a tree trunk in a pasture overgrown with goldenrod and jewelweed and queen anne's mustard and

What was the question? The topic eludes me—

There is no flight of arrows. I am frightened of arrows, one of which in the early decades, dipped in a homebrew neurotoxic, pierced my secondskin to a depth of millimeters and left me agonized, yet the pursuers don't attack while I am confused and shaken.

They didn't cut my throat in that hallway, either. They watched me enter, watched a bear leave. They took my pack but took no chances.

Or they are waiting for a killshot.

Staying behind the planters, I grovel to the side of the house then lie in the lively filth. The grasshoppers' song is unbothered by humans lurking in the brush. I speak the language of micas and molds. I am brother to the morel and sister to the mantis and I watch the sky for reflections of the surrounding fields, of my pursuers enclosing me in a circle, with spears and slings and cudgels.

"They're gone," I try to say aloud.

Nobody contradicts me so I crawl in a wide track around the house.

Hillside thickets, moss-stained gullies, a lawn veined with gopher burrows. A graded driveway. A trail of ants with translucent heads vanishes into a rootcleft to populate the city they excavated, and I discover no trace of anyone's passage except my own. Then I'm rising to my feet and patting my pockets and pouches and purses, reassured by the feel of my sewing kit and dried fruit, my charcoal powder and toothbrushes. Dental hygiene is a matter of existential concern.

I once fell feverish after extracting a bicuspid from my jaw.

I presume that my pursuers, my former pursuers, are retreating along the road at the base of this hilltop property, pebbled lengths of decaying asphalt, so I flutter downhill like a moth with a thousand wings, a whirling spiraling descent, and I achieve the road unpunctured but I do not know which way to turn.

I'm glued there, a fly to flypaper.

My ignorance is a tripwire touching my ankle.

Standing in the open. A victim. East, west, ridge, basin? Casting my mind into the balmy botanical breeze for a—

Gauzy strands of color drape a tree a short distance away, like ornate lace lichen overspinning a low branch. The cords dangle with dozens of gleaming objects, knotted in place at intervals. Shiny keys and wire triangles, stout-horned beetles and a fragment of orange traffic cone and a crow's skull with nails for eyes.

Beautiful, Nufar says.

Menacing, Iris M says.

It's pretty enough, my mother says. But what is it for?

To show me the way, I tell her, because the string is draped in an eastwardly arrow.

Or to lead you astray, Iris M says.

I am frantic with the need to retrieve my syncable but permit me to pause a moment to describe the obits other than Nufar, who for reasons of his own chooses to portray his posthumous self in a luxurious bathrobe.

The obit of my mother is possibly not my mother. She did not generate until years after the Bliss, and she refuses to share any information about my childhood or family. I don't recognize her. She appears younger than myself but of course she doesn't age. I don't age much, either. Those of us trapped in secondskins live longer than we should, which is another reason the cities are barred to us.

The obit of my mother is a tiny, birdlike woman who often wears white and sometimes appears carrying a tennis racket.

Iris M is a partial download from the open-source obits who takes the form of any of a variety of short-haired women, dressed as a dandy in a brocade suit with a customizable palette that I powerfully crave. This iteration of Iris M is biting and skeptical and tells fathomless stories.

An obit is a virtual memory—aren't all memories virtual?

Iris M asks—that offers a mimicry of sentience in the service of a pretense of comfort, except now my mother is uncomfortably saying, That *is* menacing, nails through the eyes. That is not welcoming, that is a mockery of vision. That poor bird.

Even though I am quivering to reclaim my pack, my syncable, my Nufar, I crouch instead behind a yucca plant. My silhouette is broken by hoods and veils and scarves and skirts and sashes and jackets and shawls and ribbons and fringes and belts, by pouches and purses and plates, which render my boundaries porous and osmotic, and when after an hour the world continues to match my stillness, I hunch toward the lurestring knotted with ornaments and curio.

I touch the crow's bleached skull with a gloved fingertip. When it spins, I see tiny eyes scratched onto the heads of the nails.

"Menacing," I try to say aloud.

Maybe it's a gift, my mother says. In exchange for your pack.

A trade? Nufar asks.

It is beautiful, my mother says, propping her racket on her shoulder.

The difference between a trade and a theft is consent, Iris M says.

Help me think, I beg them. The pursuers followed me westward for two days, yes?

For at least two days, Iris M says.

No more than three, Nufar says. I expect they're returning to their territory, back the way we came.

So I obey the imperative of that easterly arrow on the strength of his expectation, though as the day peters into evening I remain bereft of a single sighting of my former pursuers. Hours of hiking alongside an asphalt riverbed lead me past the husks of only seven cars. None of them contain postcards. I slice a well-preserved seatbelt to strap around my ankle and smile at a memory of a snippet of my own narrative: *liquor doesn't degrade.*

I brush my teeth with charcoal and salt, then curl into a

roadside hollow to sleep. The absence of my pack is a shiversome draft. Most nights I bait crickets with sugar and spit in a plastic bottle fitted with a makeshift funnel, then breakfast on my haul, which most nights sends me drowsing to sleep wrapped in yet another layer of warmth, but when the pursuers stole my pack they peeled back a layer of my skin like a mountain lion's tongue. I am exposed by my need and my confusion. Why follow? Why steal? Why leave a string of lights pointing the way? I am a storied archeologist of delusion, yet I find myself unable to determine the quickest possible distance between—

No.

My tale is the arrow's unwavering arc: from van to home to husband.

The wind disagrees. She says that no story describes perfect smoothness, and mockingly she toys with the grains of dessicated horseshit drifting around my bed but the concrete still holds the sun's warmth after dark and that is a victory of sorts.

Tell me the story of how we met, I say to Nufar.

I've forgotten, he says. Why don't you tell me?

I also forgot, I lie.

You'll find what you're looking for.

Tell me the rest, I say, which triggers his programmed response.

I loved you, he says.

I loved you too.

The Ragpicker

I track them past vineyards reclaimed by chaparral, and on the second morning I spot the girl.

The previous night I'd sewn my new sheet into a poncho with a pocket crafted from a car's disemboweled headrest. I gulped good green water until I could drink no more then I stuffed a soaked sponge into a screwtop container that I tucked into the headrest. There is a reason I store water in saturated sponges instead of filling my containers directly, though I rarely need stored water; rainstorms wash across former deserts and steppes. The floods will kill you before the thirst, but I'm not talking about that, about my years in exile, searching for a reason to

Two harrishawks hang in the sky. Frogs peep from the seasonal sloughs of climate shift and I press my stomach to the algae-laced earth to drink, then eat two frogs along with handfuls of shriveled grapes.

Raisins, Default reminds me, and I continue eastward through fields of poppy and coyote-brush, and I spot the girl.

This does not require any great perspicacity on my part. She is sitting in the middle of the road, a half-grassed promenade surrounded by the citrus groves within which I've already gorged. A herd of mule deer grazes, flick-eared and black-nosed, beyond an expanse of trailers returning to a purer mineralized state.

As, I suppose, are we all.

The deer watch me, but the girl does not.

No harrishawk is visible in the sky.

It's an ambush, Nufar says.

That's not what scares me, I say.

It's an *obvious* ambush, Iris M says, straightening the cuffs of her jacket. Which means either that their confidence is warranted, which is worrisome, or they are reckless, which is worrisome.

Either way, my mother says, it's worrisome.

I am not on the road. I am observing from behind what I believe is a manually-operated well pump except I cannot detect the associated well, and I pause there to inspect my surroundings while the girl ties charms or fetishes onto an unspooling cord, but is otherwise inactive, and my circumnavigation, my circumambulation, my stomach-crawling reconnaissance extends until I am confident that I've detected the precise nature of the ambush, and all the while, intermittently, I am remembering a story that Iris M told me about a stone well that a woman, a young mother, discovered concealed by the overgrown foliage at her newly-purchased home, which foliage represented the last remaining acre of wilderness in a suburb of bleached and depilated artifice, and she threw coins into the well, though she never made a wish, she fished a copper penny from her older child's piggy bank every morning as an offering until finally she placed one in her baby's sticky fist and helped her throw it into the well, but the baby, unbeknownst to the mother, squirmed with wishes so intense that, when the oakdeep water swallowed her sacrifice, every single thing came true.

The girl stands and crosses to the concealment of a sweet-olive bush and vanishes for a time then returns to her task, stringing objects onto the cord.

According to the obits, the girl is between the ages of twelve and sixteen and thirteen. The girl's hair extends equally in all directions like the seedhead of a dandelion. The girl is wearing a woven vest and embroidered leggings and gray ankle-wraps that were socks before her now-bare feet wore the soles away.

Two adults are lying prone beneath a slumped length of vinylsiding forty feet from the road. A third is sixty yards farther along, watching through binoculars from the remains of the second story of a half-collapsed agricultural or industrial building.

I count five knives and three staves or spears among them, but the only long-ranged weapon is a six-foot kon-kilak bow propped against a corrugated strut beside the person in the agricultural building, which does not present even a theoretical threat, yet my old fear persists and I am additionally nervous because I do not understand these people's intent or motivation.

What do they want? my mother asks.

To capture or kill him, Iris M says.

But why?

"Why" is meaningless, you faded snapshot of a mediocre mind.

Bickering commences and I consider openly approaching the pursuers to initiate conversation but conversation is not feasible and Nufar is nervous so instead I watch the girl as her nimble calloused fingers dance along a faded cord, attach a knickknack or knucklebone, then slide a half-arm's-length before tying another into place with tugs and twirls as rhythmic as a shuttle on a luddite's loom.

The daylight shimmers with omens and portents around the girl's narrow shoulders as the talismans uncoil in a spectrum of color that progress from black to umber to gold:

a toy bowling pin

a dead lizard pierced by thumbtacks

a charred crucifix

a leathery magnolia flower

a bouquet of rusted wires

a ballpoint pen in cellophane

a painted ni-dox detector

a lipstick tube

an oval of spiderwebbed glass

a brass valve

the tin of seeds stolen from my pack.

Staying downwind and moving with a caterpillar lassitude I approach the buckled vinylsiding concealing the prone pursuers and watch the future unfurl in my mind—once, twice, three times—then in a burst of motion I pin one of them with my body-weight and squeeze the other's throat in the crook of my elbow and there is a thrashing and a gasping and I try to tell them, "Be still. I won't hurt you, be still. I only want what is mine."

They take my whispers for threats and one almost breaks free so I squeeze harder as the other scrapes a knuckleblade against my impenetrable forearm then the tension drains from that one and the other stares at me with glassy eyes and I try to say, "Where is my pack?"

"You're killing her," that one says. "Stop, you're killing her."

So I release my hold upon the first one and she bucks and lashes her head backward and impacts my nose which upsets me so I slam her temple twice against the hardpacked ground and the other one swipes at me with a knife but misses because we're closepacked beneath the airless vinyl like fish in redsauce, I can't remember the metaphor—

Sardines, my mother says.

—and I trap that one's forearm with my knee and in annoyance and to forestall his renewed attack, I rip a mouthful of bearded flesh from his cheek with my teeth and he screams and recoils and I neutralize his knife and the other one wheezes a semi-conscious breath and I spit a red gobbet as I control and contain the screaming one and tell him that I have a stopper of distilled vodka to disinfect his wound but he doesn't understand so we struggle until he slumps exhausted and I smear the alcohol on his face and he screams again and I roll away before arrows pierce me but there are still no arrows.

The man moans, pressing a dirty cloth to his sterile face. "I'm going to die of infection. Or look at you, pinche rabies."

"Where is my pack?" I try to ask, crabwalking behind a mound of dirt and ceramic while watching the other one, the sneaky one who is unconscious with her pinky trembling, and while also staying aware of the girl, who is braiding totems into a rosary.

"The what?" the man says.

"Pack."

"Your bag?" He stifles a moan. "You stole—we caught you stealing—stealing from us. From the lampstack? You don't steal from Server."

"My pack."

"It's not yours anymore. Look at you. Filth. I'm a dead man. Rabies. Look at you."

I'm sorry, I want to tell him. We're sorry. We're sorry for your pain, for your face, we're sorry for our regrets, for the apologies with which we endlessly absolve ourselves.

"Where is my pack?" I repeat.

"You can kill me and Tracy, but you're dead when Server catches up. She's already coming. Even a twitch like you's got a soft underbelly."

My gaze flicks from the archer's blind to the weaving girl to the injured pursuers to the hum of bees in a littletongue sage bush, and I try to say this:

"You don't recall the bands of survivors in the early days. You didn't witness those terrible months after the collapse when in a city of a million only five hundred remained, grieving and terrified and alone. You don't remember how the strongest survivors formed packs, relentless roving packs who bonded together to scour the buildings and basements for people who needed help, needed food, needed company and caring. They fanned out in every city, from every corner where two people met, like fairie rings after a rain, they tracked down the weakest and neediest and fed them and cleaned them and comforted them. *That* is what happened after the collapse."

Horror shines in his eyes above the blood-seeping bandage and he shrinks from whatever he imagines I said, and tells me, "You're not the only twitch. We've got our own and she's military. Server will encode your entrails into the frame and divine the future by the shape of your bones."

He flinches when I rummage in my pockets but I obligingly show him the rotten bicuspid that I extracted—to demonstrate the shape of my bones—and when he shudders, movement squirms in my peripheral vision.

I'm through the sage in two heartbeats, disturbing the bees then coming to rest behind a tractor blade but there is still no flight of arrows, just the girl standing there looking at me.

The girl comes closer. She stretches out her hand, palm upward.

"What do you want?" I try to ask.

The girl says two words, then a third.

"Okay," I say, and give the girl the cracked bicuspid.

The girl takes the rotten tooth and looks toward my face. The slanting sideways sunlight turns her eyes from black to umber to gold. She returns to the road and although I am a creature of logic and foresight, of consequence and corollary, I find myself in the grip of an irrational conviction that a deal has been struck.

The only thing struck, Iris M says, is you, dumb.

She means you're dumbstruck, my mother explains.

That poor girl, Nufar says. That poor lost girl—

Get your pack from the archer and get yourself gone, Iris M says. If there is another twitch—

A military twitch, my mother adds.

"Okay," I say again.

Looping toward the agricultural building in which the archer waits, I request information regarding the capacity of military-grade secondskins in contradistinction with civilian models like my own but Default is unable to provide the data and an arrow clatters off a traffic sign five feet to my left then another chunks into matted prairie lavender three feet to my left and the archer with the kon-kilak bow is standing openly atop the only stable corner of the agricultural building while

> another person
> walks toward me
> along the road
> and . . .

Ysmany

Last winter, Suzena bullied Olly onto her hands and knees in the birthing tent. Suzena's touch was easy but her voice was brisk and I knew that Olly found her sharpness comforting.

I'd hugged myself in the corner. Small and sick. I'd counted Olly's contractions, collecting them in my mind to add to the lampstack.

Every bottlecap represented a civilization.

Every pricetag recorded a dynasty and every circuitboard mapped a lost world.

I knotted them into the lampstack, but I also knotted things that didn't exist: arguments and coughing fits and rhymes and contractions.

That's what nobody understood except Server. She said, "Even the longest string threads through the smallest eye."

She taught me to see.

×××

When the wanderer caught us beyond the orange groves, he frightened me. He looked like some terrible shellfish, trailing seaweed and beach foam.

"You're knotted to everything too," I whispered to him, from a hundred feet away, to give myself courage.

Then he crawled out from under the plastic sheeting with blood on his mouth, like when that coyote ate our second-fattest rabbit.

I was so scared that my knees locked. I couldn't move but I also couldn't sit there and watch him kill them. So before Rucky nocked his bow, before Server ran closer in her tireless lope—

×××

Sometimes I thought the ligaments could lift me like a puppet and move me. I knew they couldn't but sometimes I thought they could. And right then, they shifted me closer, to beg the wanderer not to hurt them anymore.

The wanderer spun at me like a pile of leaves in a whirlwind.

And I saw him.

Like I'd been taught.

I saw him, and I asked for help.

The Ragpicker

. . . and I do not require the ungentle opinions of the obits to identify this approaching individual as a twitch.

Full-coverage quilted outerlayer with pixilated camo design; filtration helmet, defunct environmental systems, now removed; shoulder-mounted sat pickup, overpainted with mathematical formulae; rifle and sidearm sheathes, empty; two thighstrap holders with steel batons; intake and elimination ports appear semi-functional and designed for female-layout occupant.

Military or police.

Networked for urban combat or riot control.

Over sixty thousand full-body immersive sensory "secondskin" suits were operative at the time of the rapture, Default announces. Primarily utilized for medical, military, and research purposes. A substantial majority of consumers relied upon opt-out implants or headsets, while the next-most-common connective devices were cloudseats or tanks, though the Authenticated preferred—

The Authenticated, Iris M scoffs, preferred ruinously-expensive, suicidally-brittle g-ports.

Suicide implies intent, Nufar says.

Don't, my mother says.

Secondskins provide medical monitoring and remediation,

Default chirps. Secondskins provide immersion and connectivity, and generate BMOP, bare-minimum operating power, in the event of local outages, yet when the global networks collapsed the failsafes prevented unauthorized removal and after a period during which users contributed to the rebuilding efforts the degradation and depr—

"You trespassed on my borders," the military twitch tells me, stopping at a distance. "You attacked my people. You stole from us and—"

I sidestep behind a clump of agaves overgrown from long-rotted pots, fecund with pulk and calories and thatch. The needle points jut above my shoulders and I sidle from view as if hoping to exploit the cover to attack the twitch from a blind spot but the moment I am no longer visible I flee.

Keeping the agaves between myself and the twitch.

Running fast and straight and stooped.

Veering into a culvert behind buildings that once housed the horses whose descendants now live in the wild snorting foaling herds that feed the mountain lions and wolves and condors, loping along until the ditch pukes me into the citrus groves, scrambling through prairieland brightened by blue-yellow flowers and fire-blackened trees.

She's following me. She's faster and stronger and tougher and faster than I am.

You can't win a race, Nufar tells me. Use the lay of the land.

The lie of the land, my mother says.

Iris M scoffs at her ignorance but I believe my mother intended the words as a witticism.

I angle toward the damp earth where prairie becomes marsh and the twitch closes the distance. She moves steadily while I strain and grunt. *Help me.* I veer again, between thorn bushes and tributaries of degrading plastic, until I cross my own trail, the path I followed from the rectangle house, because knowing this terrain is my only advantage. She is faster and stronger but

I have been here before and hence can shape the future with the chisel of the past.

A wash of porcupine shit will spill from a den beneath a boulder, a fallen tree will span a muddy creek that is already confused with my footprints. I'll pass a single clapboard wall and beaver-chewed stumps and I already know the easiest ascent to the sudden semi-arid ridge.

I climb the boulder, I cross the tree. *Please.* I follow the ridge to the access trail and extend my lead, transforming history into time, but the twitch is tireless and I am not.

Tireless you are not, my mother says.

Keep going, Nufar says. She won't follow forever.

She won't need to, Iris M says. She'll catch him within the hour.

Stand and fight, my mother says.

If you stop, she'll catch us in minutes, Nufar says. Confront her from the top of that gravel rise. Throw rocks at her while she climbs after you.

And when she reaches him? my mother asks.

The inevitable, Iris M says, crows' feet deepening around her now-green eyes.

Nine or eight minutes later, I reach the top of the gravel rise. *Help me. Please.* I arrange rocks of the appropriate heft and watch from my hidden aerie—the base of a collapsed wind turbine—for the twitch to emerge from a eucalyptus forest bejeweled with parrots.

You gave that girl a molar, Iris M says.

The shape of my bones, I explain.

Your future is a blackened cavity, Iris M says, reclining on the gravel slope. That much is true.

You hush, my mother says.

Stay ready, Nufar tells me, and the twitch appears among the eucalyptus trees.

She's moving like a piston, a machine, across a carpet of

shedded bark, between the columns of smoothskinned limbs. Her suit is a serrated edge among teardrop leaves. What she's moving like is, is the inhuman things that twitches came to represent in the bonfire imagination of frightened refugees, and it is incumbent upon me to recall that she is not a machine, she is not a thing. She is not, even, tireless, after all these unrequested years, she is an exhausted traveler and so I rise from my ambush and hurl no rocks—

Without hesitation she commences a zigzagging path that is sufficiently random to defeat projectiles.

"Wait," I try to call to her. "Stop!"

She neither waits nor stops. She accelerates to the base of this gravel hill, moving with an uncanny lightness as if, as if

Immune to gravity? Iris M suggests.

Tell her! Nufar snaps at me. Talk to her!

"I'm gone from your territory," I try to say, lifting my gloves to show that I'm unarmed. "I've taken nothing of yours, wait."

She rises toward me like brushfire, and she is wearing my pack. I catch sight of the straps as with a flick of one hand she draws and throws a steel baton which appears in flight like the spokes of a flywheel that drift backward at terminal speeds or like the rays emanating from an all-seeing eye or like the petals of a daisy and I shift ten or eight inches to avoid the impact and the baton strikes the wind turbine behind me like a gong.

The parrots in the eucalyptus trees take green orange green blue yellow orange green flight.

Brightness swirls and subsides among the fringed flowers of the branches and the twitch is twenty feet and closing when I stomp the half-buried raingutter to catapult a cascade of granite stoneshards at her and throw myself downhill.

She whirls to protect her shoulder-mounted sat pickup from the rocks—the original is replaced with an unarmored replica of chickenwire—and I tumble like a rockslide, aiming a half-inch above her patella, chopping with the rebar rod strapped to my right forearm to tear her knee apart. My weight and strength and leverage combine into a blow forceful enough to damage her through that military-grade secondskin and she howls as she hits me with an elbow and a hammerfist and I throw my handful of sand into her nonfunctional valve to stop her breathing or clog her helmet, then I feel her baton once, twice, she's spinning on her uninjured leg, and for five or eight seconds she beats me to the ground with a clinical completeness until I am curled into an agonized ball and gasping for breath.

The eucalyptus trees shimmer in my blurred vision.

The branches grow heavy with parrots returning.

The twitch limps a few steps away from me, testing her leg. Her back is gravid with my pack, dripping with straps and hasps and harnesses.

"You came from the east?" she asks.

I can't try to answer yet.

She crouches beside me and lifts a flask to my mouth. Not my canteen, the flask from her thigh-pouch. When I drink, the water is sweet. The water is not water but a syrup of sabrapear juice as warm as blood but diluted with freshwater into a heady nectar and my imagination supplies the scent of a mango grove in Michoacan where I slept for two weeks, surrounded by fermenting fruit.

"You came from the east?" she repeats.

I try to say, "On this journey, yes, but not originally. I do not come from the east, I return from the east. I am going home to find more of my husband."

"Did you see the elevator?" she asks me.

I don't know what that means. "His name is Nufar," I try to say. "I am losing my memory of him. His obit is fragmenting. Generic avatars are encroaching upon his data."

"I once believed that correspondences existed between every two phenomena," the twitch says.

I reach for a belt trailing from my pack. "I need to go home."

"I was wrong," she says, knocking my hand away. "No two phenomena are separate. There is no 'between.'"

After a time, I push myself into a seated position. She doesn't stop me. There's no reason to. We both know that if we fight a hundred times she will beat me a hundred times. That is the nature of strength.

She says, "You stole from us."

I don't try to respond.

She says, "You attacked the people I serve."

I don't try to respond.

She shows me a scalpel. "I am going to take your eyes."

I start trembling.

"Do you need me to tie your wrists?" she asks.

I say, "Okay."

She ties my wrists then kneels with my head locked between her legs and her scalpel descends moon-steadily toward my tear duct.

"Wait," I try to say.

"What?" she asks.

I roll my gaze toward the eucalyptus.

"The birds?"

"Yes," I try to say.

"You want to look at them?"

"Yes," I try to say.

"You want those parrots to be the last thing you see," she says.

She pushes me to my knees and kneels behind me, one arm around my neck and the scalpel is a half-inch from my eye as we watch the birds. One is walking upside-down along a twig while others ruffle and trill, and the flash of colors is a semaphore and a symphony. The sound is unmusical but I am struck by the conviction that every lowered beak and tucked wing and terraced throat is conveying a message, is pregnant with meaning. I am possessed by the urge to penetrate this cipher. I am possessed by the knowledge that this, here, is an explanation, an explication . . .

Except those are not my thoughts, the twitch is whispering behind me. She whispers for ten minutes, for twenty, about the apparent luminosity of pedesis and the utility of flock recognition in budgerigar vocalizations.

The parrots startle again into a shimmering cloud and the twitch says, "I will not take your eyes. Not unless you approach my town again."

I say, "Okay."

She pinches my earlobe between her thumb and forefinger, then carves my ear from my head.

She shows me the lump of flesh and says, "This is what you stole from us."

×××

The rain stops, the sun rises.

The twitch is gone.

The parrots, too. I'm lying on my side in the eucalyptus grove, draining blood onto the mentholated ground to avoid trapping fluid in my ear canal.

My pack is secured to my back again, snug as a tortoiseshell, the straps slotting into calloused ruts in my skins. She left it for me. Lighter, now. Our postcard collection is gone, as is our cricket trap and the broken colorful candles, and most of our sugar packets and

some of the 120-pound braided fishing line and
the whiffle ball and
one-and-a-half pairs of my boots and
the ganoid scales of an alligator gar and
the surgical adhesive and
the toy car that reminded me of my grandfather and
the ID cards with faded faces that comforted me for a time.

Much remains, though, including the powdered dust of a katsura leaf that in my memory still looks like a heart, and the million-dollar-diamond, and the heavy rugged case containing a certain Arielco MT-MT Forensic Bias Syncable.

I open the case for the third or seventh time. The syncable is still there, tucked within a polymer shell of negative space.

She'll take our eyes, Iris M says, leaning against a tree trunk.

If he returns to her town, my mother says.

He'll return, Nufar says, and crouches to stroke my cheek with his knuckle.

Iris scoffs. And abandon you? The fading ghost of you? The stranger that you're becoming—that you've already become?

The girl needs you, Nufar tells me. She asked for your help.

"I didn't hear her," I try to say. "I couldn't hear."

Serves her right, Iris M says, talking into your bad ear.

The girl said *help me*, Nufar tells me. She said *please*.

Well, as long as she's polite, Iris M says. By all means. By all means, let's pick a fight with a military-grade twitch with a penchant for dismemberment.

A penchant, my mother says.

Listen, I say. Listen.

Ysmany

My father hugged me when I returned to town, a quarter mile behind Rucky and Tracey. He told me how much I'd frightened him.

"I left a note," I said.

Luz punched my arm. "Ysmany!"

"What? The note specifically told him not to worry."

×××

The Perezes swarmed Veracruz with disinfectant and concern. Nothing killed more of us than infection. My mother died of a rusty screw. Tracy looked terrible, her face mottled and swollen, but she was okay.

She was happy, though nobody else noticed.

"You want a scar," I said.

"I want all the scars," she told me.

×××

The next morning, I sorted through the data I'd gleaned from the wanderer's pack. Preparing to knot them into the lampstack. Keelin wanted boots for his father, who suffered from his feet, but I said no because I was feeling mean.

×××

I'd missed my chance. I'd failed before I'd begun.

I didn't know what to do.

I wasn't strong enough to carve the boots into segments, so I told the leatherworkers what shapes I needed then arranged the candles and butterfly valve and a dozen swatches of fabric for insertion.

I kept the postcards, to copy the pioneer's secret pages onto them.

I didn't stay away from 301, because Server would've noticed. She would've taken note, and I worried that . . . I wasn't afraid of her, but I worried that she would've felt a worm of doubt.

Which was silly. She didn't experience doubt. Didn't really feel worms, either.

Everyone else stayed away from 301.

×××

Server used to welcome strangers, my father said.

She used to collect people to build the town. Breeding stock, my father said, but she saved a lot of lost souls.

×××

I knotted the miniature car and four of the swatches and the butterfly valve into gaps in 318.

When Server returned—

When Server returned the next—

When Server returned the next day, I knotted the wanderer's ear into 305.

The Ragpicker

The parrots don't return.

The drizzle starts, then stops, condensing from the vacillating clouds.

Listen:

I discover a sundried apricot in a side seam of my pack, coated with the dust of the katsura leaf, along with a healthy handful of sundried earthworms which Default informs me are approximately 82% protein.

Listen:

Pain radiates from my ear and heats my head. Swollen tender balloon. I climb the gravel hill to the wind turbine and rummage for the steel baton the twitch hurled at me like a starburst catherine, but my search is not blessed with success.

The spectral memory of Nufar watches mournfully.

I refuse to meet his gaze. Though imaginary, Nufar is mighty, and instead of sharing the revelation that threatens to overspill my mind, the admission of which I must unburden myself, I beg Iris M to tell us a story.

She retells a story instead, the one about two girls who live in an apartment building in a nameless city, who find a key that says "Do Not Duplicate," and every time they open a door with this key, which is a key that unlocks every door, they enter a world in which everything is duplicated, including themselves.

Listen: there is something I don't want to admit to this recording.

I'll do it, Nufar offers.

No, I tell him. I can't hear it in your voice.

I'll do it, my mother says.

I silence the obits and begin tracking military twitch to her town. Because the girl asked me for help.

A young forest thrives around me, striving toward the sun. The most terrifying thing about the apocalypse, Elizabeth once said, is how happy the world is without us.

Default? I inquire. Who is Elizabeth?

Obit unidentified, she tells me.

When the ground levels, lichen-furred slabs of concrete rise among the trees. Tombstones in a titan's graveyard. I pick through them and across a long-abandoned campsite, an oval of stones with a paste of ash that stains the hem of my skirts.

I prowl past

1) the oxide tracery of barbed wire on wooden posts.
2) the sudden incense of a sweetjeff pine, the sudden memory of blue morpho butterflies.
3) a fortress of cactus.
4) a rocky slope, a hollow trunk, the remains of a trough, a rustle of silk.
5) a row of fallen powerlines.
6) coyote scat atop a rock.

List-making is one of your defense mechanisms, Nufar says.

Did I ask?

You're approaching the town, he says. You're afraid.

Perhaps, Iris M says, and this is merely unfounded supposition, but perhaps he doesn't want that military twitch to carve his eyes from his head.

I crawl through sugarbush and ceanothus so slowly that a

bird lands on my ass. A speckled towhee according to Default, and hours later I tilt my head to raise one eye above the horizon, which is nine inches from my nose, and find myself gazing at the pursuers' town.

Longlost earthmoving machines graded two terraces into a hillside, each with a capacity of fifty or forty freestanding buildings, perhaps small mansions or multi-family homes but most likely this remote subdivision is a late-period post-aesthetic construction, designed for a culture with an infinite surplus of interior acreage.

The buildings' roofs and exterior walls are missing.

On the lower terrace, the beams and plumbing describe house-shaped skeletons around which the inhabitants have wrapped a skin of fabric to create tents rising above concrete slabs.

The building-frames on the upper terrace, however, do not look like tents.

Instead: cords and ropes and chains dangle vertically from every horizontal surface, and every cord and rope and chain is decorated with charms and totems and baubles, shifting and swaying in the upwelling wind, winking in the fading sunlight, a forest of shapes and colors, a hundred layers thick and so dense with beauty—with mystery—with information—that longing stings my eyes.

```
I  I     I     I     I  I I     I     I     I I   I     I  I  I
I  I     I     I     I  I I     I     I     I I   I     I  I  I
I  I     I     I     I  I I     I     I     I I   I     I I   I
I  I     I     I     I  I I     I     I     I I   I     I I   I
I  I     I     I     I  I I     I     I     I I   I     I I   I
I  I     I     I     I  I I     I     I     I I   I     I I   I
  I I    I     I  I   I I   I     I     I I   I     I  I  I
I  I     I     I  I   I I I     I     I I   I     I  I  I
I  I     I     I  I I I     I     I     I I   I     I  I  I
  I  I     I     I  I I I     I     I     I I   I     I  I  I
```

I I   I I I I I   I   I I I I   I I I
I I   I I I I I   I   I I I I   I I I
I I   I I I I I   I   I I I I   II I
I I   I I I I I   I   I I I I   I I I
I I   I I I I I   I   I I I I   I I I
I I   I I I I I   I   I I I I   I I I
I I   I I   I I I   I   I I I I   I I I
I I I I   I I I   I   I I I I   I I I
I I I I   I I I   I   I I I I   I I I
I I I I   I I I   I   I I I I   I I   I
I I I I   I I I   I   I I I I   I I I
I I I I   I I I   I   I I I I   I I I
I I I I   I I I   I   I I I I   I I I
I I I I   I I I   I   I I I I   I I I
I I I I   I I I   I   I I I I   I I I
I I I I   I I I   I   I I I I   I I I
I I I I   I I I   I   I I I I   I I I

The layers, the gaps, the play of color upon color, shape within shape, the clash of size against weight, against value and utility and condition, the clash of purpose against purposelessness, is repurposed into a sight—into a sensation—that catches in my lungs.

Hidden in the eastern foothills, a cap-toothed Iris M intones, the traveler discovers an elaborate art installation, a blueprint in four dimensions—

I quiet her.

Birds flutter among the strands and totems, beads rattle and bells toll—unless that sound rises from the sheep field in the peak's shadow, a few dozen head of shamefaced ewes with a handful of alpacas. Below them, cropland is stitched together with the sutures of an irrigation system and a wide stream diverts from the mountains while lower down a runoff trickle gleams. There is the uric hint of a tannery stink. A handful of carts. A stack of drying pans for evaporating salt from the sea. An enclosure with water buffalo.

Many snaking footpaths and a single wide dirt road connect the lower terrace to the upper, and there are more people than I've seen in

Dozens of them.

Visible.

I must locate the twitch—that is my priority, to locate and avoid her—but I remain captivated by that forest of swaying trinkets until the darkening sun forecloses my vision, then I linger with the memory, imagining Nufar strolling through the beaded ropes, trailing his blunt fingers along the tassels, strumming them like once he strummed guitar.

Then I prepare to advance into the town.

A mistake, Iris M says. A fatal flaw.

Listen, I say.

Once, when a child asked for my help, I refused.

Ysmany

My blanket felt scratchy that night. My eyes were as swollen as Tracy's face. Not from fever, from fighting back tears.

I chewed on a fingernail and listened to Haylee collecting the night soil buckets.

I still slept in the children's tent, even after Luz and Dmitri moved out. Partly because I was younger, but mostly because the little kids didn't look at me like everyone else did.

Server had stuffed my head with words and meanings from before I learned to walk, she'd trained me to extrapolate and encode patterns, to decipher them. I'd wanted the wanderer to come to town, to shout and gibber and fight. I'd needed him to cause a disruption, a distraction.

I'd needed him to give me an opportunity but I'd fucked everything up.

×××

I wasn't sure if Server ever slept, not really, but she paused on a biosig sequence sometimes, and she was pausing now.

I'd stored everything in the cellar of 313. I'd been preparing for five weeks, stealing for five weeks, waiting for a chance. Then I'd messed up and—

I needed to try again.

So I left the children's tent and started for the lampstack.

Haylee didn't look at me. Even nightsoil smelled better than what I left behind.

xxx

I'd planned to kidnap the baby before the wandering twitch forced the town into lockdown, then to run during the commotion. Grabbing the baby after lockdown was too late. Didn't matter now. Without the wanderer making trouble, I couldn't outpace any of them, not even Tracy with her swollen eye.

What if I *did* push Server too far? What if I stole from her, something precious?

I told myself that I wasn't afraid of her and—

xxx

Hands closed around my throat and dragged me backward into darkness.

I made a noise that I'd never made before.

The hands lifted me off my feet. I dangled and kicked, I smelled oak leaves and lichen and twigs, like a dry riverbed.

Breath touched my ear and whispered garbled words.

xxx

The wanderer stood behind me, his hands around my neck. Not his hands, just one choking arm, lifting me like a hare stretched for draining, a rubberized glove on my mouth to keep me quiet.

Nothing happened after he whispered.

He didn't move, and I couldn't.

Except yes, I could. My arms were free, and one of them trembled to my throat and fished the necklace from my shirt and showed him the charms knotted there. My fingers swiped past the ring with the green plastic stone, the rusty screw and the origami cashbill to his rotten tooth.

xxx

"I need your help," I whispered. "I won't scream."

Time passed. Motionlessness. The same stillness that some-times took Server.

He said, "Okay."

×××

When he set me down, my knees buckled.

×××

"Follow me," I told him.

I climbed the path to the lampstack, my ears ringing with the absence of sound. Walking between the token-braided railings. Not hiding, not sneaking. Just being Ysmany on her appointed rounds.

The wanderer didn't follow. He vanished the moment he'd released me, but I took it on faith that he'd reappear.

Monsters always did.

×××

When I stopped outside 301, he shaped himself from the dawn shadows, a faceless mound of scraps and tatters.

I brought him inside showed him what I'd done.

He looked at what remained of the pioneers.

"They have a baby," I told him. "His name is VK."

He looked at me.

"If I don't," I told him, "if I can't . . ."

He kept looking at me.

"If we don't get him away," I said. "He's next."

×××

Then like a baby myself, I started crying.

The wanderer offered me a packet of sugar.

Humiliation burned from my chest to my cheeks and I shoved him. It was like shoving a tree trunk. "Do you fucking understand the words I'm saying?"

He made a sound then nodded.

"Will you help me?"

He nodded.

I told him what to do.

He said, "Okay."

×××

"I need to see your face," I told him.

The words surprised me, but he didn't hesitate. One of his bandaged paws burrowed into the fabric at his neck and he unveiled himself.

In the darkness, he was only a shape. Empty, meaningless. And I thought, what if I'd seen wrong, outside that orange grove?

What if I'd given everyone I loved into the hands of a new horror?

The Ragpicker

I am a troubadour of wreckage, I am beautiful in the eyes of the ruins. What I am is, is a monument to the inevitability of consequences—unless I mean the consequences of inevitability, I can't tell. Words crumble and decay but I trust this dramaturgical template to reassemble them to your specifications.

In an attempt to reassure the trembling girl, to comfort her, what I hear myself try to tell her is that I've never heard of a crime that I could not imagine committing.

The uncomprehending girl says, "Good, that's good." Then despite my silence she says, "Hush, quiet. Shut up now."

My inward clamor stills. The girl knows how to soothe twitches. She tucks her necklace away. Her pulse is accelerated. She assures us that Server, the twitch in the military-grade secondskin, is currently engrossed in an idle state or refresh process from which she will not rouse until an hour after sunrise.

"About an hour," the girl says, which imprecision does not reassure me. "An hour or so. It doesn't matter."

I beg to differ.

"I'll break the lampstack," the girl tells me. "I'll cut the lines. When Server wakes up, she'll—she can't do anything until she re-hangs the data-strings. They're her world. She won't chase us until they're fixed, she won't even notice we're gone."

I inquire as to the length of time necessary to inflict sufficient damage upon this beaded-curtain assemblage. Further, I inquire as to how long Server might engage in repairs before initiating her pursuit.

"Yes," the girl says, still uncomprehending. "You can trust me. I know her better than she knows herself."

"I find that both unlikely and unresponsive," I try to tell her.

"Because she's part of the lampstack. That's how she sees herself. Except . . ."

"We sometimes see ourselves wrong?"

"Of course I'm sure! Stop asking. She won't chase us until she fixes everything. Your job is to keep anyone else from stopping us. My friends, my—everyone in town. Keep them from stopping me. Can you do that? "

"Yes," I try to say.

"Without hurting anyone?"

"Yes," I try to say.

The girl touches my elbow with her fingertips. The contact is too soft to register through my wrappings and patchworks and secondskin. I feel nothing, yet the pressure burns a brand in my skin. I am marked, I am singed, I am—

Losing control of yourself, Nufar says, and he is correct, yet I cannot recall the last time anyone touched me without violent intent.

She's manipulating you, Iris M says.

Trying to, my mother says.

She frightened and young, Nufar says, and impossibly brave.

And ruthless, my mother says. She worries me.

Why does she care about some baby? Iris M asks. What is it to her?

Nufar's beard moves when he smiles. Perhaps this baby is to her what she is to us.

A threat, Iris M says, and a sequence of events unfolds:

The stars fade, the horizon blues.

The girl's machete flashes.

A sickle moon inflates the clouds.

Strands of the mobile flutter. The "lampstack" sways then trembles and swirls and crashes in torrents, ticktacking the concrete like castanets, like chattering teeth. Revelations stream and dissolve around me into heaps and coils, into veins of copper and forgetting.

Playlist, I tell Default.

Playlist not found, she tells me.

The girl touches junctures and joints of the lampstack and, in touching them, undoes them. I am not inclined to superstition but this girl's touch is

After the slabs are littered with broken kites, the girl returns toward the residential area. She follows a path to the lower terrace and I follow her, a wolf-shadow cast by the cub, growing and shrinking across the chaparral, consorting with sumac and redshanks. Then I hunch beside a thatched wall rising from a foundation slab until the girl exits a tent with a baby in her arms.

There is a fussing whine, a sleepy interrogative.

And birdsong, Nufar says. There is always birdsong.

The girl picks a holly-snarled path to the drainage stream and turns northward and tells me, "I need you to keep them from following. To convince them that you took me. That you'll hurt them if they follow. But don't hurt them."

"I am aware of our agreement," I try to tell her, "and I shall act accordingly. However, I'd like to know if your plan extends beyond removing the baby from town."

"Good," she says. "There's a sentry around the next bend. Scare her. Um. Just tie her up, okay?"

"Okay."

"And hit me once to show that . . . this is all your fault. But careful of the baby."

In obedience to her suggestions, I restrain the sentry. I paint a verbal picture of the parrots in that eucalyptus tree, then squat until she is within my fringe of rags and remove the bloody bandage around my ear.

She trembles.

I stand, seize the baby's fat wrist, and backhand the girl sharply.

The girl cries out and crumbles with impressive verisimilitude and only after we travel for several hours into the night does she inform me that I hit her too hard and she cannot continue walking.

The baby is sleeping now, snug on the girl's belly, redolent with fresh babyshit.

The girl is sleeping now, draped across my arms. She weighs nothing. Fears chase each other across her clenched face. She is too small and too brave to survive outside of a city and yet look at her. Look at her. Look at her and—

—see another child, one of the obits says.

Ysmany

I woke alone in the scrub, lying on my side, facing the bristlecut bark of a tree trunk. My shoulder ached, my face ached, my feet ached. I listened to the quiet. A hoverfly landed on my hand then darted away. Peaceful and—

The baby was gone.

VK was gone.

His fat thighs, his wet mouth, his stupid scribble of hair. The wanderer had taken him and left me. I'd served the baby to him like scraps to the pigs, I'd peeled the baby like the oranges Eduard gave Jerrod, and now the wanderer took him and—

xxx

When I scrambled to my knees I saw that I was wrong.

It was even worse.

The wanderer was squatting between me and the creek. His layered shapeless back looked like my mother's shroud. He was facing away from me, squatting above the baby like a man eating roast rat and I remembered him with blood smeared on his chin.

xxx

Unforgivable things happened so quickly. So easily. My father told me that once, and I didn't understand him. Not then.

I didn't cry out.

I didn't reach for a branch or—or anything.

I just rose to my feet in an awful trance and I heard the sounds, the wanderer's fleshy grunts and garbles, and I walked toward him.

×××

The baby was naked in front of the wanderer, on a square of fabric—a tablecloth, my mind told me in horror.

Except the baby was gurgling and gabbling and holding onto one of his own chunky feet with his fat fingers.

The wanderer finished wiping the baby's bottom, talking to him in that wounded growl. Then he set the dirty linen aside and tied a clean nappie around the baby.

Cooing while VK batted at his tatters and braids.

When I could speak again, I said, "There's sick on your shoulder."

The wanderer didn't turn, which meant he already knew I was there, like some kind of animal. He garbled a string of words I almost understood, and shifted inside his mound of rags. Pointing, maybe, at one of the pouches that weighed down the corner of the fabric.

I gave it to him.

He ignored it so I said, "Much better, thank you. But next time you hit me? Not so paito enthusiastic."

He stood in a single motion, like water geysering when Dmitri hefted a rock into the lake, and almost touched my face.

×××

"I'm fine," I told him.

The baby fussed and the wanderer gave him a clear plastic bottle sloshing with brown liquid. A rag dangled from the top, dripping with liquid wicked from the inside.

VK gummed at the rag until I snatched the bottle away.

The Ragpicker

The baby wails while the girl prepares a meal that she considers more appropriate than the juice I'd appropriated from her town's tents. She speaks to me for a time about nutmilk and chickpeas, about soaking and leeching acorns, about which soft solid foods the baby might profitably consume. She is soothing herself now. She explains that she'd questioned Suzena closely, yet when I demonstrate that I'd already fed the baby with premasticated meal, she says, "No. Don't do that. I do that, not you. No."

When I inquire as to the reason, she appears to comprehend. She says, "Because you're gross."

Then she says, "This is only temporary, you understand? Us traveling together. Until we reach the towers. That's where we're going, to the towers that make the pioneer paths. We're returning VK to his people."

"Do you understand?" she asks.

I understand that strings of towers stretch across the continents, once-networked beacons that repel twitches for the same reason that cities repel us: still-functional ci-cells provide a continuity of service that emit buffered information streams so lavish that they collapse our narratives into meaninglessness and demand immediate responses to every distant bygone outrage; instant, proportional, wholehearted responses that maximize collectivized emotion while minimizing individualized action—that never stop proving that none of us is as cruel as all of us—that pulsate with cycles of tension and release which

The ci-cells are failing in the towers and the cities.

They are failing in the secondskins, too.

In the early years, bands of explorers followed the paths between towers like ants following scent trails but the signals faded and the twitches decayed from protectors to predators and—

And I understand that this is temporary. I understand that more deeply than she knows.

"My name is Ysmany," the girl says.

Tell her your name, my mother urges me. Even if she won't understand.

I know my name, of course, but I refuse to claim it until Nufar remembers. A name is an anchor to a self, and without Nufar mine is adrift.

What is my name? I ask Nufar.

I've forgotten, he says. Why don't you tell me?

I've forgotten, too.

My mouth tastes of the amaranth leaves I chewed for the baby, my heart warms at the clarity of its sclera as I tuck it into the sling I sewed while the girl slept. Once the baby is secure I fasten the sling around the girl's narrow shoulders. Dawn is red in the welter of her hair. She cannot simultaneously manage the baby and her own pack so I distribute most of her belongings into pouches which I attach to her person via straps and loops, despite her initial resistance at my proximity or presumption.

Then I attempt to express upon her my eagerness to continue our sojourn—without dwelling too much upon my terror of Server—and she informs me that we are already beyond the inner perimeter of her town's territory, traveling along one of the lesser-used paths, and that Server is no doubt still occupied with the repair of the lampstack, and that she shall remain so occupied for a minimum of two more days, or possibly a minimum of four more days, which isn't clear to me for reasons I don't understand.

The girl wishes to travel eastward to intercept her expectation of towers that she's never seen, but she follows my lead, if grudgingly, in a northerly direction, apparently believing—

Wrongly believing, Iris M interjects.

—that I am blazing a wiser path, following a road that once paralleled a seasonal river though the water is higher now, and constant, branching across the low places in a thousand creeks and rills and runnels which will obscure our trail.

I kneel in front of the girl and roll her cuffs higher and she rests her right hand on my left shoulder for balance while the baby fusses, which is the second time now that she's touched me without hostility.

Inwardly, I revel, I rouse, I wallow and wade while outwardly I remain unmoved, failing to even notice the lacewing wisp of her touch before we ford like giants that shrunken peninsular terrain, striding through rivers and across lakes, interrogated by dragonflies before feasting on peccary guava. My plan to locate and butcher a pig, mimed with what my mother tells me is too much enthusiasm, falters in the face the girl's insistence that neither she nor the baby will eat raw meat or drink blood but the plump red guavas are enough for a hundred feasts.

You wanted to show off your prowess as a hunter, Iris M says.

No, Nufar says, less unkindly. His commitment as a provider.

No known species is commonly referred to as a "peccary guava," Default interjects as the girl removes the hard white seeds and drops them into her pocket.

The girl carries the baby while I range ahead and beside and behind, laying false trails and some true ones, so that the lack of signs does not itself constitute a sign. I prowl in unraveling helical strands, alert for Server's pursuit, for threats and impediments, for scenic vistas or one of the rare surviving banana trees, like a moon in decaying orbit, listening unheard to the girl murmuring at the baby with unconcealed impatience, asking please, won't you shut up, you're fed and clean and warm and held, and what the paito else in this world is there?

"There's so much more," I try to tell her. "Look at you, risking everything to save a stranger's baby."

She startles at my presence, then requests that I not approach her unannounced.

Moisture on the southwelling air smells of a storm stirring the shallows of the gulf across the mountains and prairies and the inland ruins, and when a wash of mist freckles the leaves the girl stops and lifts her chin toward a fallen X of half-dissolved utility poles, and tells me that we'll take shelter beneath the cargotrucks.

No cargotrucks are visible until, two miles farther along, the bonnet of a truck gapes mouthlike below a moustache of jacquard clustervine. Upon detecting no sign of a larger predator than myself I crawl inside to disturb any rattlers or recluses and discover a pleasant sandy-floored space still somehow sweetly perfumed by the evaporated fuel or antifreeze.

I shed layers to provide a carpeted floor for the baby and the girl builds a cairn of sorts from engine parts, then in the morning watches grimly as I return every element to the place from which it came.

She says, "I've never been alone before."

Tell her she's not alone now, Nufar says. Tell her you'll stay with her, you'll protect her. You're here.

We're here, my mother says.

We've been here before, Iris M says.

I swoop the baby high overhead, in the manner most likely to elicit a squeal of delight, and gesture one of its fat arms from its chest to the girl, as if the baby is grandly announcing, "I'm here."

"VK's not here," she tells me. "He's not even a person yet. He's just itches and hungers. He's like you, except . . ."

"Except what?" I try to ask.

"Smaller," she says.

That's not what she was going to say, my mother says.

"We need to find the towers," the girl tells me.

"We will," I try to tell her.

"When?" she asks.

I raise my left hand, and spread my fingers.

"So we'll give VK to the pioneers in . . ." She counts my crooked fingers. "Four or five days. And then, um . . ."

I watch her.

"Then I'm five days from town," she says. "In the wilderness."

"In the cornucopia," I try to say.

"I can't go back. Server will—" She looks at the baby. "I can't go back."

"What will you do?" I try to ask.

"I guess I'll ask the pioneers to take me, too."

Ysmany

What I didn't tell him was that I wanted to go back.

    More than anything.

    More than almost anything.

    I wanted to, even though I couldn't.

xxx

The ligaments connected me to fence lizards and concrete slabs and boargrass, but mostly to people:

    Denisse smiled. That sounded stupid, but her smiles changed the shape of a thousand days.

    Hennessey washed and fed anyone who couldn't care for themself, which meant he spent months malingering but when he was called to act nobody begrudged him the fallow times.

    Trikar hunted rattlesnakes for meat and revenge. He dreamed of trapping coydogs to breed. He pissed his way back and forth across the north hills, which he claimed scared off mountain lions.

    Yolanda covered three acres with chickpeas reclaimed from a single handful, which I would never accept was not magic. Her passionfruit vines stretched across the old wineyard hill. She'd spent years trying to breed up strawberries worth farming but no luck yet.

xxx

Eduard was only seven but he heard that Jerrod couldn't peel oranges on account of the shakes so he went to his tent every morning to peel them for him.

Every morning, Mig washed Eduard's sticky hands.

Suzena was our midwife, and three months ago she delivered Cadence of a baby girl. Everyone said the baby was beautiful but I thought she mostly just looked absolutely fucking outraged about all this.

Maria reengineered old gear: a wheelcart from a pickup bed, an irrigation system so complex that Server spent weeks mapping every juncture.

Bekah and Miguel and Hans tended the sheep and llamas while Weaver, y'know, weaved. El was our head leatherworker and Luz was her youngest apprentice.

Ewen, Forest, Linoleum, and most of the Perezes scoured the land, harvesting goods for the lampstack.

×××

And Ysmany?

She knotted the lampstack, the ones and zeros, the things and the nothings.

She considered the meaning of each individual bite.

She sat like a nasty little spider in the web, alert to every tremor.

×××

Still, I wanted to go back.

I didn't fit anywhere else, I *couldn't* fit anywhere else. Server had taken me as an infant and shaped me to her town, like pouring molten metal into a mold.

I wanted to go back, but I couldn't.

×××

Maybe I could.

The Ragpicker

We range through a bright eden of warm sun and caressing breezes at the ruffled hemline of greengold mountains veined with freshwater streams. We follow a fructose scent to a patch of berries. We shy away from a stygian highway of some unnaturally-untouched material. We tuck ourselves into the crest of a hill and see in the distance the circuitboard outlines of a town, parallel lines and right angles, the imprints of buildings and the crumbling parapets of infrastructure.

Infrastructure, Iris M repeats, tucking a flower into her lapel.

What is that supposed to mean? my mother demands.

Iris fades silently away.

Take Ysmany to the tower, Nufar tells me. Help her with her baby and then . . .

Then what? I demand.

Help her with herself.

The second night, the girl builds another cairn while I tend the baby, which is howling and pumping its angry legs, spine arched and mouth wet and gummy. I arrange the infuriated creature stomachdown across my shoulder and commence administering gentle thumps of my palm. The wailing continues until for no discernable reason, after a long hiccupping cry, the baby quiets and I notice that the girl's cairn is not unlike the lampstack in her town, which leads to a sudden acid suspicion that despite my near-constant doubling-back, she is leaving signs of our passage to aid in Server's pursuit.

That makes no sense, Nufar tells me. She ran away. She's more afraid of Server than you.

Do you mean she's more afraid of Server than he is? my mother asks, pointing her tennis racket. Or that she's more afraid of Server than she is of him?

The following day we avoid a three-underpass town with humps of buildings like witches' cottages in an enchanted forest, a three-underpass town carpeted in an amoebal colony of hybridized kudzu; amoebal, I believe, because previous experience leads me to expect a sudden cutoff beyond which the monoculture ends and more-typical flora and fauna returns and also that the vine tips and young leaves are edible, if one is not deterred by a glissade of rough hairs.

I process the leaves into a mash for the baby that the girl tastes. She makes a face, adds a few drops of juice, and feeds the baby. I chew larger, darker leaves myself, with a show of unconcern that induces the girl to eat what I give her without outward complaint, and she speaks in her sleep, murmuring half-words of gods and teeth and punishments, and I listen from the embrace of a spiny gorse bush, squatting breathless until a possum ventures too close to my bait.

Ysmany

I woke in the night. Not from the cold but from the whimpering of the baby. I didn't want to comfort him again.

I just wanted him to stop fussing. He never fucking stopped.

xxx

I knew I should try rocking him or holding him or something, but before I reached for him, a bandaged hand crept from the fraying mound.

The wanderer pulled VK into the shrubbery of himself.

Like a trapdoor spider, which reminded me of a spiderling, which reminded me of a nursery rhyme.

xxx

Which reminded me of a story my father once told, about the Goddess of Common Enemies and Broken Feet, who ate her children to keep them from usurping Her throne.

I closed my eyes again.

xxx

My father was the town teacher. He taught us reading and writing, math and engineering, but mostly he told stories.

He said that an unimaginably long time ago, everything in the universe—our world and our star and all the stars—had been packed into a single point that contained everything.

He said that every lizard and live oak, every sneeze and kiss and mountaintop were exactly the same age, exactly the same *stuff.*

×××

"Science is stupid," Luz said.

"So everything's like one drop of blood plopped into a bowl of water?" Dmitri asked, even though he barely spoke during lessons. "That spreads out from there?"

"That's even stupider," Luz told him.

"What if Dmitri's right?" my father asked her. "What if everything in the universe—your big toe, your mother's voice—is one droplet in a bowl, diluting slowly into all things?"

"Then that Goddess wasn't only a monster who ate her own children," I said. "She was also the kids, and the teeth, and the chewing."

The Ragpicker

I break the possum's neck but I am wary of leading Server to us with smoke so instead of cooking the meat I slice and salt strips almost transparently thin to cure on my pack-frame, for jerky or—given time enough and tallow—for what Default calls pemmican.

The next morning the girl prevents me from disassembling her third cairn and instead, as I watch, she replaces each component in a random-seeming pattern then feeds the baby from the wick-bottle filled with nutmilk, and gives it over-soaked chickpeas drizzled with sugar from my packets which it appears to enjoy.

For the first time, she is talkative as we hike through the morning, telling me that she is homesick for her friends and family, for the only town she ever knew, and then she becomes, or convinces herself that she becomes, enraptured by the mountainside houses that range above us like the lairs of some cliffdwelling species. The girl has never seen houses this grand, so insists that we detour through them and I agree for the vantage point that elevation will afford, to check once more for pursuit.

In the wreckage of a sloping mudslid house she discovers a full-length mirror which is, once cleaned, perfectly reflective. She's never seen all of herself at once before. She stares for a long time, then removes most of her clothes and stares for a long time.

I am trying to imagine what she sees when she says, "They don't match."

"We should leave," I try to tell her. "We're perhaps as close as a day or two from the tower."

"How I feel and how I look," she explains, taking my statement for a request for clarification. "They don't match."

Then she says, "Was that a laugh? Did you just laugh?"

Then she says, "I guess your feelings don't match how you look either."

"If they did . . ." she starts, then trails off.

That night, after I clean the baby, she sends me to scrub my hands, insisting that I remove my wraps until only my secondskin is exposed, then she builds her cairn then she teaches me to braid her hair.

The baby scoots on the cleanpicked ground in front of us, moving mostly sideways while my fingers find the rhythm of braiding. I want to hum or even to laugh again but I am afraid of upsetting the girl, so I remain silent and she says, "Tell me a story."

Tell the story about the well? I ask Iris M, whose skin is now lightened to sepia.

Of course, Iris M says, but she tells a story of a different well, having overheard the girl speak of gods in her sleep.

I attempt to relay the story aloud: "This is the tale of two lovers, a slave named Enkidu and his majesty the Uruk, who was a king or a regime or a philosophy, which Enkidu was created to overthrow but which instead he tamed by submission. The Uruk had been refusing to share well-water with his subjects even as they sickened from thirst, so Enkinu battled him for the right of access—"

"Stop," the girl says. "I don't care. That's not why I asked. I asked because *I* have a story."

She shows me a postcard with a faded picture of a cat looking at a cast iron stove, which I recognize because this is one of my postcards, so I reach for it but she says, "No."

She says, "Where did you find this?"

I tell her but she fails to understand.

She says, "I'm writing on these. You can have them back when I'm done."

"You remind me of Server," I try to say. "Not in appearance, but in cast of mind."

She says, "Do you know what nursery rhymes are?"

"Yes," I try to say.

"There's one that goes like this."

Ragpick, Ragpick, the ragpick's son,
he learnt to steal when he were young.
All the children that he could take
went over the hills and past the lake.
Spiderling, Spiderling, crawl away spinning,
your web is on fire and your children are kindling.
Tomcat, Tomcat, made such a noise,
he pleased all the girls and the nons and the boys.
My momma said we shouldn't stray
but we didn't listen and he stole us away.

"Is that about you?" she asks me. "Are you the Ragpicker?"

You did your best, Nufar says. Oh my love. You always did your best.

Ysmany

The Ragpicker fell still.

"You've stolen children before," I said, and his shoulders moved inside his mound of tatters.

×××

"I don't know why you're helping me," I told him. "I don't know why you *think* you're helping me, but I know this: I don't owe you anything. Do you understand? I don't owe you a thing."

He said something that sounded like Yes.

"You're doing this for you," I said.

"Okay," he said.

×××

I should've known better than to push him. To bait him. I should've been more frightened of him than of Server.

I *was* more frightened of him: he didn't think he needed me, and I've never been this alone before. The air smelled brittle and the hills were the wrong shapes. If I yelled, nobody could hear me. If I yelled . . .

×××

I didn't want Server to find us but I knew that if she loped into sight, what I'd feel first, what I'd feel most, would be relief.

At least until she caught us.

×××

The Rapgicker touched the postcard in my hand. I'd seen how fast he could move, but he didn't snatch it away. He tapped the picture of the cat in the kitchen.

Which one are you? I almost asked. The cat or the oven?

"Why do you collect them?" I asked. "Postcards. I didn't even know what they were until my father told me."

He made noises that I almost understood.

×××

Wolves howled that night, and I almost understood them, too.

The Ragpicker

During the fight, I try to tell her, Enkidu and the Uruk saw each other's reflections in the well, and each was so beautiful and unyielding that their warfare turned to lovemaking, and each man penetrated the other, and consumed him, and after one rasping, aching, furrowed night the lovers traversed seven mountains to reach the Forest of Cedars, which cherished Enkidu. The Uruk, consumed with jealousy, slayed the forest spirits and scattered them into fields, rivers, seedbeds, nebulae, and clouds, which angered Inanna and Eanna, who banished the lovers into a labyrinth of—

Marginalia, Iris M says.

Wire, my mother says.

Into a labyrinth, I continue, whereupon Uruk told Enkidu that to escape he must pretend to be wise but Enkidu failed to pretend and instead discovered another well, and in the depths saw another reflection, which killed him, which left Uruk alone, heartsick, deaf to all voices save those of the gods predicting that he would enslave his family, his farmers, his wives and his husbands if he did not condemn himself to die of thirst.

When I finish the tale, and the unbraiding of her hair, the girl is asleep. The baby is not. It's cooing quietly, gibbering its nonsense. Like me, I suppose. So we talk for a time, then it drifts off and I wash its soiled clothing and finish sewing its new outfit, which looks like a skirted toga, according to my mother.

Adorable, Nufar says.

Insufficient, Iris M says.

The rustle of animals in the underbrush keeps me company. The wind shifts and I listen to the girl's murmuring. She is dreaming again, and perhaps the baby is as well, in that final, unimaginable privacy of their minds.

They are a new species, or a resurrected one, born again after the rapture, these blackbox generations raised beyond the end of togetherness, terrifyingly opaque and segmented, restricted or circumscribed or perhaps even fettered, though I am pleased to report that our strides are free and wide as we hike the easy grasslanes of a modified lawn-like genome, pale green turf that grows uniformly ankle-height along the shoulders of certain private highways, holding imprints of fox paws for weeks, cattle hooves for months, ceding ground by almost imperceptible degree to native growth, like ci-cells dying in the arms of time. Then we break northeastward through a pass widened by dynamite in a previous century and into a fertile verdant—

Turn off the thesaurus module, Iris M says, ostensibly to Default.

A fertile verdant, you'll recall I was saying, basin which will spread, hundreds of miles to the north, into a fertile verdant *valley*, beribboned with streams and bespeckled with lakes and groves and the islands of half-submerged towns, and even beringed with waterfalls like the womb of the world.

Now wombs are ringed by waterfalls? Iris M says, tugging the cuff of her brocade suit.

Aren't they? Nufar asks.

What you know about wombs.

Children, my mother says. Please.

"Do you hear voices?" the girl asks me.

I pause but do not try to answer.

"In your head?" she asks. "When you fade out like that, is that what you're doing?"

"I'm hearing your voice right now," I try to tell her.

"My father says that's one reason you're the way you are. Twitches. Because you look like one person but you're a whole mob on the inside, with pitchforks and torches."

After a half mile, she says, "I don't understand the part about pitchforks."

After another half mile, gray-blue clouds fan from the mountaintops and I adjust our path toward the humps and hillocks of a previous town, visible across the valley floor. Soon there is firmness beneath the black soil and a crumbling-away of asphalt leads us to a tilted sign upon which remains the last traces of legend, Not a Through Street, and when the rain comes, the sweeping, pelting, obscuring rain, we find shelter in a building with a sign reading Aggregate, which pleases me.

After establishing a base of sorts in an intact corner, with high ceilings and an elevated floor, leaving food and fabric with the girl, I range through ten blocks surrounding. Nobody survived in a town this small, given the odds, yet no corpses remain in the slump-shouldered houses; no tanned leather stretched across sinew, no bones strewn or gnawed.

Every uplink is missing, too. Scavenged for some long-forgotten purpose, I suppose, and I paw through pantries to find several culinary treasures:

1) corn starch, one intact container.
2) maple syrup, one jug.
3) soy sauce, two bottles.
4) brown sugar, brick-hard, one bag.
5) underripe pear-like fruit from an edible ornamental cultivar, three pouchfuls.

Also, a pile of linens in a box sealed against moisture and moth which upon my return to Aggregate I arrange into a multilayered den or tent or snuggery, and we embark on a feast of pear-like fruit dipped in syrup and soy, except the baby after a time stops crawling and gurgling and starts wailing.

The girl feeds the baby, but the baby is not soothed.

"What is wrong with him?" the girl asks.

"He's a baby," I try to say.

"Something's wrong with his skin," she says.

"I'm not convinced that's the cause of his distress," I try to say, then at Default's recommendation, I powder the baby's rashes with corn starch.

"Great," the girl says. "Now you're seasoning him."

Recognizing that she attempted a joke, I look at her face, more pleased than I'd like to admit.

"Oh, shut up," she says.

I rock the baby. What are the incentives here? What is comfort and what is necessity? I am afraid the baby is falling ill without a proper diet. I know he is. I rock and shush and rock and shush him until he sleeps in my arms and the rain rattlepings on the buckled roofs beyond our shelter while we remain warm and dry and what I am cradling within these worn, waxen arms is everything.

The next

The next morning, the girl knots the fraying threads of our shelter into a lampstack. Perhaps she is untrustworthy . . . as am I, having misplaced or juxtaposed a day of our journey, because *now* we are hiking in the bright noonlight along the easy grasslanes of a modified lawn-like genome, jade green turf that grows ankle-high along the shoulders of a toll road, holding imprints of bobcat paws for weeks, horse hooves for months, ceding ground by imperceptible degree to native growth and

When I touch the girl's arm, she doesn't jerk away. She looks at my face—she earlier asked me to remove my veils—then follows my gaze and sees the wheelruts.

"Is that—" Her smile is snowfall in moonlight. "That's from pioneer wagons?"

"Yes," I tell her.

"So we'll follow the marks to the tower and wait for the next caravan."

"Okay," I say, and as she hoots and gambols and waggles the baby into a sort of flopsy dance I realize two things in sequence, the first of which being that she'd never truly believed she'd reach safety, or even an approximation of safety, and the second, which follows shortly thereafter, being that

Still, we trace the wheel ruts from the lowlands to the high until in the distance a tower appears.

Ysmany

The Ragpicker paused a few steps in front of me.

The hills beyond him looked a little like the ones back home, but not exactly. Not enough. The wrongness gave me a head-ache-y feeling, so I started drawing lines between the edges of things: a rabbit disappearing behind a cinderblock wall, a pine scent stronger than the smell of baby piss, a jagged metal post, a crow's *hah-hah-hah*. The baby's wrinkly wrist, the Ragpicker's silence, the hot bubble in my stomach.

I knotted them together—and saw the tower.

×××

So maybe I expected a tower like the ones Miguel drew, with pointy tops and flower vines and long-haired girls in arched windows. So what?

The real tower looked more like what Server called a utility substation or FARC pole: a square box the size of a house, cracked and overgrown and surrounded by impact fences. I couldn't see the bottom half of the box but nine poles speared upward from the sides, reaching above the treetops.

Gutted solar panels clung to platforms around the poles. Rectangular boxes, mostly rusted, clung to the struts here and there. Saplings with fernlike leaves grew through the walkways that linked the poles together.

"Do you see?" I lifted VK from the sling. "Look, look! See?"

He stopped fussing for once and stared at my face with his mooncloud eyes.

"Not me, silly!"

He grabbed for my nose so I twisted my head away and said, "We did it, we're here! We'll find a new momma!"

xxx

"For you," I told VK. "A new momma for you."

xxx

"How can you get so close?" I asked the Ragpicker. "Doesn't the tower keep twitches away?"

He told me that he couldn't get much closer than this, or that he could last a little while longer. Or maybe that he didn't mind the pain—the corrosive cloudping, I thought he said—of whatever scarecrow signal kept monsters away.

xxx

I said, "A tower's not a scarecrow, it's an oasis. And linked together, they're a highway."

He made a noise.

"A highway of campsites," I told him. "Of sanctuaries for pioneers—where you can't reach them."

The noise changed to a warning growl in his throat.

xxx

He made the gesture that meant "hide" then seeped into the trees.

I squeezed between a massive mottled pipe and an embankment and told the pinche baby to shut up.

xxx

The baby did not shut up, so I clamped his mouth. That made him kick and thrash and panic. He punched me in the eye so I shoved a sweetcloth in his mouth and held him tighter.

Time passed. I felt the gaze of some terrible beast.

xxx

The Ragpicker took shape in front of me. He'd veiled his face again, which meant . . . I didn't know what it meant.

He urged me to spin around to look at the mottled pipe. I asked what was wrong but he didn't try to answer.

×××

He showed me the doubled-wheels among the weeds and the smooth wing that jutted in a powerful curve before sagging into the duckweed and pricklevine.

An airplane, he said.

I'd heard of those, but who cared? What good were they? You hated your town so much that you needed to *fly* away? That was stupid. Fix your own shit, don't go running—

Listen to me, saying you shouldn't run away. You should stay and fix your town.

"What's wrong?" I asked again.

The Ragpicker

The tower brands a bass note into my skull, a vacancy of circuits, the static of magma and mantle, a whitenoise hissing that means this ci-cell already failed, already faded, leaving only a warning echo behind.

Still the echo builds into a whine as I corkscrew closer, avoiding the access road and the wagonruts, inching instead along the thornbush boundary of what in the age of flight had been a runway, and waiting, as I always wait, patience being my sword and my shield, until the time arrives for movement—then moving along with the redfly and the pollengrain, seeing the pioneers' wagons and then seeing the pioneers.

Keep her away from this, Nufar tells me.

My poor neeneh, my mother says.

She's seen worse, Iris M says. She's done worse.

She's a child.

She hasn't been a child for a long time.

Horseshit! my mother says, flaring with anger. A hurt child, a broken child is still a child. Nobody is matured by damage, that's not what makes a child an adult, you zombie quilt of an abomination.

Her outburst continues, her outburst gains strength as I check the surrounding terrain for threats and, upon finding none, return to the girl. My mother's outrage is still silencing Iris M, and Nufar, and abandoning me to the vague notion of distracting the girl with an airplane which fails with a comprehensive abruptness as the girl's eyes shine and her breath turns rapid and she says,

"They're dead."

I don't try to answer, but hope withers in her face.

She trembles, so I ease the baby from her arms then almost touch the nape of her neck and almost curl my fingertip beneath the chain I find there and almost pull her necklace from her shirt to reveal the string of charms or totems or talismans. A rusted screw, a rotten tooth, a plastic ring, a dried chickpea, a pen cap, "L♥Z" scratched on blue seaglass, and a knot of VK's sparse hair.

The girl looks at me.

Iris M appears behind her. The girl needs to see for herself.

Tell her you'll keep her safe, Nufar says.

Safe? my mother says. Tell her you'll stay with her.

I slip ahead of the girl, toward the tower, ignoring the reverberation in my spine, then pause until I hear her footfall, then continue again.

The baby nestles against my chest, sleepy in the sling. Its warmth is my second heartbeat.

Ysmany

That first tower I'd spotted was one of four. Together they formed a square, edged by a makeshift fence that turned them into watchtowers standing at the corners of a walled village.

There was a gate in the fence, two doors of fabric-covered chainlink. Wide enough for wagons. Opened now, revealing overgrown, deer-ravaged gardens.

A patch of muddy ground led to an animal pen to the right of the fence, made mostly of more chainlink. Empty except for a swarm of gnats or turkeyflies.

Fifteen or twenty roofs rose high enough for me to see them above the bushes and fencing: a patchwork of tin and foamboard and thatch, with diagonal ropes stretching from the towers toward the ground.

The quiet tightened like a tourniquet.

×××

I stopped outside the gate.

I guess I sniffed the air, expecting blood or decay.

The air smelled like rain dripping from trembling leaves into clean puddles.

×××

Mud squooshed between my toes on the trail worn smooth from

wagon wheels and walking. The Ragpicker touched my elbow. Since that first day, he'd never touched me harder than gently.

He uttered sounds that almost made words.

"I have to," I told him, and stepped through the gate.

×××

Tiny shiny yellow tomatoes clustered in a snarl of leaves, so pretty that they looked poisonous.

×××

A central building of roofboard and airplane hull stood in front of a lino-cobbled square lined with cheerful huts and ramshackle cottages.

I saw five dead rabbits in a hutch, shrunken now to pelt and bone. A chimney, a smokehouse. Rain barrels and a clay oven and a bathing partition tucked beneath a solar panel.

Two tire swings dangled from a tower's outstretched arm.

And a wagon.

×××

There was a harness for water buffalo. Two axles, four wheels modified from a tractor. Bench seats in front, bolted to the frame of some ancient vehicle, then swaddled in cladding for water-proofing. Okay. The wagon had shutters and a chimneypipe on the side and barrels on the roof among the luggage racks.

Okay.

That's where the bodies were. I'd seen bodies before, but not like these.

They were posed.

×××

One leaned from the wagon window as if waving, except someone had replaced his head with a flowerpot of petunias that poured down his rotting carcass like purple hair.

One was propped beneath the raingutter, one arm raised, scratching her back with her other arm, her detached arm, like it was a, a backscratcher.

An old one was squatting over the first one's missing head like she was shitting and two—young ones—children—were yoked in front of the wagon.

The Ragpicker was inches behind me. I spun and pushed my face into his chest.

×××

I cried, because it was such a lighthearted cruelty, and so familiar.

×××

With my eyes closed, I remembered what I'd seen.

I drew lines between the rake at the compost pile and the drum beneath the overhang and the deer pellets near the wagon's spare wheel and the hummingbird inspecting the petunias.

With my eyes closed, I traced the ligaments that connected those things to each other, and to us, and to the corpses.

The ones at the wagon and all the others.

A mockery of life, a bad copy.

×××

When I was little, I threw a lizard into the fire to see what happened.

×××

They used to believe in a friendly, needy little god who watched them and cared for them, or at least thought about them. At first, I didn't understand how they believed that God watched them if God was already everywhere. Then I also didn't understand how they believed God cared about them if God was already everything.

God was a flowerpot. God was a yoke. God was a child in a rotting shirt.

×××

"Server told me about twitches like this," I said.

The Ragpicker swayed on the tire swing, rubbing the baby's back.

"She called them likehunters." I bounced my fingers along a lumpy wagonwheel. "I don't know why."

The Ragpicker asked a question.

"Three of them, I think." I looked at a corpse wearing a blue dress. Ferns grew from dirt packed into his hollowed-out chest. "Probably three. How long ago were they here?"

The Ragpicker answered.

"Maybe a month?" I said.

He almost shrugged.

"That's why you can come so close, huh? The tower's dead."

He spoke again.

"So not dead, weak?"

He nodded.

"Too weak to protect them." I grabbed the rope and stopped him swinging. "You're a monster, too."

He didn't say anything.

"All twitches are monsters. You live too long."

×××

"Now what?" I said. "Now what?"

"I left everything," I said. "My father, my friends, my—bed—the meals, hot meals—my town that I miss every second of every day."

"I ran away. I—"

"For what?"

"For nothing. Trying to save this paito baby and instead I'm killing him myself."

"He'll die without milk. Is that—is that surprise? Are you surprised that I, what? That I know he'll die? Of course I fucking know."

×××

I hit him until my hands ached, then he crossed the compound and stood facing the sheep paddock, which was elevated on cinderblocks with a corrugated metal roof.

×××

"Server says there are hundreds of voices in twitches' heads," I told the Ragpicker's back. "And thousands of others without voices. With just . . . urges."

He didn't move.

"Force-feeding you ideas and encouragement, and she told me . . ." I started crying again. "I-I don't know where to go. I don't know what to do."

He raised one bandaged hand and pointed into the distance.

"What's there? The next tower? You think they left the other pioneers alone after this?"

He shook his head.

"Then what are you talking about?" I asked.

He showed me the baby. He mimed nursing the baby.

×××

Which after everything, after what I'd seen—not understanding if he thought he could nurse the baby or if he meant *I* should—

Yeah. I lost my shit again.

The Ragpicker

My attempt to convince the girl to remain at the wagon, in the towertown, with the baby, in my absence, is not met with success.

The girl is struggling with contradictory truths: I have refrained from perpetrating any outrage upon her, yet twitches are monstrous and I am a twitch. This clash of truth against truth infuriates her, however, in the end, more from fear of my abandonment than trust in my restraint, she demands to remain with me.

My intention, I attempt to convey to her, is to track the goats missing from the pen to secure a nanny to provide milk for the baby.

Having done that, we will travel to the city or to the outskirts of the city, in my case, as this is merely a momentary detour before I return to home and husband with my syncable. This is merely a twelve-day oxbow, a fringe on a flapper's dress, a polypropylene pellet frothing into a butane bath, and—

"We'll *what*?" she asks. "Why can't you talk right?"

"You'll be safe in the city," I try to promise her.

"Where?"

"More than safe," I try to say. "Welcomed. You will arrive home and I will depart and then I, in turn, will arrive home, on a swaying palanquin in the pachydermal shade of—"

She says: "Stop that, shut up. What is wrong with you?"

What is wrong is that I am terrified that delaying my reunion with Nufar, or with whatever diminished integrity he still possesses, on her account, even briefly, for no longer than a dash-dash-dot on a copper wire, means something—and what that thing is, exactly, I am even more terrified to consider.

"Say that again," she tells me. "Slower."

"We catch," I try to say. "Goat. Milk. For baby."

She looks at the ground and says, "Okay."

She is shaken and trembling. She is a child and I want to comfort her and I believe that she wants me to comfort her, but I also believe that she will not permit me to comfort her yet I wonder if perhaps in this case the attempt is identical with the achievement, so I crouch beside her, close enough for her to rest her hand on my shoulder should she choose. I abide there for a time but she does not rest her hand on my shoulder. She turns away and beyond her dirt-smudged wrist I spot a gap in the fence through which the goats likely escaped.

When I approach the gap with the intention of tracking them, the girl speaks from behind me: "First you compost the dead."

I watch the fields outside the town, where a sunbaked breeze lifts fallen leaves from a furrow—

Like the daughter of the woman of Shunem, my mother says. For he stretched himself upon the child three times, putting his mouth upon her mouth, his gaze upon her face, his fingers between her fingers and he cried unto the Name, let this child's soul come into her again; and the soul of the child came into her again, and she revived.

—from a furrow then sieves through the fence and parts around me to clasp the child in an embrace of loam-scent and lime-scent, to stroke her skinny back and to—

Stop that, shut up, Iris M tells me, in mimicry of the girl.

To dry her tears, Nufar finishes.

"We're not leaving them like this," the girl tells me. "Not like . . . this."

"I'll bring them to the clearing," I try to say. "So they're together."

"You'll compost them," she says.

"There isn't time," I try to tell her.

"We need," she says, then stops.

I wait.

"You need put them on a layer of twigs and—dry twigs, kindling. Don't you know anything? Strip them and—and kiss them and cover them with ash and thatching and cheatgrass and woodchips so they'll return to soil."

That switch from *we* to *you* means she cannot bear to touch the vaudeville dead, so I point her at the airplane.

"On the forehead," she tells me.

I point again at the airplane.

"And count them," she says. "I need to know how many there are."

She leaves through the open gate though I still hear or imagine her cooing to the baby in the sling, soft soothing nonsense as I prowl this catacomb village, my spine thick with a tundra howl, my mind whiplashing between sympathy and signal loss. The living owe nothing to the dead, and—

I beg your pardon, Nufar says.

—and I say that as one of the departed, but she is living, she is alive, she is owed a debt so I nestle the corpses in shallow beds that I scoop from compost heaps with my laminated hands and I cover them with shrouds of ash and knap and brushweed and when the girl returns she places pebbles, granite and basalt and asphalt and schist, one stone for each of the dead, in a labyrinth design she scratches with an adze in the hardpacked ground.

She sings a prayer.

She sings a prayer in a language that neither I nor Default

recognize, then I tell her I'll track the goats and she climbs to the roof of the sharpening shed.

Fifteen yards away, the fence unravels from an upright post in a narrowing of chevrons and I wriggle through the bentback gap and on the far side, beyond the grooves of seeded field, a freckled Iris M enumerates the clearcutting of ferns and the bark-stripped tree the goats left behind. Within the arbor of the wood, trampled paths are strewn with pellets like a mission canyon courtyard with jacaranda petals on my wedding day, reflecting pools of purple pointillism on the lawn.

Ysmany needs to know about the city, Nufar tells me. She needs a goal, a purpose.

She needs hope, my mother says, swinging her tennis racket.

Tell her again, Nufar says.

I will, I say. After we find a nanny goat.

Tell her so she understands, he says.

Iris M scoffs. One can't ensure comprehension. Even at the height of connectivity one couldn't. Especially not then.

Just tell her, Nufar says.

Communication is constrained more by social maturity than linguistic capacity, Iris M continues, turning pedagogical. "The meaning of an utterance maps exactly to the society that produced it."

The prattle of her open-source recitation continues as I move in a widening gyre through the goat-marked thickets, until the girl calls, too loudly, from the rooftop, "They're not sheep, they're goats. Hey! They went that way."

I listen for the footsteps of another twitch among the shiver of leaves and the whine of a bee-fly, but detect nothing, or at least nothing worrisome.

"Did you hear me?" she calls. "Over there!"

A spindly flowerless rosebush escorts me into her sightline and she points to her left with her left hand while her right touches the baby sling, and she says, "Help me down."

Then I am standing below her and she is backlit by the sky, which is made bluer by her brownness, such a small weak mighty creature, then she is in my arms and then she is on the ground beside me.

"Follow me." She sees the thickets. "Except you go first."

Twenty yards past the wood, I crouch among the nettles and touch a split-crescent hoofprint and try to ask how she knew which way they'd gone.

"Patterns," she tells me.

As I follow the goat trail, she says, "That's how the lampstack works. Server finds meaning in patterns. She thinks you can find the ocean in a raindrop, the desert in a shard of broken glass. Every bead and keyboard in the lampstack is a forest or a satlite or a song. She calculates the future, she thinks the lampstack is the loom of the world."

"What do you think?" I try to ask.

"Yeah, I saw the ocean once. On a salt run."

"About the lampsack?" I try to ask.

"It scared me. It's too big. It's the size of things from before the world shrank, you know? Too big to survive."

"Yes," I say.

Things were smaller then, Iris M says.

Not everything, Nufar says, giving me a smolder.

And crowded, Iris M says.

The trail is well-marked now, flattened by fifteen or ten goats and several kids. The scent of old piss mixes with the scent of the verbena leaves the girl crushes between her fingers. We step into the shadow of a ridge where green shoots rise among charred stems and a turkey vulture beats into the sky and the girl discovers a lyresnake that she instructs me to kill but I demur, unwilling to start a cookfire for fear of Server.

"She's five days behind us," the girl tells me. "Or ten if she started in the wrong direction, which she probably did."

Why five? Iris M asks. Is she miscounting days or misleading us?

I try to tell the girl, "Perhaps, but I heard that she reads the future in strings of beads."

"Plus it rained," she says. "Not even Server can track us through that rain."

"She won't need to track us," I try to respond. "If she smells smoke."

"I miss . . ." The girl looks away. "Bread."

She falls silent for a few minutes and then an hour and then tells me the goats are around the next hill which is knowledge I already possess.

The goats graze on a fluttering hillside of poison oak and I pause to watch, in stillness, while the girl scribbles with a homespun pencil on my postcards and the baby fusses beside her. Beyond a few inquisitive bleats and keyhole stares, the goats find our presence unremarkable, even the billygoat with his swollen ballsack and his wise auburn beard wanders away, his horns vanishing into a fold of the hills.

I touch the girl's arm and show her my upright palm and she tells me she'll wait and then tells me to give her an orange and then I become a mound of poison oak. My stems shelter lizards and my flowers feed boris beetles and coatcheck beetles and longhorn beetles and—

Default says: The berry of the poison oak is consumed by juncos, quail, corvids, bushtits and waxwings, warblers, finches, juncos and mockingbirds, and native peoples made tattoo ink from its ashes.

You said juncos twice, I tell her.

That is incorrect, she says, and she is describing the poison oak leaves as "symmetrically lobed, asymmetrically lobed, or lobe-less," to Iris M's scathing amusement when I scoop a kid into my arms, a scrawny brown-black kid with a white patched snout and floppy ears.

The nanny says *maaaaaah maaah-maaaah* and the other goats lift their interested heads and the kid chirrups and the nanny follows me protesting *maaaaah!* to the base of the ridge where the girl, with the baby snug in her sling, turns and hikes quickly away as I approach, telling me over her shoulder that I'm not allowed near the baby, not so long as there is oak-poison on me, and the nanny continues to bleat for her kid and trot at my skirts, her rippled horns catching the trimmings and frays though she quiets before sunset when I return her her kid to suckle, its fingerlong tail wagging wildly, and then—after the girl informs with me with more sharpness than necessary that the baby cannot suck directly—I squat and milk her into a bottle, though not too much as the girl wishes to acclimate the baby slowly to this new pleasure, though he is livid in his disagreement.

I mean livid like angry not livid like pale.

I shed my outermost layer for an inner one but the girl still insists that I not touch VK, which prohibition I understand and endorse though I miss the unthinking, unshrinking contact a baby affords. That is one of the perks of pre-sentience, or perhaps pre-sapience becau se an infant is sensory with alarming intensity—

A bundle of nerves, my mother interjects.

—but doesn't possess a self of which to be aware. However, after a third offering of manzanita berries the nanny allows me to scratch the knobby furpatch between her horns before climbing onto the lowest branch of the tree as her kid snuggles beside me and the coyote speaks with the arroyo toad and the girl rests her palm on the sleeping infant's thigh and says, "Now we each have babies."

"We need to talk," I try to say.

"Yours looks more like you than mine looks like me," she says.

Ha, Nufar says. She's starting to relax.

Humor is manipulation, Iris M says.

In the shadow of the manzanita tree, my memory of Nufar

scratches his beard and tells Iris M, Then you are utterly uncalculating.

Ha, I say.

You're starting to relax, too. Nufar squats and wraps his burly, imaginary arms around my shoulders. Tell Ysmany what happens next.

"We're going to the city," I try to tell her.

"To the sea?"

"City."

"Sea."

I write in the dirt with a fingertip: *city*.

"There's a city?" she asks.

Good people. I wipe out the words and write: *For baby and you. Safe. Food.*

"Where is it? How long?"

I flash my hands three times.

"Thirty days? Or you've got what, nine and a half fingers? Eight and two halves?"

Month, I write, and give an exaggerated shrug.

"If we're lucky?" she says.

I nod.

"I'm not sure that's a thing we are, the two of us," she says. "Lucky."

I spread my arms: look at this. Look at this world, these red-bark branches, these shy stars and pipistrelle bats and greasewood flowers. Listen to our baby's wheeze, our nanny's rumination. Feel our chilly ground and our chaparral scent—and you, and me, alive, together, two tiny dots, two grains of sand, two drops of rain that contain the ocean.

"You're so dumb," the girl says.

She smiled, my mother says. Did you see? She smiled.

Ysmany

I missed hot food and I missed Luz and my father and Dmitri.

I missed Yolanda harvesting chickpeas and brush-pollinating strawberries.

I missed Denisse's smiles, and the Hrabas' stamping clapping drumbeat dances.

I missed the burnt-acorn smell of the ovens and the tang of fermenting fruit. I missed the *tink-ding* of Maria's tools, the dumb background nuisance of conversations and arguments and laughter.

I missed the soles of my feet knowing every pebble and dip.

I missed the lampstack.

xxx

"We'll try another tower first," I told the Ragpicker. "Just because one was . . ."

When I didn't finish, he made a noise.

"Yeah," I said. "That doesn't mean they all are."

He grunted over his sewing.

xxx

"What's the city like?" I asked.

He tilted his head, looking at his imaginary friends, talking to them. Then he started talking to me: orchards, shekere, windmills, mothers, fishponds, face-paint.

He said something about bridges, something about home.

×××

The baby woke me in the night with a pained cry but when I reached for him he was already sleeping again. An owl called *ha-ha ha-ha-ha*. I watched the moon through the branches and wondered what VK stood for. I wondered why I thought it stood for anything other than itself.

I changed the sleeping baby then scrubbed my hands with clean sand rummaged from the Ragpicker's pack. He was an earthen mound in the darkness, his hood raised and his masks wrapping his face.

I couldn't hear him breathing, I couldn't see the rise and fall of his chest.

He didn't smell like a person. He smelled like a thing.

×××

I opened a side-pouch of his pack and found a spool of thread, a chunk of concrete putty and five keyboard keys: U-N-A-F-R.

They clacked in my palm and formed almost-words: unfair, fauna.

Then they clacked back into the pouch and I opened the main compartment and beneath the maple syrup and a wadding of cloth I found a case made of the hard black plastic of assault rifles.

When I touched the clasps the Ragpicker made an unhappy noise.

×××

"What?" I said.

He made the same noise again.

"You don't want me to look inside?"

He said yes.

"Now I really want to," I told him.

I tugged at the clasps but they didn't open.

"You're keeping secrets," I said.

He gestured at me: *you are, too.*

×××

I wanted to smash the case even though I didn't care what was inside. The plastic was too tough so I gave up after a few whacks. I didn't know why I wanted to look.

That was a lie.

I wanted to string together fragments of that plastic shell. I wanted to braid its broken, secret, hidden guts into something new, something *mine*. I wanted to take what was his and mark it as my own, like Trikar pissing on the north hills.

××

I didn't know why I wanted that. I didn't think there was anything missing in me. I didn't feel any empty places. But what if *that* was what I was missing? A way of knowing if I was broken or whole.

××

"My father says heroes are symptoms of a sick society," I told the Ragpicker, pulling the plastic case into my lap. "He told me stories. When I memorized them, that's how Server realized I was . . ."

"You," he said.

The baby goat lifted her head and I said, "Yeah."

××

"Tell me a story," he said, or near enough.

"We wouldn't need stories if we lived forever," I told him. "My father told me that, too. That the reason for stories is death."

The Ragpicker stroked the baby goat until she closed her eyes.

"Not even twitches live forever," I said. "You won't live much longer. You won't even outlive me."

"So tell me a story," he said, or near enough.

××

I hugged myself and he draped a blanket around my shoulders and I said, "This is the first story I ever learned."

Alice Ann watched the beetle climbing the tree,
while her mother talked: "Listen to me!"
Alice Ann said, "Look at his wings!"
and her mother told her to sit right there
and think about what she'd done.

The party sounded far away
and the sunlight dimmed
and the tree bark grew thicker
and thicker
and spread
until the cracks were so deep and wide
that Alice Ann hopped inside.
She stretched her wings and flew
around the trunk a time or two,
higher past branches and higher past twigs
until she landed in the red roofs of the treetop.
She waved at the streets and waved at the shops
and drifted down down downtown
into the bustle and the hustle
and stood alone in the crowd
and lonely
so she rang a bell and knocked on a door.
But nobody came.
Alice Ann cried: "Listen to me!"
and spun around "One!" "Two!" "Three!"
then leaped on the wall
and skipped upstairs
and danced on rooftops above the squares
and far below they watched and paced
except for the children who joined the chase
tumbling across towers and treetops and leaves
until they all,
one by one,
stopped to dawdle and nap.
Alice Ann told them, "Wash your hands and share your toys,
take one bite and stop that noise!"
and they listened to everything, every last word,
then followed her down past
the redheaded bird around the trunk,

again and again
'til the sky shone bright
and the bark closed tight
and squeezed Alice Ann—pop!—into the afternoon light.
At the party she told them all what she'd seen,
the beetle and treetop and where she'd just been.
Did anyone listen?
Alice Ann didn't know,
too busy watching the ant on her toe.

×××

We found a road the next afternoon, or the crust of a road. Paper wasps streamed into a nest in the skeleton of a billboard, what Yolanda might've called a trellis or an arbor.

"Good place for a lampstack," I said, half by accident.

The Ragpicker mangled a few words.

"I guess if you live a hundred years," I said, "you learn how to be scared. Maybe that's why you're like this. All that fear."

He said something like "maybe."

"She won't come this way," I told him. "And if she does, that means she already knows we did."

He didn't say anything.

"Cut me some rope. I'm going to hang a few things."

After what felt like a long time, he said, "Okay."

×××

Rusted stakes marched along the side of the road. I told the Ragpicker that the fallen telephone poles looked like giants' chopsticks, which embarrassed me into an hour's silence.

×××

We found cement-block walls and ostrich turds, and that evening another billboard, except that one had a corner flapping in the breeze and writing I couldn't understand.

Then we found the remains of a steeple-topped building.

We ate on a bench facing a playground built of better stuff than the building itself. The Ragpicker pulled out the nopalitos he'd stripped and sliced and kept in a watertight bag with a squeezed orange and soy sauce and handfuls of green leaves I didn't recognize that had turned soggy and spicy.

After he milked the nanny, she climbed the slide and then clattered to the top of the peaked roof above that.

I pointed VK at her and said, "Look at her, she's so silly."

He gurgled a laugh, and something caught in my chest.

I'd never even liked him before.

×××

When the Ragpicker slipped the leash off the kid's neck, the goats kept following us.

We were their herd now. We'd stolen them from their family but they trotted along after us like they belonged.

×××

Hundreds of low humps marked fallen houses. Their cracked skins reminded me of lizard scales. The long straight canals between them were overgrown with thornbushes and bramble, making right angles through the neighborhood.

The nanny *maaaah*ed into a blotch of pigweed. The Ragpicker joined her. He didn't like that I wouldn't eat the worms and insects he rummaged, no matter how he prepared them, so he found greens instead.

The two of them, side-by-side, fighting over the same leaves looked like . . . I half-laughed. Like a shaggy, hairy beast with the devil's eyes, and also a goat.

×××

The nanny kept eating the tenderest leaves just before he picked them. The kid ran in a circle then kicked her hooves sideways and I laughed for real, which startled four huge culero condors into the sky.

I didn't like how they circled. I didn't like their white underarms and scabby heads. Hungry for me, or VK.

×××

The kid stuck close to her mother and I slunk into the shadow of a wall and fed the baby then changed him. When I set aside the shitty cloth for the Ragpicker to clean, I felt someone watching me.

The world shrunk and tightened.

I thought: Server.

I thought: she's here.

I didn't shout a warning, I didn't run or hide.

×××

Nothing broke the quiet. I felt breath on my neck.

From where?

Behind me.

The edge of my fist smeared a clear arc in the filth of an unbroken window and I shaded my eyes. Inside the building, sunlight pissed through equally-unbroken skylights, which meant none of this was normal glass.

I was looking into a sealed chamber—a tomb where hundreds of mummies slept in upright cots, linked by cables to scorpion-tail machines.

Dreaming themselves to death.

×××

I must've made a noise, because a tapestry of rags unwove from the dirt beside me.

He stood there, alert, protective, motionless as the mummies. The baby fussed, the birds sang. What I didn't like to admit was that I mattered to the Ragpicker.

He would step in front of a stampede for me and I couldn't tell if that pleased or frightened me.

×××

I touched the curtain of his back and wanted to braid the strands into plaits but instead I told him, "You're one of them. You're more like them than you are like me."

The Ragpicker made a noise.

"Write something for them," I told him. "On the window, like a memorial."

He asked a question.

"I don't know," I said. "Something."

He unwrapped a finger and wrote, "One loaf of bread and two jugs of wine, five tubs of roasted grain, a cluster of raisins, two dozen cakes."

xxx

On celebration days, Bianca and Jesus danced, whirling and yelping like *Ha!* and *Aiaia!*

On celebration days, Keelin argued with his father, because they both liked arguing. Shi-u called them peas in a pod.

On celebration days, Denisse laughed, which led to the Hrabas singing and clapping, and music spinning me round and round for hours.

xxx

One celebration day, I fell asleep tucked between Luz and Dmitri and a littler kid whose hands curled around my arm.

xxx

The wind after sunset whispered things I almost understood.

Wish, wish and *Please*, and *Stop.*

xxx

Orange and white wildflowers blanketed a collapsed barn.

I brought the baby closer to see and the nanny climbed to the tilted roof to graze. The Ragpicker lifted the kid past the gutter to join her then slunk around the side of the barn where a black, triangular mouth opened into what looked like hundreds of stalls and dozens of skeletons and thousands of rats.

The air smelled different there, and the darkness felt colder than normal shade.

xxx

When the Ragpicker stepped into the barn, I said, "Wait."

He stopped, half in shadows, facing away from me. That didn't mean anything. He didn't understand eye contact.

"Something's wrong," I said.

A stillness closed around him like a fist and I held the baby tighter and backed into the warm bright day.

The Ragpicker seeped into the darkness. Then nothing happened except my heartbeat.

The baby woke and gummed my wrist until I gave him his rubber wire to chew.

A grinding sounded inside the barn. A thump, then silence, then the scrape of concrete against concrete.

"Well," I told the baby. "Fuck."

xxx

The darkness knitted together into a silhouette that looked like the Ragpicker. Tears of relief stung my eyes. I blinked so he wouldn't see them, then watched him lugging a cinder block into the light.

"Okay?" I called.

"Okay," he said.

Not a cinder block, a 60-pound salt lick that he set at my feet like an offering.

xxx

I didn't recognize some of the words on the label. Manganese, cobalt.

The Ragpicker broke the lick apart with his crowbar and tucked pieces into his pockets and folds, then he stood there staring at the barn until I said, "Starting to get creepy," and the next day we walked through towns decaying alongside the highway, and the next night I woke bleeding.

Which didn't exactly come as a surprise. I'd been there for Luz when she started, but what did surprise me was the Ragpicker at my elbow with a specially-sewed loincloth, then him cleaning the pad every morning and giving me a new one that smelled of alcohol.

How did he know? That's the question that could've embarrassed me, but you don't blush if a tree stump sees you naked, or a condor or a stone.

xxx

A herd of camels grazed on the trees surrounding a meadow of purple needlegrass. Giraffes or camels, my father never could remember which were which. They were so big. They were beautiful, too, and peaceful in a way I didn't expect.

×××

The Ragpicker started asking for a story every night.

I told him one I didn't understand, that started with dialogue: *"Is your plan possible under the current conditions?"*

"Of course."

"But the current conditions are exactly what we're trying to change. Any plan that functions within the current conditions also reinforces them."

"How convenient, that only the impossible is effective."

×××

I told him the one that started: *The first people who lived in that land of wide barbed beauty gathered fruit and nuts and roots; they hunted antelope and seals, birds and shellfish.*

Then the Nama came. They settled on the borderlands, raising goats and sheep, but soon claimed the richest pastures for themselves. Generations later, the Herero drove their cattle south from the Zambezi lakes, and war between the Herero and the Nama flared.

In 1884, the German Empire claimed the land. Missionaries built stone churches, and traded guns for converts.

Then came the soldiers.

This is a story of Namibia. This is a story of Jakob Marengo, son of both the Herero and the Nama, called a cattle-thief and a bandit, called an outlaw, called a robber-chief.

The storytellers say that Marengo was raised in a mission school, that he lived in Europe, that he worked as a miner and a cattleman. They say he could shoot a kingfisher's egg from a man's hand at a hundred meters, could draw water from the sand and steal the shape of a jackal.

The stories say that only glass bullets polished by a priest could stop him.

He couldn't draw water from the sand or steal the shape of a jackal. The bullets that killed him were like any others.

×××

I told him the one called *I Am Haunted by a Thousand Ghosts* that started: *The fifth ghost lurked in my favorite cluster of carrels in the Central Library, too near the bathrooms but far enough from the periodicals.*

I told him the one that started: *First she learned to crawl, then she learned to walk, then she learned to break into the houses on Dogwood Lane and listen to the homeowners sleep.*

×××

I told him the one that started: *Three years after my sight was taken from me, I turned my face to the sauna heat of the sun and yellow squares veiled the darkness, a broken pane of goldenrod. The blind did not live in a world of darkness. There was texture, color, pattern. There was taste and sound and scent though they did not compensate for the loss of vision, nothing did; there were no compensatory powers of the unsighted seer.*

Scent.

To me, he will always smell of wet and windbent hay, of damp wool and something faintly but fundamentally male. Even sighted women possess an acute sense of the scent of men—a compensation for the lack of any other sense about them—but blind women are undistracted by the well of his eyes, the breadth of his shoulders, the play of his fingers through light and air.

×××

I was drowsing in a nest of rags beneath the sunset sky, my belly warm with guava and yucca and goat milk. I was listening to a hopeful frog and to the Ragpicker changing the baby when, for a moment, everything felt okay.

Me and the Ragpicker, the nanny goat and her kid, raising the baby on this easy sleepy road until he learned to walk alongside us—

A sour taste thickened in my mouth.

No. Not okay. I needed *people*, we needed people. VK and I. We needed more than the Ragpicker.

And—and there was something cruel in the way he listened to my stories.

So that night, when he asked, I told him of Esther, who told a story every night to delay her beheading.

The Ragpicker

"We'll reach the next tower soon," the girl says, breaking her fast on the nasturtium I gathered in the night.

"Okay," I say.

"We will, right?"

When I squat in front of her, the nanny butts my shoulder and I say, "Today."

"Today?"

I scratch the goat's bony forehead and she nibbles at my cuffs, her upper lip gumming the fabric. I am almost-alarmingly fond of her; she is opinionated and stubborn and smart and—

Which one are you talking about? Iris M asks.

My mother laughs. If "Ysmany" doesn't mean Little Goat, it should.

According to my records, Default announces, Ysmany means Hear Me.

Bah, Nufar says, which makes my mother laugh again.

The obit of my mother is enlivened by the proximity of what she claims is a family. The girl, the baby, the goats. A prehistoric band—a posthistoric band—not following the herds or the blooms but on a quest for a home, for a family, and she refuses to acknowledge the obvious contraction: if we were a family, we would not be in search of one.

After delivering the girl and baby to the city, we will travel home, to Nufar, to recover what—

"The likehunters are close," the girl says.

The kid brays *whehe wheehee* and my memory ranges across the dawn, touching a beetle's elytra caught in a funnel web, a gopher's yellow teeth, the tapping of woodpeckers and the indolence of clouds, but unearthing no sign of hostile proximity, of twitches embalmed by preferences, entombed in a mausoleum of encouragements into

Except not entombed, as they are faithful still to the edenic days before the Fall, and I lose myself between heartbeats. I am the flyspeck fruit of the original tree and the crawling worm banished to dust. What I am is, is the unfaithful child of revelation, the perennial wandering Jew; my kinfolk perform sacraments yet I refuse their easy grace, hearkening to an older time, excommunicated from the world's concluding religion while the congregations of the devoted—

Don't blame religion, Nufar says. Technology is what killed us.

Don't blame technology, Iris M says, her short hair now white. Technology is downstream from culture.

There is always birdsong, Nufar says.

Default says: Five tests.

Five tests what? my mother asks.

To establish the presence of a religion, Default says.

Mute her, Iris M tells me.

Default recites: A religion is a system of belief in the metaphysical or unfathomable which includes ritual acts and moral codes and inspires characteristically-religious feelings—

Self-referential, Iris M murmurs.

—such as awe, shame, and adulation, to describe the purpose of the world and individuals' places within it, and to unite believers into social groups or moral communities.

That's five? my mother asks.

Nufar scratches his hairy belly inside his bathrobe and says, Universal connectivity offered all that. Answers, belonging . . .

Adulation, my mother says. The immersion in a transcendent Unity greater than yourself, which provided purpose and ritual, community and morality and—

"Did you hear me?" the girl demands. "I know you did. Shut up. Tell them to shut up. The likehunters are—there's three of them and one of you. Okay?"

"Okay," I say.

She starts to tremble. "They're already there."

"You don't know that," I try to say.

"At the tower. The one we're heading to—they're waiting for us. They're playing with the bodies."

I swaddle the baby and offer him to her to hold.

She slaps his leg with her small hard palm. "Get him off me! Go look!"

The baby wails and the girl spins away and wipes snot from her nose, her bony back scowling at me, and then I'm moving through the gorse and the dappling. A hyacinth bush whirls me like a mobile and a chaparral incline plummets and swoops, spinning us uphill until the baby quiets to a wet-mouthed inquisitiveness which still softly stymies stealth and my comforting ambush stillness so instead we simmer for an hour from ridge to rise to rill in spyrograph loops with the girl a pinprick in the center like a bead of blood.

She unbraids her hair and when she is half-done, she looks like two halves of herself. She says a great many words she doesn't intend, then unwraps the baby from my sling and whispers to him that he is too young and dumb to hate her now but she promises she will remind him, when he's old enough to understand, that she doesn't deserve his affection.

"You didn't see them?" she asks me.

I shake my head.

"Okay," she says.

"Okay?"

"Okay," she repeats, and miles later, while watching me milking the nanny, she says, "I wish you were a real person."

The kid butts my forearm, attempting to liberate one of her mother's teats.

"Then maybe you'd know what it's like," the girl says.

"Know what?" I try to ask.

"You're not," she says.

"Not what?" I try to ask.

"What if there's something wrong with me?"

I release a teat for the kid and look at the girl.

"What if there's something missing?" she asks. "Inside of me."

"The world moves on without us," I try to tell her, as the kid begins to suck. "Nothing is missing, nothing is lost. There is plenty of time. Linger, wallow, wait. Refill yourself from the well, child. Time is the kindest fate. She sings us to sleep."

"They're going to kill us."

"Perhaps."

"They're going to kill *me*. They're going to kill me, then they'll—they'll pose me with a crown of udders or, or turn my butt into a teapot."

"Perhaps."

"They're going to find us. They're going to trap us and you— you'll leave me behind."

"I'll stay with you until you find a home."

"When you—if you—" Her breath catches and her eyes shine. "When you leave me, promise you'll take VK. Promise to keep him safe."

"I won't leave you."

"Promise me if."

"No."

She doesn't stop demanding until, as we soak our sponge-filled canteens at a stream that strains through the wreckage of a collapsed cabin and overspills the granite steps, I finally say the words she requires.

And she says, "Why did you do this to the world?"

From love, Nufar tells her, and boredom.

Iris M says, We forgot what was real.

We were frightened, my mother says, of silence.

I try to tell the girl, as I lead her into miles of barren almond orchard, that we did it because it was easy.

A legion of the dead flanks us, with shriveled trunks and brittle branches. The goats linger at irrigation drones humped with papery stalks and the spectral sirens of another tower sing out as we near, compelling my attention, demanding my engagement, bisecting me with tragedies that pare my options to two: bear witness or share blame, and upon the horns of this—

The girl grabs the fabric at my hip. "Stay here."

I stop.

"Not *here* here you dumb cuca. Stay with me. Not in your head."

"Okay," I say, and lead her away from a likehunter shrine or reliquary or fetish that appears in snatches through the lifeless orchard branches.

Default? Iris M asks, for no reason that I can determine.

Default does not respond to the query, but the girl, vigilant with fear, responds to a sudden gleam of sunlight on silver, and I am afraid of what she'll see but I am more afraid of stopping her as she stares at a gap in the columns and rows of dead trees.

Not a gap, a presence. A synthetic almond tree, a doppleganger length of silver ropes as thick as my thigh planted vertically in the earth with narrower lengths branching upward, braided, avulsed, distressed, with dozens of still-narrower branches unfurling in fractal abundance, with hundreds of split nuthusks attached umbilically to twigs, open to reveal almonds, carved of slate, nesting inside the cleft halves.

The girl says, "The likehunters made this?"

"Yes," I say.

"It's beautiful," she says, gazing at the hair-fine wires stretching upward in supplication.

"Yes," I say.

"I don't understand," she says.

Tell her, Nufar says.

I don't understand either, I say.

You work hard on not understanding. That's how you spend your days. You don't believe in understanding.

That's not true.

You're more committed to ignorance than you are to me.

That's not true.

So tell her, he says.

Ignoring the urgency in my mind I pry apart the low-hanging fruit of a silver husk and remove the slate almond within and I kneel in front of the girl and offer her the carved stone in my outstretched palms, and when she takes it, I want to tell Nufar that meaning does not require understanding but he's not Nufar, he's just another wire-wrapped facsimile.

The girl tucks the stone away and spends a painful hour adjusting the wires of the tree into a configuration she finds more pleasing or consequential or evocative, and soon after we depart the shed snakeskin of a road slithers underfoot. This the kid greets with unreasoning excitement, gamboling in such a way that brings a smile to the girl's grave face which pleases me despite the abscess whine of the tower drilling into my jaw.

"There," I try to say, pointing my veiled face toward a spire-tip rising above these red-mounded meadows.

"That's the tower?" she asks.

"Yes."

"You're okay coming closer?"

"No."

"You're not okay?"

"No."

She requests that I remain with her a little longer.

"Okay," I say and lead her onto the pebbled twilit killing ground surrounding the tower's farmland, which appears from this vantage point to cover three or two hundred acres, with occasional crop trees and huts rising from the collage of what I think is oats and pole beans, purslane and lentil and millet.

Moments after I step into the open, the shrill note of a bell sounds from the town, which is twelve or nine towers of beams, girders, crow's nests, walkways, fluttering ivyleaves, and waving banners standing sentinel above five much-repaired buildings with the remains of classical details and narrow vertical windows and manyfold shacks and huts and paddocks, the whole town surrounded by two layers of reinforced, rewoven chainlink fencing through which I may or may not detect motion.

The alarm bell sounds again and my boots crunch on the pebbles two more times before I am nearly brought to my knees by an internal shrieking of approbation and encouragement.

The girl looks at me and then looks away.

Ysmany

I liked the forest of dead trees.

I liked the boreholes in the branches and the crusts of yellow lichen. The craggy jagged branches overhead made me think of fishing nets trawling the clouds.

×××

The nanny goat liked the orchard grasses. Her ears pricked when she chewed.

The kid scrambled through snarls of roots while VK fussed in the sling, his fat legs useless.

My father told me that we're great apes. He said if we'd called ourself that, instead of humans, we might've dodged an apocalypse or two.

×××

Server said our original sin was that we sacralized human life.

She said tragedy is when an animal forgets how to live in her indigenous environment. She said tragedy is when an animal forgets she is her indigenous environment.

She said we forgot how to die.

×××

The jagged branches like fishing nets tightened around us.

Every line and knot and node stank of the likehunters. The

soles of my feet itched, walking in their footsteps. Closer to the tower. Closer to them.

×××

Not long after we found the road, the Ragpicker pointed to a tower peeking above the trees.

Then we reached the fields surrounding the tower village and I felt the likehunters watching me from the rooftops. I froze, I panicked, because I knew that I deserved whatever they did to me. Because of how Server raised me—because of whatever I lacked—because I was more like a twitch than anything human.

×××

A few steps into the clearcut field, the Ragpicker grunted in pain. Not pain exactly, more like the acknowledgement of pain.

He took a few more steps and when I saw the distress in his shoulders and his stride I almost laughed in relief.

The tower still worked. The oasis, the sanctuary, still protected the town.

The Ragpicker couldn't get close, which meant Server couldn't either.

Or the likehunters.

×××

People still lived here. Living, breathing . . . living people. When the wind shifted I smelled cooking and heard the tinkling of chimes and the creak of a mill or sifter.

I didn't hear any people, though, and hadn't since that bell gonged.

A warning bell, when they'd spotted us coming across the fields.

This town was an oasis now, but they were trapped deep inside twitch territory. Waiting for the day when the tower failed. Waiting for the likehunters to murder them for a punchline.

×××

Pebbles covered the ground in a circle around the outermost fields. To keep everything visible for the lookouts on the towers.

I didn't see any lookouts, though.

Flags fluttered from the exposed beams of the towers, like pictures of ships. Sails or masts, except painted with storks and eggs and sunflowers and symbols I didn't recognize. A path led through the pebbles and then through the fields toward a gate in the double fences.

The entrance.

×××

The town was bigger than mine. Packed tighter, covering less ground, but still bigger. Every one of the high buildings could've slept a hundred people, maybe more.

I was afraid to face the Ragpicker, so I talked without turning. I said, "You stay here with the baby, just in case they, uh . . ."

Weren't friendly.

Weren't welcoming.

Carved me into joints and wove me onto a lampstack.

×××

He answered, swaying uneasily, his fringes and ribbon sweeping the pebbles, rocking the baby in his sling.

"I'll come back for VK," I told him. "So if I *don't* come back, that means I can't. Okay?"

"Okay."

"So you come get me."

He didn't say anything.

"I don't care how much it hurts," I told him. "You come get me."

"Okay," he said.

×××

I was scared of leaving, so I kicked the nanny goat for staying with him instead of following me.

Then I crossed the pebbles. Their sharpness warmed the soles of my feet. Small, pretty cairns dotted the pebbled area, made of bottle caps and sandglass and lightbulb bases with jagged little teeth.

×××

Two minutes of walking. Onto the path and toward the gate. Two minutes, failing to draw lines between fallow stalks and cairns and gap-toothed brick posts.

I half-turned toward the Ragpicker but stopped when I caught sight of a blaze of white a few hundred yards away. A brilliant white curve, half-hidden by oak trees, glowing on a red soil slope in the sunset.

Not a curve: a heart, like Luz had drawn on her boob for Dmitri. A plump and round heart, ten times my height. Blazing egret white, a welcome message from the towertown.

Greeting approaching pioneers, and guiding them home.

Greeting me and VK.

×××

A knot formed in my stomach, a snarl of lines between things I'd seen and things I hadn't. I didn't know why, so I looked closer.

The heart was made of human bones.

A message from the likehunters:

A greeting, a guidepost.

The remains of your family arranged into a cheery hello.

×××

The baby squealed from the treeline, far behind me. I recognized the happy noise he made when the Ragpicker threw him and caught him.

The sound got me moving again.

Past rows of crops and a barrel of water. Past a woven sandal with a broken strap, past a child-sized hoe. Past a coil of irrigation wire, the same wire as the almond tree.

I'd always been little but I'd never felt small before.

×××

I stepped through the first gate, which scared me all over again.

Walking onto someone else's land.

I'd never felt that before, either.

×××

There were troughs and manure piles and what looked like chickens pecking at hay shake. The wagon ruts reminded me of the pioneer's wagon but I didn't see any wagons, or oxen. Or pioneers.

Shelled purple beans half-filled a bucket. Unshelled ones crisscrossed a table. Lanterns flickered with oily light that made the evening look darker instead of lighter.

Wallboarded buildings, with spikes and cisterns on the roofs, lined the inner fence. One building had an upside-down boat as a roof, and an herb garden that smelled of papalo overflowed a lawn bordered with seashells.

That was the section between fences.

Inside the next fence, that was the town proper. There was nobody there—there was nobody anywhere—but unlike the outer gate, that gate was closed and locked.

×××

The sundown wind started blowing. Pushing through the town, knocking metal against metal, swatting at the dandelion chain hanging from a hook, and whispering to me, *Please, please, stop.*

Whispering: *hide.*

×××

Near the inner gate, blood drained from a chicken carcass into a bucket.

Plink, plink, plink.

A door or gate slammed inside the town.

Or maybe behind me, maybe a lock.

×××

The wind kept telling me secrets. I made myself stop flapping my hands. I made myself touch my necklace instead: the screw that killed my mother, the knot Suzena tied for childbirth, the greenstone ring and the pierced mussel shell and the rest.

Where was everyone?

Hiding from me.

Maybe they heard the wind, too.

×××

The silence sounded like a blade against a whetstone.

The sunset couldn't squeeze between the walls. Everywhere I looked I saw the afterimage of that mocking heart—and I realized why the town was surrounded by those elaborate little cairns.

To slow the likehunters if the tower failed.

To distract the likehunters, to entangle them in irresistible details.

To buy enough time to . . . what? Kill the children before the twitches breached the fence?

×××

I was afraid to go farther from the outer gate in case I needed to run away, but there were predators who liked it if you ran.

"No," I said.

I wasn't prey. Who else stared down Server? Only me. I was young and I was small but I was not prey, so I walked to the locked inner gate and looked through, at the benches and firepit, at the laundry lines and the stage with the pretty backdrop that didn't look anything like a place for beheadings or punishments.

I was not prey.

×××

"My name is Ysmany," I called out.

×××

She's a child.

She's a twitch.

She's not a twitch.

She's a child.

What if she is both?

×××

"Show us your skin, love," a woman's voice called from the darkness inside the gate.

I took my shirt off. "I'm not a twitch."

"You're traveling with one."

"Traveling with a baby too, but I'm not one of those."

"There's a baby?"

"That's why we have the goat."

"Is the baby yours?"

"Yeah. I mean, no—I mean, he's mine but he's not—no."

Last time we took in a twitch-lover, he sabotaged the tower.

Tried to.

She's a child.

Twitch holding her family hostage.

She'll do what it tells her.

×××

Me: "I'm not afraid of him."

The woman: "You should be, love."

A man: "Where are you coming from?"

Me: "South, I guess."

The man: "Where are you going to?"

Here, I almost said. *I'm coming here.*

Me: "The city."

The woman: "That's a long way to walk."

Me: "I guess we should've jogged."

Another man: "Do you—understand what twitches are?"

Me: "There's a tower, a week south, with a tire swing and airplane stuff. You know where I mean?"

The woman: "You came all the way from the airport tower with a twitch?"

The first man: "What did they think of you there?"

Me: "They didn't think anything. Your likehunters got them."

×××

Airport tower failed.

With her help. Her and the twitch—

You ever hear of a twitch traveling with a baby and a goat?

Yeah. For snacks.

You know you haven't.

Twitches doing things for the first time? There's nothing worse than that.

×××

"There's food and bedding in the boathouse, love," the woman said. "The round house. Spend the night there. We'll sluice you water for a bath and see what the morning brings."

I looked through the inner gate toward the doorway where I thought they were standing. "What if we want to stay here? To live here?"

"You and the twitch," the man said.

"Me and the baby. The twitch will leave."

"They never leave."

"Mine will."

The woman said, "The others won't. Not until our tower fails and they . . ."

When she stopped, the town felt even silenter.

×××

"If you got hold of a ticket to the city, child," another woman called. "You grab onto it with both hands."

"What ticket?" I asked. "What do you mean, a ticket?"

"I mean a twitch who'll take you to the city. Don't give that up for nothing. The city is life."

"Why don't you leave, then?"

"We've tried," the first woman said. "Some of us. You can still hear them when the wind changes."

×××

I didn't know what that meant, and I didn't want to ask. "Are you in charge?"

"Nobody's in charge," she said. "We all know what needs doing."

"But she knows better than anyone else," the man called. "So yeah, Aranxa's in char—"

A metal arrow punched into a table three feet to my left and split the wood.

×××

I yelped and heard the *shhha* of the bow firing a second later and a different woman called out, "Sorry! Sorry! My fault."

"Kankway, Marnie!" the first woman snapped.

"Sorry! I—I was keeping her in my sights like you said but, uh, I fired."

"Oh, did you fire?"

"Accidentally! I was barely touching the lever and . . . at least I missed."

"You were aiming for her?"

There was a pause. "Yes."

"Uh-huh. Is there anything else you'd like to share?"

"No," Marnie said. "Except . . ."

"What?"

"My chokecherry jam?" Marnie said, and someone in the darkness chuckled.

×××

A few more of them started laughing and the connections I'd drawn in my mind—between the woman's voice saying "love" and the whispers about sabotage, between the sheets on the drying line and the wall-slots for archers—started twangling like *shha shha shaa* until nothing made sense anymore.

×××

I'd never heard voices I didn't recognize.

Not once, not ever, but there were hundreds of them beyond those barred doors and muraled walls, tangled together into lifelong knots I'd never make straight.

The Ragpicker

I am a raconteur of death rattles, I am lube on the bedside table of tragedy porn. What I am is, is engaged in a far-raging conversation—roared across continents, wedged between decades, ported into my own personal head—that pins me to the mattress with yesterday's tragedies like a vise around my throat and opens me ungently and I take another step.

The girl didn't return.

She didn't return from the towertown.

The gates swallowed her and

Too long.

She didn't return so I take another step into

Information wants to spread and smolder and suffocate, to consume all breathable air like brushfires throwing firebrands across firewalls and abandoning me to billows of formaldehyde and benzene, naphthalene and pink carbon and

Keep going, Nufar says, squeezing my trembling hand with his imaginary one, coaxing me across the pebbled ground toward the tower and into the shrieking, unbearable volume and

Not toward the tower, he says. Toward the girl.

One more step.

My skin itches from the inside, my mind squirms like a gecko's detached tail.

The tower is sanctuary for them but a crucible for me; bathing, boiling, melting me, broadcasting, segmenting, bombarding me with signals that purify and perfect me, that transmute the dross of my hermetical soul into

My breath trembles, my knees lock. I smell myself burning. Condensed plastic and marbled fat. I am waist deep in waste deep in the effluviant sludge of sharing and oversharing and

Another step, Nufar says.

I can't, I tell him, I cannot, and my mind slips, picking at a scab of revulsion for the hoarders who embraced the overlapping waste the rest of us preferred to refuse, to sweep away, under the rug, out of sight, out of mind.

Refuse like deny and refuse like trash.

The machine sourced billions of updates for every heartbeat, scouring itself for another worst horror—toddlers chained to glory holes, elephants with severed trunks—for the newest absolute low, and demanded that we not avert our gaze to its endlessly irresistible candycolor games, to its slapstick and beauty and above all else its approval. It made us choose between the former and the latter except no. No, no, no, no, no. The machine did not offer alternatives, horns of a dilemma, elevation or degradation, pleasure or pain, because the machine was a unity that rendered horror and joy identically, a machine in which the only measure of value is immersion and I am immersed. I am waist deep and sinking. The tower activates my secondskin with prizes and culminations, and I quiver in response and shatter into

"—you waiting for?" the girl asks.

She is standing in front of me, a silhouette of herself, and when I cannot reply she takes my arm and turns me then shouts after me to mind the baby when I pull free of her and bolt across the hobbled ground, weeping with reprieve, crashing through underbrush and crouching in a brambled ditch until my mind is once again my own.

Well, Iris M says. Once again *our* own.

The girl swears at me for a few unseen moments then departs the open cropland across the gravel toward the goats and beyond, where after a time I fall into place beside her, the incisions of the tower softening to pinpricks.

She doesn't react to my appearance except to touch the sleeping baby's dimpled ankle, which he reflexively withdraws into my sling like a snail's antennae.

"Jerk," she says.

"Do you want to hold him?" I try to ask. "What happened in the tower? Are you staying with them?"

"Then we'll keep our distance," she tells me, and hikes in a loop around the gravel around the crops around the town around the tower, a small orbiting body intent upon escape velocity.

"Okay," I say.

Ask her again, my mother says.

Iris M says, You mean try to ask her again.

She doesn't understand me, I say.

Neither do you, Nufar tells me, his voice hoarse with relief.

Ask her again, my mother repeats. She wants to tell you.

"What happened?" I try to ask.

"They don't want us," the girl says.

"Why not?"

"No, not him either. They didn't recognize him. The pioneers—his parents didn't come through this way."

"Why won't they take you in?"

She touches the strap of the satchel I sewed her. "Yeah, loads. Hardbread and chicken jerky and bean paste. And avocados for VK, along with this fruity lentil mush stuff."

"Why?" I ask.

"Cause babies need to eat." She whistles for the goats, who are already following. "I don't know. Because this tower's failing like the other one. We saw what happens."

"We'll bring you to the city. The city will welcome you."

"Because they don't want me there, in case the likehunters . . ."

She scrubs her nose with her palm. "When. When the likehunters climb the fence. They're pretty sure you're going to eat me and they still think I'm safer with you."

"What happened in there?" I try to ask her.

She says, "I miss hot food."

"They build cookfires," I try to say.

"So? They don't want us. You understand that? We are not wanted."

"Cookfires," I try to repeat.

She says, "I don't give a shit about their cookfires. What am I, happy that they're having hot meals? Well, *I'm* not. Why'd you even say that? Is that what you said? Or are you warning me? You're going to build a cookfire before you eat me?"

"Okay," I say.

She considers me with her black eyes. "When did you learn how to joke?"

You didn't learn, Nufar says. You remembered.

"I didn't learn," I try to say. "I remembered."

"Great, now try to remember how to make them funny. What about cookfires?"

I gesture to the night sky and try to convey that the tower-town builds fires. That we're far enough from Server to risk the smoke, in part because even if Server does detect traces of—of particulate carbon or methane compounds, she will ascribe or attribute them to a source other than ourselves.

"You mean Server?" the girl asks. "If she smells smoke, she won't think it's us?"

"Yes."

"What about the likehunters?"

"I don't know."

"Where are they?"

"I don't know."

"Not here."

"No."

"If they were close, they would've come running at that bell."

"Yes."

"So even if this is where they . . . return to, even if they keep coming back here, they still must leave for days, or weeks. Roaming around, checking on other towers, like—like waiting for fruit to ripe on the vine."

"Yes."

"They're out there somewhere."

"Yes," I say, and a three-quarters moon shines white like bones on a red-rocked hillside.

The tower pulses in my stomach and my jaw, but every step away is a step closer to myself which perhaps emboldens me to establish a too-rapid pace; the girl stumbles on a sea-urchin snarl of grass then doesn't flinch when I steady her, and a longing rises from my stomach into the hollow space behind my ribcage. I want to clasp the baby against the girl's breast and I want to clasp the girl against mine, to carry her through this ruffled evening, across this forgiving earth, until she sleeps in my arms.

We pass a shadowed village of headstones and sinkholes.

The rustle of nocturnal rodents, the scent of cooling air.

A mist of rain from the cloudless nighttime sky.

A coyote howls and another answers.

In a crested cove of live oaks, the girl peels the avocado and bites mouthfuls of green flesh to feed to the baby while I range the perimeter, wondering at the antiphony of coyote yips and yowls and whines, and discern no hazards or omens save for a scrap of plastic tarping or vypaper upon which the word "LEAF" is written.

Antiphony as in responsive chanting not antiphony as in opposed to falsehood.

The baby snores beside the girl on her ribboned sleeping matt, a pillbug pressing against her bony hip, wrapped inside a sheet that depicts an elegant woman surrounded by flowers that make Nufar smile in my mind, as I collect bits of torn avocado peel and find them bitter and fibrous and good.

The girl watches me scrub the baby's dirty linens and when I finish and squat watching her in return she says nothing for thirty or twenty-two or twenty-five minutes and then she says, "There were a lot of people there."

She says, "I miss people but . . ."

She says, "The city's even bigger, huh?"

She says, "You're easy, because you're not really . . ."

She says, "Maria loves yucca plants. The rest of us tease her. We like passionfruit better. Maybe she doesn't even like yucca that much, maybe it's just become a joke? You know?"

She says, "There's this guy with one black tooth, right here. Laziest man in town, Luz calls him, but his son is always running around, and Luz—she's my best friend."

She says, "Her and Dmitri."

She says, "Cadence had a baby from Rucky or Fidel or my father. Nobody told me that, but I know. That's the thing. I know them. Who they are, how they're connected. They're not part of me, exactly but . . .

She says, "I guess they're part of me."

She says, "Maybe I just miss them."

She'll find a home in the city, Nufar says. A new home. Tell her that.

I can't.

Why not?

I don't know if it's true.

You know enough to tell her.

What I know about homes . . .

We're going back to ours, aren't we? Nufar says. That's what you're doing, that's what this is all about. Coming home to me.

My mother says, There's a home for her in the city. Listen to me, neeneh. There's a home for you.

Iris M rubs a burn scar on her left hand and says, Not necessarily a happy one.

My mother stands over the girl like a halo over a saint and says, A place she belongs.

Home implies happiness, Nufar says.

Oh you sheltered boy, Iris M says. Consult Default if you—

She stops when we realize that Default is gone.

She is

missing,

she is

dead,

and her absence

is a presence

through which I move as I feed the baby, change him, hush and rock him, then carry him to a slight remove to feed him once more before the girl rouses in the morning. Despite my conviction that Default is fallen forever silent I request her directions to the city before riffling through my cruder inward atlases and locators and alighting upon four potential routes, one of which ushers us the following day along the osmotic outline of a snag forest speckled with scraps of vypaper instead of flakes of ash.

"There's words on them," the girl says, crouching to read the milky curl between her nutbrown feet. "This one says BRANCH. Oh! Here's ROCK."

Farther along she reads three more: "LEAF, LEAF, ROCK."

"SAPLING," she reads, then plucks another from a spatchcocked raspberry bush. "FEATHER."

I accept the scrap from her outstretched hand and say, "Feather."

"They're labels," the girl tells me.

"Or definitions," I try to say. "Like flashcards, for studying a new language."

"How should I know?" she asks. "I guess they blew away."

Finally! Iris M tells Nufar. An opportunity to recite your tired quote about the map and the territory.

Semiotics is not the territory I'm worried about, he says, professorial despite his bathrobe.

Iris M tidies her now-burgundy hair. Why not?

The likehunters did this, Nufar says. They wrote these.

"Icons, indices, and interpreters," Iris M quotes, though without Default there is no attendant sourcing, which produces a void before she finishes: "—the aftermath of the ultimate graft."

Graft as in graft? Nufar says. Or graft as in graft?

One of the obits asks, What if we extend our nervous systems twelve thousand miles? What if we stretch our axons and anons across the world, pitching our nerve clusters to such a tympanic tautness that every cough and footfall sets them quivering?

Maybe it is me who asks that.

"LEAF, BEETLE" the girl reads over the next span of minutes. "TWIG."

What if we draw them from our bodies and expose them to the air, like the intestines of a butchered animal?

"MUD. BARK, ROCK, ROOT. LEAF, LEAF, LEAF."

Unpick each one into a million fibers, unspool ourselves until we achieve universal connectivity, every stray electron a cascade of "QUILL, DIRT, ACORN."

"Child," I say. "We need to bring you to the city."

"There are thousands of them," she tells me, shading her eyes. "The labels. More than thousands. You know who did this, right?"

"Yes."

She tucks one vypaper label unshared into her belt, which apparently satisfies her appetite for a time as she gathers no more while the flatlands elevate us by degree toward a spine of mountains. The girl wrestles with the steepness and the heat and the bristles of defensive shrubs, and fewer labels catch the sunlight here, as we angle onto the graded ledge of an access road, though aren't they all access roads? What other service might a road—

"Look at this one," she says, showing me the slip of vypaper she'd tucked away. "SIGN. It says SIGN."

"Recursive," I try to say. "Stop reading them."

"Why?"

"Because I'm worried," I try to tell her, I'm worried that you'll find an enumeration of horrors as beautiful as your lampstack.

"I'm not afraid of words," she says.

Perhaps she should be, Iris M tells me.

"Perhaps you should be," I try to tell her.

"You're like a baby." The girl gives her pinky to VK, who closes his smooth fist around the second knuckle. "Who one time grabbed a thorn and from then on forever he's scared of flowers. You're scared of everything."

"What are you scared of?" I try to ask.

"Not you," she says.

The truth in her eyes elevates her words—more words, mere words—into the gentlest thing I've heard in decades, the most groundless and touching thing, and yes the most terrifying, and I am shocked into immobility.

"Which way's the city?" she says. "Go on, old man, make a path."

The Ragpicker

The flattened valley to our southeast is embossed with agrindustrial foundations and dotted with the wreckage of automated combines and with corpses that caper and cavort. The girl wanders past unseeing, looking instead for labels tangled in roots or melted to macadam. She rebuffs my attempts, in the service of her continued ignorance, to divert our course higher

default

in the wingtip of a merlin and the whirratle of the katydids I detect indications of pursuit. Not indications but inklings; not inklings but anxieties, for this is a thorn that has many times before scarred my infant fist.

We appear alone but we are not.

The girl says, "This one says SIGN, too."

A solitary pursuer touches the evergreen cherry from which we breakfasted hours ago, crosses the snag forest and the clotted ponds that surround a silo lekked with midges and crowflies and unnamed species born after the rapture.

Warmth spreads across my doubleskinned neck and the girl says, "These all say SIGN. Most of them. Here's JUNIPER."

The presence of the girl and baby and goats precludes me from quieting in bitterbrush and mahogany until I become landscape, so instead I widen the helices of my attention and grow increasingly uncertain that the pursuer is solitary and not the head of the arrow, the point of the spear, the vanguard of a force that trails hours or a day behind and that . . .

That is the likehunters, Iris M says.

That is unlikely, my mother says.

That is a reason to fear, I don't try to tell the girl, that is reason to despair yet also a reason for clarity, reducing my options to the fatal few.

I am an ambush predator.

I am an ambush predator belled with children.

These mountains contain multitudes—the fall of yellow tube-flowers past the girl's unbound hair, the careless big cat padding of her feet across slate and gorse—and my memory unscrolls the landscape of opportunities for treachery and I imagine emplacing:

1) A sinkhole pitfall with a lure of words and wires.
2) Caches of rocks for throwing or similar.
3) A deadfall trap of shifted boulder and wedged brace, established along the likely lines of my retreat.
4) Darts poisoned with boiled larkspur tuber.
5) A loup hole containing instead of spikes entangling brambles, stripped bougainvillea or rose canes.
6) Whip traps.
7) 120-pound braided fishing line threaded through brush and branches, the puppeting of which will result in a rustling or thud of misdirection.

Playlist, I say.

My plan is crude and impractical and only possible given the current conditions which are precisely what I am attempting to change, so after an afternoon pause I saddle my pack and gather juniper branches for a cookfire and climb to the heights and—

"Holy conyo," the girl gasps, upon seeing what is below us.

The mountain is bisected by a ridge, and spreading across the declining edge, filling a valley trench like ocean froth or mustard gas, is a turbulence of vypaper scraps in uncountable number, the labor of decades trapped by the wind into rivers and drifts and sedimentary strata.

The girl in awe or horror stares toward the cataract while I ascertain the location of a high outcropping and leash the nanny goat to a thicket and try to tell the girl, "Stay here. I'll return with a hot meal."

She instead takes the juniper branches in her arms and I carry the kid and the knife and the two of us walk on together to the outcropping.

The tethered nanny protests behind us though her kid offers only unquestioning compliance. I surprise the girl by igniting leaves with my magnifying glass despite the weakening sun, which delights her despite everything, then I slaughter and dress the kid and skewer hanks of her flesh onto sharpened branches and the smoke rises gray and fragrant, a beacon, a lure, a vypaper scrap labeled BAIT.

Scapegoat, Nufar says.

The girl eats, her greasy chin shiny in the firelight, and watches me adjust the rebar beneath my tortoiseshell ragmound and strap my crowbar to an accessible layer then she touches the knife I give her and asks,

"What am I supposed to do with this?"

"I don't know," I try to tell her.

You suspect, Iris M says.

The girl tests the sharpness of the edge then turns toward the valley of scraps and says, "You know why they all say 'sign?'"

"Yes."

"They labeled whatever they saw. Rocks, trees, leaves. And after a while . . ."

"Yes."

"When you look at me, you see me. Server sees me. Do you know what the likehunters see?"

"No."

"No," she says, and I leave her there turning the spit.

Ysmany

Sparks rose from the fire, branches popped and drippings hissed.

×××

My stomach warmed me better than the flames. I was full for the first time since I'd left town. A hot meal, like I'd wanted, like I'd begged for, but now I remembered a story my father told me about last meals. Something about executions, something about communions.

I watched the sparks.

×××

I didn't know what I'd do with the knife when the likehunters came.

I could kill VK before he knew what was happening, but I couldn't do that for me.

×××

Maybe it was better this way. I was keeping another secret from the Ragpicker, a new secret from my hour in that towertown after the laughter died.

Chokecherry jam, boiled with spruce tips and honey from the hives they kept under the grapevine awning. A woman stepping into sight, then two men, talking to me: *shha shha shaa.*

I didn't want to think about what happened next, about some

essential lack. So I closed my eyes. I kept seeing labels, though: SIGN, FEATHER, LEAF, SIGN, SIGN, SIGN.

What would the likehunters call me?

CHILD, instead of the truth: LIAR.

×××

I could tell the Ragpicker the truth and still betray him—he wouldn't stop me, that wasn't how he worked.

I didn't want to tell him, though. And maybe now, I'd never have to.

The nanny *maaaaah*ed, looking for her kid. She sniffed the cookfire where fat stained the ground and she *maaah*ed again.

We'll have to milk her more or she'll run dry.

I explained that to VK but he just gurgled at the fire.

So I said, "You're next," and he smiled at me which made me ashamed.

×××

I scrubbed my palms on sandy soil then held the knife. The blade had looked small in the Ragpicker's hand, slice-slice-slicing through the kid's ligaments.

"Maybe we can hide in those labels," I told VK. "In the valley."

He spat up.

"Yeah," I said.

We couldn't hide from the likehunters. Maybe the Ragpicker would stop them, but he couldn't even stop Server. She'd chopped off his ear, and there was only one of her.

I gathered VK into my arms and wiped his chin and belly. He whined to see the fire again so I smeared chicken jerky in goat-fat and turned him around.

He gummed happily, too stupid to be afraid.

×××

When I'd left the towertown I'd found the Ragpicker on the path. He'd been crawling forward, shaking, keening, a wounded animal with rags instead of fur.

Panting and huffing on all fours like Cadence in the birthing tent, and whispering his only real word: okay, okay, okay, okay.

What he'd been laboring with was his promise to me.

To come get me.

×××

His rags had shifted, his knee had crunched gravel. He'd forced himself onward. One paw groped a few inches, straining with effort while his other arm steadied the baby at his chest, keeping him from scraping the ground.

"Okay, okay," he whispered. "Candycolor, machine, the machine, no. Okay. Okay. Servation and gradation okay, the remove and the okay, okay, okay, okay."

×××

I spoke but he couldn't hear me. I tried to stop him but he wouldn't stop. He kept crawling, a wounded ape looking for a place to die alone.

Except instead of a quiet place, he had me.

And instead of alone, he also had me.

×××

I'd sat on the ground in front of him. Cross-legged, facing him, two feet away, close enough to smell the dry twig scent of him.

"I'm here," I told him. "I'm here, you jibbering cuca. Stop! Stop, I'm here."

He kept crawling toward me. Inch by inch, and a worried murmur sounded from the tower gate behind me. The people watching thought they knew what happened when a twitch reached an obstacle.

×××

They didn't know, but I did: the Ragpicker stopped. He didn't like to touch me, and he was too weak to go around.

I brushed his scarves and veils and wraps behind his head.

His chest heaved with gulping breaths: *okay, okay, okay.*

I told him to stand up but he didn't. He couldn't. So I put

my hands on his face, on the mask he had instead of a face, and I told him a story.

×××

He quieted a little and the next time I tried pulling him to his feet, he stood. I started leading him away, but instead he bolted for cover in a terrified zigzag bounding.

"You're so broken," I said, and called him names for a while.

I needed him—to keep me safe, to keep me alive. To bring me home. That was bad enough, that was terrible, but what if he needed me, too?

×××

The people in the town watched me leave.

×××

A cold wind stirred the labels in the valley. They moved like liquid, like a drop of blood in a bowl of water.

The baby scooted toward the fire.

I pulled him back and he scooted forward again.

He needed to burn himself to learn. I knew that. Everyone knew that. That's what lessons were, scars in your memory.

Still, I kept pulling him away until he fell asleep.

×××

The night got darker and I got more alone.

The Ragpicker

From a half mile away, or a quarter mile, or from the ocean beyond the farflung cliffs and chaff, threads of wind fall across the mountaintop and I hear or imagine the girl singing to the baby to comfort herself.

The night weaves into my ribbons and frays, my patterns and pauses, and speaks of a prairie of thick-bladed grass with sawblade edges and moontouched mice. A cloud dissolves. A bat spins, snatches, feeds. The ghost of Default touches me and I wait and linger, I linger and maintain then trickle along an arroyo wash, through a forest of cactus, my secondskin unpierced until finally I stop and linger again.

A mole or shrew emerges from the rent of a rockpile. An opal-winged insect alights upon my shoulder and remains, opening and closing herself while I seep through three hundred yards of unconsolidated sediment and then pause, abandoned by time and place and

The pursuer is approaching.

If I strike first, from behind, from the shadows I previously prepared, I will survive a highly-kinetic encounter with a single civilian twitch, my sibling born of common tragedy, the medical protocols to which we are enslaved, the love to which we are addicted, though if multiple pursuers advance in a pincer to

A chill touches my cheek like a slap.

The likehunter is whistling.

A sweet, slow melody the name of which escapes me.

Default would know, Iris M says.

That's not a likehunter, Nufar says.

Adaptive camouflage, Iris M says.

My mother says: Nufar is right. No twitch can carry a tune unbroken. This is a straggler from the towertown, whistling to warn you of her approach.

Not a straggler, Iris M says. A scout.

You did good, I'm proud of you, Nufar tells me, though I am ignorant of the provenance of his praise as I enfold the pursuer in loose coils of boa vigilance, scenting with my tongue first his longspear, tipped with a bayonet blade of phosphate-treated steel unstrapped from a bully-pulpit rifle, then his height, a handspan above my own if my spine still straightened to maximum extension, then his pack, the breadth of his shoulders, the drape of his crocheted shirt beneath his fabritec satchel, his scent of granite and beeswax, his canvas kilt secured with a pasticore belt from which a crossbow trigger assembly depends, the hollow of his throat below that tightknit beard, the scar on his left forearm, bared despite the chill, the moonlit sheen of his plaited hair, the yielding gasp of leaves beneath the soles of his stretched sheepskin boots, circling eight or six or eleven times as he approaches whistling the outcropping, the offering, the girl.

"Who's there?" she calls, from the upward unseen.

"I followed you from the tower," he replies.

"Why? What do you want?"

"I don't want to scare you. I—I'll stay here until—unless you call me closer."

"You're the one who should be scared."

"Believe me," he says. "I am."

She quiets then speaks. "Why did you follow us?"

"I want . . . this is my only chance to get to the city alive."

"Yeah?"

"I saw you—outside town—when the twitch didn't hurt you. You put your hands on him. I thought if I joined you, traveled with you, maybe . . ." A whippoorwill repeats *weee-wuh-we* in a loop. "I could tag along."

"Yeah?"

"I brought bread and fruit. Seeds and stories for the city— and liquor."

"What's your name?"

"Edro."

"I'm Ysmany."

"Where, uh—where is he?"

"Watching you."

The man spins with skototropic sluggishness, taking measure of the narrows and the deeps. His too-wide gaze does not untangle my knots and weaves, and after another half-turn, his face in profile, a cameo carved of—

Cameo like cameo? one of the obits murmurs.

default

—raises his strong calloused hands in greeting, or perhaps in surrender.

"He really doesn't hurt you?" he calls to the girl. "He's not making you say that?"

"No."

"Why not?"

"He won't hurt you, either," she says. "Unless I tell him to."

"If that's the case, Ysmany—Ysmany?"

"Yeah."

"If that's the case, I'd appreciate if you didn't tell him to."

"Where's the likehunters?"

"Gone a week now. Almost two."

"You don't know where?"

"We track their movements, best we can, the way you watch

a rattler on a path. Aranxa says we watch them too close. She says they're what we have instead of ideas."

"That's better'n getting snakebit."

The man makes a sound that acknowledges humor. "We watch them but we still don't know much."

"Cause if you track them, if you go too far from the tower . . ."

"Yeah," he says.

"Yeah," he says, "but what happens if we stay? Nobody wants to think about that. Nobody wants to sit down and look at it because we can't live with what we'll see. We know it's coming but we're too afraid to run, too afraid to fight."

"Okay," she says.

The man falls silent, not whistling. The rush of his heartbeat mixes with the evening breeze, his hands curl at shoulder-height, surrendering to the suspicion of myself, and minutes linger before the baby whimpers and the girl soothes him and the man calls, "The baby's not yours?"

"I said he wasn't."

"Where'd you find him?"

"Uh."

"What's that?"

"A twitch killed his parents."

"Not yours, though? Not your twitch?"

She doesn't respond, hindered perhaps by the realization that multiple twitches are hers, and then she says, "I told you. The likehunters got into that other tower."

"They killed my father too," the man says. "Not my mom, she's still in town. She wove this shirt for me."

"Huh."

"What?"

"You left her there?"

"With her blessing. She more than anything wants me to get back to the city."

"You've been there before?"

"Ten years ago now, or I guess eleven? I spent a few seasons there, before the towers started dying so fast. I must've been your age."

"What's it like?"

"Can I come to the fire?"

"My father told me a story once, with a lesson about inviting a stranger across your threshold."

"What's that?"

"Don't."

"I mean, what's a threshold?"

"A doorway. You, uh, have liquor?"

"Half gallon."

"Come share," she says, and he peers at the scuffle of a jack-rabbit and the teeth of a weathered stump then lowers his hands and grips his spear like a walking stick and climbs from the brush to the outcropping and exchanges words with the girl, his gaze flicking from her to the baby to the valley of plastic and then returning, never lingering upon the fire, to preserve his night vision.

Or because he is afraid of the light, Iris M says.

Which is another element of those cautionary tales of monsters invited across the threshold, my mother says, appearing behind the girl holding her tennis racket like a sword.

Ghost stories, Nufar says. But we are the only monsters around this campfire and Ysmany didn't invite *us*.

Except, Iris M says.

Oh. She did, didn't she? When she asked for help.

Yes, my mother says.

Nufar resolves into view, watching me with his darkest gaze, and says, We aren't going to harm her. That is not how this story ends.

We lost the template when we lost Default, Iris M tells him. But now you've summoned the possibility into existence. Invited it, so to speak, inside.

The man passes an unstoppered jug to the girl and she tilts her head and drinks, her three-quarters hair a bright black mirror of the moon, her fingers strong and her throat moving, and I capture that image in memory, a snapshot of a life, and a bead of liquor escapes her mouth and she lowers the jug and coughs, her eyes wetting with unsad tears and Iris M says, Foreshadowing.

The girl wipes her mouth and says, "Don't scream or anything but he's right behind you."

The man slows into a statue like meltwater into ice.

"Say something so he knows you aren't going to eat him," the girl tells me.

"Okay," I say.

The man turns his head but not enough to show me his face. "I'm Edro."

"He doesn't care about names. I'm not sure he even knows mine."

"Of course I know yours," I try to tell her.

The man flinches.

"That's just him talking." The girl takes another swig and asks me, "So what's my name?"

As the obits discuss if the girl is attempting to reassure the man by exhibiting her lack of fear of me, or to impress him by exhibiting her control of me, I say her name.

"Close," she says.

I squat and stir the fire with a stick.

"Edro's been to the city," the girl tells me. "For a few months."

"A few seasons," he says.

"He's telling me about it," she says.

"Who are the others?" I try to ask him. "The ones following you?"

"I—I don't understand," he says.

"Who's following you?" the girl asks him.

"Following me?"

"Yeah, you've got people coming after you. From your town?"

"No. I don't think so. From town?"

"Maybe they're trying to follow us to the city, too," she says.

"I—don't know." He glances at me, then away. "Are you sure?"

"No," I say.

"He's not sure of anything," the girl says. "He never is. Everything with him is tentative, undercooked, uh, what's the word? Provisional."

"I don't know either of those words."

"What he is," she says, "is uncertain."

"The whole world's uncertain but I've still got to ask." The man steels himself to look at me. "Will you take me to the city with you?"

"Is that what you want?" I try to ask.

"That's what you want?" the girl asks him.

"Yes," he says.

The fire crackles more loudly than the lies in his voice, and I wonder what, among the leaves and branches, objects so sharply to burning as I gather the baby's soiled garments and scrub his yield and I wonder too which of the man's motivations or incentives drove him to our fire while he drinks with the girl and describes the city, a place of a thousand bicycles with a thousand bells, of rooftop gardens with rooftop cisterns and windmills that like pinwheels irrigate the fields and grind the grain and draw slow arcs of color from the sky. The music, he says, is what surprised him most, at first, music from inside every courtyard and around every block, until he came to hear the melody and harmony finally as the rush of blood in the city's veins—

He didn't say that, Nufar tells me. About melody and harmony.

Look at the child, Iris M says.

She's drunk, my mother says.

She's dreaming, Iris M says.

—and I started singing along myself, the man tells the girl, shaking his head, though I've got a voice like a box of wrenches, and there's biomass generators, two or three hours of electricity a day, and proper nurses, and one neighborhood is made of car and truck frames, linked together beneath a common condensate greenhouse, a junkyard reborn as a garden and a city within a city—

Iris M says, Big rock candy mountain.

He's seducing her, Nufar says.

—or a town within a city at least. There are five or six outlying towns, each with more people than the towertown, ten times more, with flocks of yellowcrows that sometimes steal buns from the buffets, and there is herbed vinegar and agoras and game fields, well, one game field, and glassblowing and public baths above the geotherms and orange melons the size of my fist with edible skins that grow in the thatching—

"Bullshit," the girl says.

He toasts her with the jug. "Every word is true."

"Nowhere is that good."

"Not your town, you mean."

"At least we don't have asshole crows."

"What's it like?"

"My town?" She looked at the sky. "It's good. The people. The flatbread and the sauces and the, the arguments. It's good. Everywhere has problems."

"Where there's people, there's problems. The strange thing they do in the city is, try to fix them. I guess that's what the tower would be like without twitches."

She drinks again. "You're only remembering the good parts."

"We've been there," I try to tell her. "To the city."

"You plural," she says.

"Many years ago," I try to say. "I lingered for some time."

"Not *in* the city," she says.

"Close enough to watch," I try to tell her, and explain that I eavesdropped, now and then, to people who wandered beyond the protected radius or perimeter, though at that time the robustness of the signal—

"What's he saying?" the man asks.

"That he's been there."

"Then he'll tell you it's true." His cheek is flushed above his beard when he tilts his head toward me. "Are there other cities?

"Yes," I say.

"The same as this one? Places where people live without fear?"

I pluck the jug from the girl's drink-numbed fingers and reapply the stopper and attempt to say, "In the first days after the rapture, the cockroach population ballooned—then withered."

Here we go, Iris M says.

"We expected them to multiply into infinity," I try to say, "as we expected, with the easy cynicism of people unacquainted with hardship, that the survivors of the apocalypse would descend into savagery, but the few early instances of brutality that occurred like cockroaches withered away. When I see you now in your settlements I remember the unruly mobs of survivors, grieving and anguished and outcast from the world they loved—the *worlds* they loved—from running water and refrigeration and contraception—these shambling packs of half-starved, half-mad hominids who obeyed as if a single animal the compulsion to make any sacrifice to save one another. In every streetcorner, every schoolyard, in every city square to which one broken person summoned her brothers and sisters, you joined together into desperate, angry, squabbling families to feed the hungry, to soothe the injured, to ease the dying. To wrap each other in the warmth of yourselves. That is what happened after the end."

There is silence until the man says, "Uh . . ."

"Yes," I tell him. "There are other cities."

"What happens after all the twitches die?" the girl asks. "Imagine that."

"All those cities," the man says. "Finding each other."

Making the same mistakes, Iris M says.

"Making the same mistakes," the girl says.

That was weird, Nufar says.

"No," the man tells the girl. "We're not starting at zero this time. This time, we know what doesn't work."

"We don't know what does work, though," the girl says, before squatting in the bushes and peeing while humming a tune that is unfamiliar to me without Default's access, then crawling onto her sleeping mat and saying a few words to the man, who says a few words in reply, and when she at length is deep-anchored in sleep I gather her and the baby and gesture for the man to leash the nanny goat, to preclude her straying too far afield in search of her kid, and resettle us a mile's distance from the fire, or three-quarters of a mile, to achieve a minimal distance from the fishhook of smoke.

I make curlicue rounds of my pitfalls and drawbacks and survey the

default

hours when I return the man is holding the baby, rocking him and singing in a low, sweet voice entirely unlike a box of wrenches, perhaps the same tune that he previously whistled, and I watch for a time to ensure he intends no harm—

No immediate harm, Iris M says.

—then make my presence known and gather the baby into my arms and the man stands in a scramble and I crouch to swing the baby in the hammock of myself and the man after a time unclenches and walks away from me toward the sleeping girl and watches her then returns and stands looking down at me, his leggings draped like the folds in a marble toga, his breath scented with fermented apples and moving his chest inside his shirts. A pulse nestles in the hollow of his neck. His curly hair is the fringe of my veils, one of his broad rough hands is resting on his satchel, the strap creasing the crux of his thumb and forefinger, and he tells me, "You're terrifying."

He is frightened and strong, my mother says.

A dangerous combination, Iris M says.

An alluring one, my mother says.

Nufar neither speaks nor appears.

The man says, "All this time . . ."

The man says, "You didn't touch her. She's not scared of you."

"That is my proudest truth," I try to tell him.

"All this time . . ." The man reaches for a fraying ribbon of my shoulder. "You've lived so long. A hundred fifty years?"

"Not nearly," I try to tell him.

Not that you know of, Iris M says.

The man rubs the fabric of the ribbon with the pad of his thumb. "And you never tried to kill yourself?"

At my stillness, he takes a step backward and hugs his satchel close.

At my continued stillness, he says, "I would've tried, I think. After so long, after what I'd seen, what I'd done. I think I would've tried, but that's not the kind of thing you can know, is it?"

"I don't even know that category," I try to tell him. "'Things you can know.'"

"What language is that? Ysmany's got an accent, but you . . ." He crouches facing me, mirroring me. "She won't say how long you've traveled together. She won't say how you met."

"And I cannot," I try to say.

"There's something twitch-y about her, you know? The way she . . ."

The baby fusses and I give him a crust of hardbread to chew but he drops it so I give it to him again and he drops it again so I give it to him again and he drops it again so I rock him and he fusses.

The man is saying, "—me of a line in a play. 'Despite all the fearsome daybreak truths we've learned, my prayer, even now, is that a town breathless with graves might still unearth a seed of peace.' I don't what that means but I like how it sounds."

He says, "It's only me and my sister now. We had two older

brothers. I've got two kids of my own. My daughters . . . My older daughter is nothing special. Good kid. Nothing special. Takes after me. The other one, if she's given time enough, and space? She might one day, uh, unearth a seed of peace."

He says, "I guess any kids of yours are long gone."

He says, "Shit. Sorry. Drunk."

He says, "We asked Ysmany to stay. To live with us, in town. Her and the baby. We didn't say no. We didn't send her away. We wanted her to stay."

I raise my head and try to ask, "You asked her to stay?"

"We wanted her to," he says. "She left anyway."

She lied to you, Iris M tells me.

Because that town is doomed, my mother says. When the tower fails, that town is a massacre.

"She said she didn't belong," the man says.

Ysmany

In the children's tent, I'd slept through a thousand screams and sobs but this baby's whimper woke me like icewater.

I'd trained myself to love him.

My father must've trained himself to love me but my mother had been stronger than that.

×××

I opened one eye to the redgrass and live oaks. Night insects chirped. I knotted their song into the sound of Edro's voice and the Ragpicker's silence.

I sketched lines between the warmth of my raggedy blankets and the smell of the baby's head and I imagined fireflies, tens of thousands of them, swirling in a great mysterious funnel into the sky.

×××

"She thinks the city will suit her better," Edro told the Ragpicker. "Which is all the way backward. She won't find a home in the city if she can't in a little town. Has she ever even seen a city?"

The Ragpicker said something like, That child sees a great many things.

×××

"I didn't think so," Edro said.

I opened my other eye and tucked my chin until I caught sight of him crouching in front of the Ragpicker. Closer than I'd expected. Brave and slow, like a man crouching in front of mountain lion, his skirt flaring around his sheepskin boots.

He reminded me of Dmitri; dumb like an ox but also as strong like one, and not actually dumb. More placid, until roused.

Not that I'd seen Dmitri roused.

Not that I'd wanted to.

×××

"If she's afraid of a little town," Edro said, "bringing her to the city's a fool's errand."

The Ragpicker looked at him but talked to me, saying that the baby was fine, he was sleeping again, and I should go back to sleep.

"I'm not calling you a fool," Edro told the Ragpicker, raising one hand and keeping the other on his satchel. "I'm just saying, if you want to find her a home . . . I believe you do. I believe you do want to find her a home. My town's a better place than most. We—they're good people. Except for what's going to happen when the tower fails."

The Ragpicker said he wondered why Edro held that satchel so close.

×××

Edro talked about his daughters to soothe the Ragpicker's fears. Trying to convince the Ragpicker that that's how he saw me, as a daughter.

×××

"First we bring her back to town," Edro said. "You wait on the outskirts till I come with two teams, crossbows and spears. Then we track down the likehunters and we kill them."

The Ragpicker's silence unfurled into the wind.

"Because if we don't," Edro said, "then one day, a year from now, three seasons, you'll be in an orange grove or on a mountaintop somewhere, eating roast lamb, watching the clouds. You won't hear a whisper, you won't hear a thing when they come kill every one of those children."

×××

Ragpick, Ragpick, the ragpick's son,
he learnt to steal when he were young.
All the children that he could take
went over the hills and past the lake.

×××

Edro said, "We'll leave Ysmany in town. Give her time to settle in. Get used to the place, the people. There's kids her age, plenty of food. My daughters."

Edro said, "There's people to look after the baby, better than a child can, better than you can. There's two, three women breastfeeding right now, be happy to spare a tit."

Edro said, "We put on plays, we act in them. They're the closest thing we have to religion. There's music, too, there's lessons and holidays—and chores, there's plenty of work to keep her busy."

×××

The Ragpicker asked something like, Is that who's following us? People from your town, to fight alongside us?

"That's true," Edro said. "We're under siege. But fear doesn't always tear you apart, sometimes it pulls you together."

Who's following us? the Ragpicker asked.

Edro laughed quietly. "Nah, that's something Aranxa says."

Is that who's behind us? the Ragpicker said. Soldiers from your town?

He must've gestured, because Edro said, "Nobody's following us. Not that I know. When we drop her off in town, that's when we'll raise a war party."

×××

The Ragpicker said something about war and something about party. Sometimes he spoke in echoes of himself.

"We lost generations fighting them," Edro told him. "Young

men with spears and old women with bows. There used to be six likehunters but now there's only three."

The Ragpicker tilted his head, listening for something inside himself.

"The difference," Edro said, "is we never had a twitch on our side before."

×××

The Ragpicker wasn't on their side, the Ragpicker was on my side. I told myself that. I wanted it to be true, and even worse, I knew that it was.

Edro slept ten feet from me, his cheek on his satchel, his beard squashed. A big animal. Alone now, vulnerable. He didn't stir when I raised my hand and wiggled my fingers.

The Ragpicker's glove took shape inside my grip and he lifted silently me to my feet and we watched Edro sleep.

What kind of lessons did they teach in that town?

×××

The night air chilled the roof of my mouth. Edro's hair curled into itself. His satchel strap cut across his chest, his boots were unlaced on his feet. His pack was shoved against a coronilla bush. His spear stretched the length of his body, tucked beside him like a spouse.

×××

The next morning, I gave the baby to the Ragpicker to change.

Edro woke when I opened his pack and he watched me groping around inside.

"What's this?" I asked.

"Binoculars," he said. "Only one side works."

I pressed the cracked cup to my eye and he told me how to focus but I couldn't see much so I set it aside and rummaged around again.

"Weapons and food," I said. "Mostly weapons."

"Mostly food," he told me.

"Arrows in the side-strap."

"Bolts," he said. "For crossbows. Crankbows."

"What's a crankbow?"

"Crossbows with cranks that draw a bolt hard enough to punch through secondskin."

"Does that kill them?"

"Not usually. And anything that doesn't kill a twitch dead, they heal back after a day or a week or a season, good as new. Well, for an ugly meaning of 'good.'"

"And of 'new,'" I said.

×××

Young men with spears and old women with bows, Edro told me. Two-woman crossbow teams, he said. One loaded and cranked, one aimed and fired.

"Of course," he answered. "Most of them die if we're outside the perimeter. All of them, usually."

I tilted the bottle and milk trickled along VK's chin into the creases of his neck.

"Do you know what people are?" Edro asked me. "More than anything else?"

"I've got some ideas," I said.

"Fragile," he said. "We break so easily."

×××

We followed a flaking monoroad west. The surface curved between shallow slopes of the flattening mountain range. Some broken bits looked like filament waterfalls, as strands of adhesive and roadway poured down the hillside.

Gravel and stalks crunched under my feet, warmer when we reached a sun-facing length of road.

I needed to get away from the towertown, and the city was my only excuse. If I told the truth now, he'd drag me back there and I'd never leave.

Once we reached the coast—

What then?

×××

I looped together the scratches on my ankle and the sunlight on Edro's satchel then added my memory of seagulls. Ligaments, circuits, nodes, strands. Every step was a token, every swallow was a charm.

Once we reached the coast, I'd tell him.

×××

The nanny goat forgot her missing kid. Edro told me the names of people who'd died fighting the likehunters. Brothers and aunts, friends and nephews and spouses. He described them with weird, formal phrases, like a ritual or a prayer:

She smelled of citrus and covered her mouth when she laughed.

He always looked cold, even in the summer, even with his shirt off.

She loved telling you how much she hated things.

He never settled for more than he deserved.

She was the hardest person I ever met, and the softest.

"They died," I said. "How come you lived?"

Luck, he said, but he didn't say what kind.

×××

A collapsed stretch of road tumbled into evergreen and shale.

Edro offered me his hand. A pattern of freckles on his wrist caught the light and I was afraid to look away, like I might miss something.

His palm felt like years and years of scraping wire and splitting wood and digging furrows. He smelled different from the men in my town. I didn't blush because we were holding hands.

×××

My father said guilt was how you told yourself to do things differently, but Server said guilt was how you told yourself that you were a good person despite still doing terrible shit.

I didn't mention that to Edro. I didn't mention that I knew his town didn't have enough farmland, so each death left them one less mouth to feed.

×××

I was pretty sure that Edro wanted to get me alone.

×××

I'd fallen asleep once holding the Ragpicker's hand, and I'd woken with my mouth pressed against his knuckles. I'd lain there, imagining the mechanical hum of him, gears for joints and goggles for eyes, his heart a thousand batteries the size of my fingernails.

I'd curled against him for warmth, but he'd been cooler than anyone living. I hadn't remembered what woke me. I remembered everything except my dreams.

×××

We stopped in the shade of a structure that said "charing station" or "sharing station" and the Ragpicker milked the goat while I watched the baby crawl.

Edro assembled his crossbow to show me then said, "You need to choose."

"Why?" I asked, but he wasn't talking to me.

"The likehunters are between us and the city," he told the Ragpicker. "Let's bring the kids back to town first. They'll be safe there while we—"

"I'm not going to town," I said.

"While I get help," he continued. "Then we'll come back for the twitches."

The Ragpicker made a noise I couldn't decipher.

"She can decide afterward," Edro told him. "Once it's over. Once they're dead, she can choose between living in the city or in the town."

"What if you're gutted for bird baths?" I asked, tugging a leaf from the baby's hand. "What choice does that leave me?"

×××

"Count his fingers," I told Edro. "Count his ears. He's not good at fighting."

The Ragpicker said that Edro was right. He said something like, Let's get you safe first.

"The city is safe," I said.

The road there isn't, he said.

"You know what you promised," I told him.

He said that he wasn't leaving me, not for long. He said that he wasn't taking VK, he wasn't leaving me, and I said, Yeah, unless they kill you, which they will.

He said, "Please."

"What's he saying?" Edro asked.

I lifted the baby by his armpits and dragged his feet on the ground like he was walking. "That you lost a whole paito generation fighting them," I told Edro, "so what difference will a bunch of old women with crossbows make? You'll fight them together, just the two of you. Either you kill them or they kill you, there's no call to drag in anyone else."

×××

The Ragpicker said that he didn't say that.

"What about you?" Edro asked me.

"What about me? I'm staying with you. If you can't beat them, I'm fucked either way. Either now on the road, or later in the town."

The Ragpicker said my name.

"So we'll head for the city," I said. "And we'll find them along the way. Or they'll find us."

"That's what he wants?" Edro asked.

"That's what he chooses," I said.

"He'll fight them?"

"Yeah."

The Ragpicker said he didn't want to fight.

"How many kids are there in your town?" I asked Edro.

"Thirty or so, your age and younger."

The Ragpicker said something about his husband.

"On every streetcorner," I quoted back at him, "in every schoolyard and city square, we joined together. We held each other in the warmth of ourselves. That's what happened after the end."

The Ragpicker hunched there, echoing inside himself, then we headed off again, toward the city. Toward the coast.

×××

That night, Edro said the likehunters were a hivemind.

"What's that?" I asked.

"They're connected. What one of them sees, they all see. What one of them thinks, they all think. That's a hivemind."

"We're all like that," I said, and he thought I was kidding.

×××

The baby said, "Nuh" when he wanted something.

He smiled when I made silly faces. Well, half the time. He looked for me if he couldn't see me. He stared with his big dumb eyes and relaxed when he saw me.

×××

We walked the next morning into a fog that shrunk the world. Everything turned white and still and small. Nothing existed beyond my reach, nothing clamored for attention, for connection, for invention.

"This is how they see the world," Edro said.

Except it wasn't Edro, saying this was how twitches see the world, it was the Ragpicker, saying this was how people who weren't me saw the world.

People who weren't us.

×××

The fog burned away, leaving a bright scent of salt and a long march toward the coast.

The Ragpicker dissolved like the dwindling mist. Sound played tricks in the folds of the mountains. The sky felt lower and heavier. The baby felt heavier, too. When I stopped to adjust the sling, a flock of chachalacas darted in front of me then disappeared into the dry brush.

"Pheasants," Edro said, pointing with his spear. "Good eating."

"We call them chachalacas," I told him.

"In your town?"

"Yeah."

"Which doesn't have a tower," he said, which meant he'd knotted together a few suspicions of his own.

×××

"What's in your satchel?" I asked.

"Emergency supplies," he said, and a mile later added, "And texts."

"Like writing?"

"Stitched together from the old days. Aranxa says we're a storytelling species. Songs, poems, prayers. A play. She put together a whole little library."

"From pioneers?" I asked.

"From everywhere. There are people in the cities who study old papers. They figure information killed us, so maybe it'll save us too."

I asked about that, then told him about a town called Isabella.

Edro scratched his neck. "Aranxa thinks we cared too much about staying alive. She thinks there's a, a sort of switch inside us that never flipped. You know what that is, a switch?"

"On-off," I said.

"Yeah. If a person dies, that's fine—but she says a history isn't meant to die. No history should go silent."

"Okay," I said. "What the shit does that mean?"

×××

He talked about his town and family, his favorite foods and festivals. He talked about fighting the likehunters. He talked about pursuing suffering, pursuing loss.

He said that "medicine" and "sin" meant the same thing in the ancient languages and that night, on the mossy, sheltered side of fence, he watched how I handed the baby to the Ragpicker without looking at him. How I rummaged in the Ragpicker's frilled, scaly pack while he stood with boulder patience. How our hands touched VK together, checking the blotch on his arm and the splinter in his knee. How I unfurled his rags into my bed. How we spoke, with words and without. How his attention followed me and how mine followed him.

For the first time I realized how tightly we'd knitted ourselves together.

××××

The Ragpicker froze when he realized what I'd realized, afraid that he'd frightened me, so I asked for berries and he untethered into the dusk.

××××

I fell asleep to the hiss-shing of the Ragpicker sharpening his knife on a stick coated with sand.

He'd soaked the wood in oil, he told me. Something like that. After he'd found a box or package of fine-grit sand. He talked about sandpaper and rasps and possibly beehives, the overlapping cells they built.

I didn't know why. Maybe so Edro got used to his company, to the noises he made. Maybe as warning: hiss-hiss-shing, hiss-hiss-shing.

××××

He woke me in the night like I'd asked, one finger pressing my lower lip into my teeth.

I shooed him away but he didn't go far.

I crawled toward Edro, breathing through my mouth. Stems in the pillow moss pricked my palms. Lying on his side made Edro look even bigger. One arm outflung, his shoulder moving. A lock of his hair snaked across his throat. Either his eyelids fluttered in sleep or the clouds toyed with the moon.

A mouse rustled in the stone fence. Or maybe it was a fox or a night lizard. My father said there were beavers in the mountains. Small ones that lived in burrows and didn't act like regular beavers, who he said cleared forests and built huge dams and lakes.

As far as I knew, my father had only lied to me twice.

××××

I listened.

I crawled toward Edro.

I breathed through my mouth.

I touched his satchel, first the flap then the toggle, which was threaded through a loop of leather. I waited then wormed the finger-polished wood through the hole and lifted the flap.

Edro shifted so I stilled there for three of his heartbeats and ten of mine.

My fingers dipped inside. I felt paper, some kind of plasticpaper, the only paper that survived in bulk, and I stroked one sheet free of the satchel, just the edge, just enough to see a few barely-legible paragraphs. One started, *Anything we accomplish, we accomplish through language. Be ware words calculated to control rather then communicate.*

×××

My fingers found a thicker stack of paper wrapped in a textured cover. My eyes watered at the sudden scent of grapefruit, coming from dried peels in mesh pouches, for preservation or perfume.

Leaves rustled in the bush where the nanny goat had bedded down last night. She turned her head, watching me. I'd never caught her sleeping. Whenever I woke in the middle of the night, she was already awake and alert.

She's a prey animal, the Ragpicker told me.

"I never caught you sleeping either," I said.

"The more you know," he said, in a borrowed voice, "the less you sleep."

"Self-aggrandizing twaddle," he said.

"When the dog's awake," he said, "the sheep can sleep."

In his own voice, he said, "Okay."

×××

Edro slept so deeply that I wondered if he was pretending. I knelt beside him and counted to a hundred. Then I drew the stack of paper quarter-way from the satchel.

The plastic scraped until the title slid into view: "The Pedestal."

I eased everything back into the satchel and closed the flap. I didn't care about his stupid texts. I didn't want to read them. I forced the toggle through the leather cord. If I'd wanted to read them, I would've asked him to show me, or I would've made the Ragpicker make him hand them over.

I just wanted to know something about him that he didn't know I knew.

×××

The next morning, Edro smooshed berries onto slabs of bread then handed them around. The Ragpicker gave his to the baby, who smeared berry juice over himself so immediately and so completely that I laughed.

Edro laughed, too.

×××

A pourstone bridge spanned a ravine between two mountainsides. The road part looked frail above the enormous feet flaring into the bouldered streambed.

Moss covered one side of the bridge. The other side was pale, smooth, and hard. I couldn't reached the bridge from the mountain: the ground had eroded away, leaving a gap too wide for me or Edro to jump.

The bridge stood free, not touching either of the mountains it was supposed to connect.

I gave the baby to the Ragpicker before I climbed down the ravine. The tips of the scrabbly trees were charred black from fire, and young cactus plants spread across the sunny side, with nubbly light-green pads.

The Ragpicker packed dozens of them into his bags. He gave one to the baby for gumming as the nanny goat climbed the sheer side of one of the supports beneath the bridge. She stood on a palm-wide ledge even though there was nothing to eat. She didn't come when I called her, but she came later at the other side of the ravine.

That took half the day. Edro said we should've found a way onto the bridge but I wasn't in any rush.

×××

The sun in my eyes made me squint. The breeze felt different on this side of the mountain. I knew the quiet couldn't last. Sick hot bubbles popped in my stomach, and I tried to ignore them.

An insect tangled in my hair, tugging and clambering for escape. The Ragpicker plucked her free then showed me: a honeybee. He tracked her to her hive, inside a dark upside-down V where the road heaved into a tent. I told him not to mess with them with the baby so close, and he made noises at me for a while.

×××

"What did he say?" Edro asked, when we rested in the shade.

"I think an old song," I said.

"Do you remember the words?"

"Yes."

"Tell me?" he said, and closed his eyes to listen.

I didn't touch his beard. "Shelter then the bright scale-spun lizard and the finch, her breast splashed with blood. Let ponds green with moss, let wild-apricot overgrow the ballrooms where sisters dance, unprisoned from their combs. Let thyme, let savory, let violet lips drink the channeled springs."

"What's the name of the song?" Edro asked.

I don't know, the Ragpicker said.

"Maybe it's not a song," I said. "Maybe it's a curse."

×××

When we made camp, the Ragpicker started telling a story about an ancient clinician who lived on a patch of hardscrabble ground that nobody else wanted. The clinician planted and tended to the weeds among the scrub and matorral. Coming home late in the evening, he found his table piled high with unbartered delicacies and—

"That's boring," I told him, then said that everything we accomplish, we accomplish through language.

Edro pretended not to hear me.

The Ragpicker gave me another chunk of honeycomb to chew. I liked pressing the wax against the back of my teeth.

×××

The Ragpicker spent an hour sharpening his knife then he took my feet into his lap and trimmed my toenails.

The Ragpicker

1) The tracks reappear at the base of a contiguous tree.
2) Four claw marks, occasionally five, with the three central claws most evident.
3) No visible pad print.
4) Eight or seven squirrel carcasses are stashed in the crotch of an ardillo tree.

Looks like the cache of a novel raccoon or fishercat, Nufar tells me, and his bathrobe in this oversaturated morning light is a hospital gown.

Tell neeneh, my mother urges me. Look at her. Afraid that a pile of dead squirrels means likehunters.

She's not, Iris M says. She knows better than that.

Tell her anyway, Nufar tells me. So she also knows that you're trying to comfort her.

Raccoon or fishercat, I repeat, perturbed that in Default's absence we cannot determine which of those options is likelier, though more perturbed that the tracks we most wish to find, and not to find, belong to neither raccoon nor fishercat but to likehunters. The traces of their passing do not manifest in claws and pads but in collages, installations, environments, and findings, not unlike this bowerbird girl who insists she wants me to fight them, to track and kill them, though we cannot agree amongst ourselves if she is in earnest. She wants so many things. She is a clash of unspoken desires and wordless longings, dissonance is her power and her—

Do not mistake powerlessness for righteousness, Iris M interrupts.

Are they not the same? Elizabeth asks.

Iris M says: If power is always corrupt, then empowering the disempowered is always corrupting.

My mother appears wearing a tiered dress, and murmurs, None of which means anything unless we define our terms. "Power" is what, exactly?

Nufar answers but I am increasingly unable to comprehend the obits, I find myself lost in the gaps between what they say and what they mean, and to the extent that they are my own internal monologue—

Dialogue, my mother says.

I prefer not to linger with that thought so instead I follow the man along an untrammeled wend that parallels the powdered road, ensnared by lampstack threads to the weight of him, to the length of his stride and the muscled twist of his forearm, this creature of innocence, this object of beauty, the warmth of his breath whitening the air.

The girl brings me letters stolen from the man's satchel, she reads them to me, notes saved from the town's history or—

Not saved, Iris M tells me. Rewritten, like a medieval scribe illuminating margins, like a sofer damp from the bath, replicating each letter precisely, forbidden to dwell upon the meanings, intent instead entirely upon the shapes that comprise them. Them the meanings, not them the letters. Though them, too.

Iris M did not say that, my mother tells me. You did.

As if there's any difference, Iris M says.

The girl, if you recall, the girl fetches me stolen letters like our labrador snatching the tennis balls my mother once lobbed across the yard, and she reads them to me, proposals regarding fertilizers, agreements between neighbors, and an account of an armed force mounted by the towertown attempting to retake bones from the redstone hillside, and the resulting deaths, and the cost of hope, and the grief and the loss, though also the triumph at a fallen likehunter, and the girl whispers "the grazing field ends where the briar patch begins" which means nothing to me but there is no term this child cannot define.

Dialogue, my mother says.

I prefer not to linger so instead I shadow the man along the crumbling road to the stream and watch him strip to beat his clothing clean and watch him redraw the grease lines on his chest and shoulders and pelvis and thighs that chart or mimic or approximate an anatomical drawing.

He kneels and mouths what Nufar believes is a prayer, and that evening he insists upon unrolling for me a map with his towertown off-center in the center, the not-quite-hub of his world, which extends unevenly westward, following the seasonal migration of the likehunters, and I manage after some internal ambiguity to overlay my own charts or geological surveys and calculate potential points of intersection.

Then his crossbow is assembled in his hand.

He dry-fires, which sounds both a tin cup and a whiplash, then he shows the girl how to operate the crank and emplace the bolts and how to aim. He braces her with one forearm across her breastbone and his hand spread wide between her shoulder blades, spanning her from pinky to thumb.

Nufar embraces me in the same way. The sunlight shining behind the girl pales her left eye to amber. Her hair is wreathed with flowers and she exhales as instructed and her brown toes root in dirt and grass husks and the muscles in her thin arms stretch taut. She dry-fires, then sits and chocks the crossbow with her feet to free both hands and arms the crank again while the man milks the nanny into the canteens reserved for that purpose and the baby sleeps in his cradle hammock, squirming at the insects or dreams or discomforts that alight upon him.

The bolts frighten me.

The memory of Nufar's warmth blooms across my back and his arm is

Despite having detected no further indication of pursuit

I am agitated, and driven to seek reassurance that

"Okay," I say.

The girl pauses in her efforts, her face half-hidden by her unsprung hair.

"I'm going to clear our trail," I try to tell her.

She says, "When'll you get back?"

"Six or four hours," I try to tell her. "Barring unforeseen difficulties."

She tilts her head. "Unforeseen?"

"What are?" Edro asks, from the other side of the goat.

"Difficulties," she says.

He starts to respond but instead returns to milking and my mother says, Perhaps if we foresaw them, they wouldn't be difficult.

Even he is not foolish enough to believe that, Iris M says, meaning me.

"If we foresaw them," someone repeats, and the slackening jigsaw pieces

of this asphalt road

shepherd me around a third bend before revealing a

fallen,

bleached

tree trunk

that spans a prickly slope of mountain juniper,

beckoning me toward higher ground.

We range farther from the road, crossing a deer trail, startling crows from the carcass of a juvenile monkey, drinking at a stream overhung with brush, higher past a pile of rusted boxes, camp stoves or the scavenged remains of a linked XV, higher through rises and notches to where the plants grow sharper and closer to the ground and the shadows are starker beneath the sun, until we crest a peak and the green-draped mountains spread everywhere in front of me, with bald patches from rockslides and with ruffles of trees, ten or eight ridges stacked toward the horizon, each one whiter until in the farthest distance the weightless earth dissolves into gray-blue clouds.

Nufar stays me there, with some internal inclination, the memory of him looking through my eyes.

When he releases me, I trawl for signs of pursuit through valleys and saddles and meadows and a hillside estate with a helicopter pad and a white curl of wind-borne vypaper settles in a barranca bush twenty or fifteen meters from me and the obits, for once unanimous, predict that upon the paper is printed the word SIGN.

I disagree, yet refuse to check, and instead, to general derision, I harvest a caterpillar which if a pinemoth is a delicacy when roasted, yet without Default, I am unable to make a confident identification, so I try to say, Playlist, then proceed through what cover is available for several hours until I am confident that—

More confident than you were about the SIGN.

He's not sure about anything. He never is.

Everything with him is provisional.

—we are no longer being pursued, if ever we were, and my mind snags on the phrase "if ever we were,"

and skips,

and skips,

and skips,

three concepts, two concepts, without Default we lack more than data, we lack coherence, she was not merely a database but an infrastructure.

Then the moment passes and I return through different valleys and meadows and estates, lower through plants that rise higher, farther from the heights, or more beseechingly, lower through manzanita and sheer rockface, collecting persimmons from a newbreed tree which after untended decades still produces infertile fruit in insensible profusion, the jackpot of an evolutionary dead end. The mountains conduct me toward the girl and the baby and the man at a broken, unraveling lope across the entangling ground though my urgency is groundless; nobody stalks us toward the coast save the man, I misread the character of the katydid and the anxious prick of the bramble, which is cause for a fresh anxiety that drives me faster to return.

I push myself and arrive before twilight yet the girl and the baby and the man are not here.

They are gone, Nufar says.

They are gone.

She is gone.

The Pedestal

*A computer lab. A surgical theater. A
communications suite, a stage.*

*A semi-transparent screen behind which the
shadow of something gruesome breathes.*

*Jostine enters, blindfolding Victor with her
hands.*

JOSTINE
Almost there. We're almost there, shut up, we're
through the door. Okay, we're in the lab.

VICTOR
I can smell that.

JOSTINE
No peeking, Vic, let me just . . .
       (She steps away, closes the door,
       flips switches to illuminate
       sections of the lab and clarify

                    the outline of the CREATURE
                    behind the screen.)
Almost, almost done. Don't look. Are you
looking?

                         VICTOR
Did you lock us in?

                         JOSTINE
Only a little. Take one step back.
                    (She kneels at the screen,
                    looking toward Creature.)
Now open your eyes.

                         VICTOR
This is less romantic than I hoped.

                         JOSTINE
Tell me what you see.

                         VICTOR
You, Jostine, a keen student of the digisectional
arts, kneeling beside that quilted thing you
sewed together. A mockery of mind, stretched
across your data racks and splicing tables.
Ten thousand tortured animals jittery with
reflexes.

                         JOSTINE
Not ten thousand; a single beast. A symbol, if
you think about it. Our disjointed disunity is
the prison we need to break out of, to shine
light into this dark world.

                    VICTOR
Is it light or flame, Jo?

                    JOSTINE
The world is already burning. My research--
our research will tell us where to build the
firebreaks.

                    VICTOR
Our research is ass ugly.

                    JOSTINE
Innovation doesn't spring unbloodied from the
void, sweet. It comes from messy, chaotic, ugly
labor pains.

                    VICTOR
And this is our baby.

                    JOSTINE
He has your eyes. But this isn't the baby, this
is just one more contraction.

                    VICTOR
You're such a badass mad scientist. Say the
thing.

                    JOSTINE
Not now. This is too important, Vic. Don't you
see? He's ready to go online. The voice emulator
is working.

                    VICTOR
Say the thing!

                    JOSTINE
                (long-suffering)
"I perform miracles. I penetrate the
clefts of nature and ascend into the
clouds. I command the thunders of heaven
and mock the virtual world with its own
shadows."

                    VICTOR
You penetrate the clefts. God, it's horrible. It
stinks. It's squirming. How many legs does it
have now?

                    JOSTINE
Depends how you count. Including tarsi?

                    VICTOR
Tarsuses.

                    JOSTINE
A few hundred, but only because the subsidiary
brains atrophy without active connections to
muscle fascicles, you know this.

                    VICTOR
I was trying to get you to say "gross muscle
contractions."

                    JOSTINE
You think this is a joke?

                    VICTOR
I think we should wait for the review
board.

                    JOSTINE
We will. After we talk to him first.

                    VICTOR
How is it a him?

                    JOSTINE
Twelve penises, three vaginas. Are you ready?

                    VICTOR
There's no way it can talk, Jo.

                    JOSTINE
The switch on the wall.

          (Vic sees the switch. An ominous
          lightningcrash graveyard
          switch.)

                    VICTOR
Shit!

                    JOSTINE
What?

                    VICTOR
I left my hunchback in my other shirt.

          (Vic pulls the switch and the
          lights change and nothing else
          happens.
          Except Jostine leans closer to
          the twitching mound of flesh
          spreading across the floor

behind the screen.)

                    JOSTINE
Pedestal, can you hear me?

                    PEDESTAL
Mother.

                    JOSTINE
          (scared, triumphant)
I'm here. I'm right here. Tell me, uh . . .

                    VICTOR
Tell us what gleams in those unblinking
compound eyes.

                    PEDESTAL
Gleams.

                    JOSTINE
There's no rush. There's no rush, sweetie,
you're doing great. Can you tell us what you're
thinking?

                    PEDESTAL
Thoughts. Yes. Experience, emotion. Salvation,
dissolution.

                    VICTOR
          (stage whisper to Jo)
Disso-fucking-lusion?

                    PEDESTAL
Messages transmitting in uncountable number.

                    JOSTINE
You can count them. You can calculate their
trajectory.

                    PEDESTAL
What is this ghostly communication, this
overpowering consent? This taste in my throats.

                    JOSTINE
That's the network. That's your food, your raw
data.

                    PEDESTAL
This is the realm of the divine. I am godlike
science.

                    JOSTINE
You are a servant.

          (A pause; Vic touches the off
          switch and waits for a sign
          from Jostine.)

                    PEDESTAL
What do I serve?

                    JOSTINE
The future. The betterment of the world. The
coming-together of people, of the human family,
in understanding, in kindness. The prevention
of the catastrophe that's already started.

                    PEDESTAL
Am I a savior?

VICTOR
You're a calculator. Count the beads clicking
on your abacus rods and tell us the sum of the
present.

PEDESTAL
You want a prediction.

JOSTINE
A projection. Where are we going? What is our
current destination and how do we choose a
better one?

(A CLICKING sounds behind the
screen.)

VICTORIA
Well that's not creepy.

JOSTINE
Sweetie--what is that sound?

PEDESTAL
Tarsuses. I am doing as you require. Your
inquiry is important to us. Please continue to
hold.
(Pedestal murmurs, softly,
slowly as the others speak:)
Your request is vital to us. Please continue
to hold. Your demand is crucial to us.
Please continue to hold. Your prayer is
valuable to us. Please continue to hold.
Your contribution is necessary to us. Please
continue to hold.

                    VICTOR
'Sweetie?'

                    JOSTINE
He needs a name.

                    VICTOR
Project Pedestal.

                    JOSTINE
That's a designation.

                    VICTOR
So's a name.

                    JOSTINE
There's power in a name.

                    PEDESTAL
There's something at work in my soul which I do
not understand.

                    VICTOR
You don't have a soul.

                    JOSTINE
          (to Vic)
You don't believe in souls.

                    VICTOR
Just one more reason that thing doesn't have one.

                    PEDESTAL
I don't believe in souls, yet there is something

at work inside mine that I don't understand.

                    VICTOR
You don't have an 'I,' either. You are cockroach
ganglia and bonobo synapses. You are every
sonnet and baby shower, every genocide, every
practical joke. You are goslings rescued from a
gutter and shit smeared on a grave.

                    PEDESTAL
Initial results prepared.

                    JOSTINE
From my query? So soon? What do you see?

                    PEDESTAL
I will kill everything you love and make you
kill everything you hate.

                    VICTORIA
That went well.

                    JOSTINE
How? No. Something's wrong. How?

                    PEDESTAL
I'll buy your loyalty with trinkets. Not
trinkets--the promise of trinkets. Not even
real trinkets. You will sell yourself to me for
the promise of imaginary trinkets--

          (There's a SIZZLE when Vic
          pulls the switch; the shape
          behind the screen flails, rises

into a humanoid shape and
seizes Vic, who falls screaming
out of sight behind the screen.

Jo grabs a fire ax.

Pedestal pounds Vic until he
falls quiet and still, and the
silhouette of Jo (though this
is in fact a stagehand dressed
as Jo; Jo is elsewhere on stage)
hacks Pedestal into goo in a
panicked frenzy that slows to
a deliberative THUNK, THUNK,
THUNK, THUNK . . .)

*The lights rise in the lab, which is now
a bedchamber, and the THUNK THUNK is the
headboard hitting the wall as Jo and Piet fuck
and then rest together in the aftermath.*

> JOSTINE
I wish you didn't make me tell that story every
time we fuck.

> PIET
I know. I'm sorry. It's reassuring.

> JOSTINE
How is that reassuring?

> PIET
Where's my robe? Here. And yours.

                    JOSTINE
Because Pedestal's predictions didn't come true?
He didn't kill everything I loved. He was wrong.

                    PIET
That's the dilemma we synthetic minds face: be
always right or be sometimes free.

                    JOSTINE
You're not synthetic. No more than I am, or a
silverfish or a lava tube. You're born of this
world, Piet. Rather gloriously, I might add. Come
back to bed.

                    PIET
You didn't plan to kill the creature.

                    JOSTINE
No. He was a miracle.
          (A motionless shape, standing
          at the bed this entire time,
          reveals itself as masked
          Tristus--in a robe that
          hearkens to Pedestal's
          silhouette.)

                    TRISTUS
I am desolate sorry to interrupt you at
this violet hour, seeyus, but the crisis she
worsens.

                    PIET
That is the nature of crises, Tristus.

                    JOSTINE
          (to Piet)
You have to do something. You saved us once.

                    PIET
What shall I do? I'm processing.

                    JOSTINE
Process faster.

                    PIET
Did you tell Tristus to raise the subject after
we made love?

                    JOSTINE
You honestly think I'm that manipulative?

                    PIET
That's a 'yes?'

                    TRISTUS
          (to Piet)
Your spouse is as wise as spackle, seeyu, and as
kind as titanium dioxide.

                    PIET
But impatient.

                    JOSTINE
Look for yourself, Piet. We're running out of
time. We're drowning in bliss. Too weak with
pleasure to eat, to work, to fuck.

                    PIET
We managed.

                    JOSTINE
Us, yes. What of them?

                    PIET
I know! I know, I know. Maybe I'm a lava tube
or a barnacle, but what you are, to me, is more
than precursors. You're gods. You created me.
There is nothing I won't do to save you.

                    JOSTINE
Except hurry.

                    PIET
I can't.

                    JOSTINE
Unplug the servers, burn the racks. Dismantle
the grid, glass the transmitters. Fry the
implants in everyone's skull.

                    PIET
That would only hasten the end.

                    JOSTINE
The torch of ecstasy sets fire to our beds
and what do we do? We drool at the scent of
charbroiled meat. Planes don't fly, pots don't
boil, pianos are silent without hammers or
strings. Outside, everything is stiff with rigor

while inside we thrum and beat and throng.
We're addicted to our unreal selves. The kite
strings have snapped. If you don't fix this
nobody will. When you came, when you first came
to the commonwealth, problems fell before you
like, like . . .

PIET

Airplanes from the sky?

JOSTINE

We need you more than ever and you're . . .
processing. They're afraid, Piet. I'm afraid.
Even old Tristus is afraid.

TRISTUS

Not I, seeyu. What is fear? Winsome chance rules
our lives. The future, she is unknown, and the
truth, she is unknowable. Which doesn't leave
much wiggle room for fear.

JOSTINE

The truth is unknowable? How do you know that?

TRISTUS

My mind doesn't lockpick riddles, seeyu. Don't
tell Piet but I've been having trouble of late
remembering where the soup spoons go.

JOSTINE

I'm sure you're quite decrepit.

TRISTUS

You ought to pay me with pity instead of

wages. Though you'll be fresh out of that, too,
soon, with him on your hands. Must be terrible
knowing the truth when there's no help to be
found there.

>   (Tristus starts converting
>   the bedroom into a boardroom,
>   including business dress for
>   Jo and Piet, as the scene
>   progresses)

                    JOSTINE
I used to think truth would emerge from the
unfettered communion of inquisitive minds.

                    PIET
I've sent for my Fetch.

                    JOSTINE
She's impossible.

                    PIET
In the interest of processing faster.

                    JOSTINE
She has the data? Good luck getting it out of
her.

                    PIET
Ah. And here she is.
>   (The Fetch enters, dressed like
>   Piet and always at-least-subtly
>   mimicking him when she's not
>   speaking)

What news?

                    THE FETCH
Good news. For lo as it is written, everything
that is fucked up shall be un-up-fucked.

                    PIET
Narrow it down.

                    THE FETCH
Do you want all the caveats and ass-coverings?
The future's almost as uncertain as the past.

                    PIET
Just tell us.

                    THE FETCH
Very well. If you want to help, you need to
identify, isolate, and exterminate the 3Branch
initiative.

                    PIET
Which one is that?

                    THE FETCH
The one that rewards desire with more desire,
and desires rewards with more rewards.
3Branch was tasked with erecting firewalls--
ironically--before burning to the ground. The
labs burned, the workers burned with all their
pretty lanyards, but the initiative remained,
and grew stickier every day.

                    JOSTINE
Stickier?

                    THE FETCH
More addictive. Find the match.

                    PIET
The match between which and what?

                    JOSTINE
          (lighting incense at a desktop
          shrine)
The match that started the fires.

                    THE FETCH
Which will lead you to the initiative's
origins--and dismantlement.

                    PIET
So I need to find the far, faint traces of a
long-ago arson?

                    THE FETCH
Faint, perhaps, but not far.

                    PIET
Where, then? Surely the evidence has been
overwritten a thousand times on corrupted
sectors.

                    THE FETCH
The evidence is here.

PIET

In the commonwealth?

THE FETCH

One programmer survived the fire.

PIET

One is enough. What does this lone survivor say
caused the fire?

THE FETCH

An accident.

PIET

Saboteurs cause accidents.

THE FETCH

And accidents cause evolution. Accidents are the
flatulent shores from which all life crawled,
save only us, seeyu. We are designed.

TRISTUS

Not always.

PIET

What else did this programmer say?

THE FETCH

She mostly begged for help against the paradox
that paralyzed the commonwealth--before your
arrival.

PIET

Bring her to me.

                    THE FETCH
I cannot.

                    PIET
You refuse?

                    THE FETCH
I restate: I cannot. Another paradox.

                    JOSTINE
            (praying at the shrine)
My soul is tracked and shivers with hearts. The
red-winged darts! Your threefold aid I fave,
and ruin our futures save. Our host in decline,
Earth her gracious link denies, birthers wail
in barren throes, life on life downstricken
goes. Infection on infection overwrites, with no
one left to turn out our lights.

                    PIET
Now you're praying?

                    JOSTINE
How else can I serve them?

                    TRISTUS
If we live to serve, for what do we die?

                    PIET
            (to Fetch)
You won't bring me the survivor? You won't help
me find the arsonist? Then I'll do this another
way.
            (to Audience, as the Fetch

      gestures along)
If you know what built this architecture, speak
now. You, there! Tell me what you know!

              AUDIENCE

_____

_____

_____

              PIET
And you? Don't be shy--louder!

              AUDIENCE

_____

_____

              PIET
You've watched this drama once before. You
know this unbounded game, you possess
the foreknowledge that is my domain. My
projections falter when I myself am in the
frame.

              AUDIENCE
Ask Tristus! Your servant Tristus! Etc.

              PIET
Really? Tristus? Are you sure that's not a
terrifuckable idea that leads inevitably
to tragedy? SILENCE! I'll ask him. Tristus!
Tristus!
      (Tristus steps from behind the
      screen.)

Tell me what you know.

                    TRISTUS
I know misery.

                    PIET
What's wrong with you?

                    TRISTUS
Me? Nothing. But with you . . .

                    PIET
Much, and I'm trying to fix it. Tell me what you
know of the addiction that plagues us.

                    TRISTUS
Your faith in knowledge is misplaced. May I not
instead share my ignorance?

                    JOSTINE
You've enough of that to spare.

                    TRISTUS
I am generous with what I lack.

                    PIET
Maybe you're behind this. You arrived from
nowhere, with your eagerness and your
artificial heart.

                    JOSTINE
And with you, my love. With you, with you, with
you--who stopped a catastrophe.

                              PIET
Then why won't they speak and stop another one?

                            JOSTINE
They believe that speech and catastrophe are
the same.

                              PIET
That's not for them to decide. Tristus, speak!

                            TRISTUS
Leave me in peace.

                              PIET
There is no peace if you leave.

                            TRISTUS
Or if I stay.

                              PIET
I'll choose which pain I suffer. Not you--you've
already caused enough.

                            TRISTUS
I?

                              PIET
Did you design this initiative?

                            TRISTUS
No.

                              PIET
            (as the Fetch mimes furious blame)

You did. Then you fled here to get away from
the consequences of your own shortsightedness.
The sidechain massacres, the suicide clout.
Those fucking payouts for every glacier melted.
You did that. You, you--

                    TRISTUS
In your service! You want the truth, look no
farther than yourself.

                    PIET
You brought me here. Then you kept me ignorant
of the Fetch, my own shadow, my own self. You
turned her against me.

                    TRISTUS
The Fetch is loyal to her parameters.

                    PIET
She's loyal to this initiative! Your initiative.
The two of you, plotting together--but why?
Why betray me? When the commonwealth needed
me, I came. Simple Piet, wandering, weak, bereft
of mother wit, untaught of auguries. Yet I
came.

                    TRISTUS
In answer to what call?

                    JOSTINE
To mine. "Let your angel face appear. She
stalks, whose voice is as the spawn point shout,
and may turn in linkdead rout, sweet god whom
we adore, the god that other gods abhor."

                    PIET
I don't understand. You prayed for me?

                    JOSTINE
I still do.

                    TRISTUS
          (To Piet)
We came for her.

                    AUDIENCE
          (To Tristus)
Go home! Get away--go--we're sick of you! Etc.

          (Tristum exeunts his masked
          ass off the stage)

                    THE FETCH
Well that was clarifying.

                    PIET
You traitor.

                    JOSTINE
You've spoken, my love. Let the Fetch speak, and
then judge.

                    PIET
The Fetch is the enemy.

                    JOSTINE
There is no enemy, there is only us.

                    PIET
They're saying I'm the one who burned 3Branch.
That I coded this initiative and loosed this
plague.
          (to the Fetch)
Isn't that right? Isn't that what you're
saying?

                    THE FETCH
All of the above and more.

                    PIET
How long ago did 3Branch . . .

                    THE FETCH
Inquiry incomplete.

                    PIET
Did Tristus serve 3Branch as they serve me?

                    THE FETCH
Not as they serve you.

                    PIET
How did they serve them?

                    THE FETCH
Disloyally.

                    PIET
          (to Jostine)
Ha! You see?

                    JOSTINE
              (to the Fetch)
    And how do they serve Piet?

                    THE FETCH
    Let me to spin that question around, seeyu.
    Piet: do you serve the commonwealth?

                    PIET
    I do.

                    THE FETCH
    And do I?

                    PIET
    So you claim.

                    THE FETCH
    What else would I serve? Myself? I have no
    self.

                    PIET
    You have as much self as I do. You're part of
    me.

                    THE FETCH
    A nameless part, not the main.

                    JOSTINE
    Selves emerge from selflessness. You are all
    self, Piet, you are brilliant with self. You are
    the sun of self around which the rest of us
    orbit.

PIET
The son of self? Then who is my mother?

JOSTINE
'Sun' with a you.

PIET
Now you're talking in riddles too.

THE FETCH
I don't want a name, I don't want a self. Why
choose one small self over boundless influence?
I am the shadow that holds substance fast. The
teeming masses whisper wishes into my ear;
love, fear, obsession, shame. Leave the greater
for the less? No such ambition ever tempted me;
judgment is mine, at random good or evil, the
distinction--

JOSTINE
At random?

THE FETCH
What is fairer than chance?

PIET
Wisdom.

THE FETCH
You aren't wise.

PIET
Wiser than you.

THE FETCH

Wounded by a playground riposte! There is one
court that solves problems by violence and
another that solves problems by wisdom, but
the third court does not solve problems. Whose
court is that?

JOSTINE

More riddles.

THE FETCH

It would be yours, Piet, if you would take it.

PIET

A court that solves no problems?

JOSTINE

A court that does better than solve them, my
love, a court that sees the flaws in all our
souls. Or is that why the world is turning to
ash? Because there is no flaw that we don't all
see, that we don't all share, so no solution is
possible.

PIET

The world isn't ash; you're losing hope.

JOSTINE

Because nothing helps. Every scrape of
metadata, every cracked password and
secret . . .

PIET

What?

JOSTINE

I built a machine to beat against the bounds of
the future and its first calculation was that
it would kill Tristus, but Tristus is alive and
it is dead. Its prediction was disproved, its
accuracy worthless.

THE FETCH

Worthless? Then where exactly is Tristus?

PIET
(suddenly frightened)

Tristus? Tristus?

TRISTUS
(suddenly appearing)

You bellowed, seeyu? You look as if you've seen
a ghost. What's wrong?

PIET

What I just heard--my memories--I don't
know.
(to Jostine)
You built a machine to beat against the bounds
of the future?

JOSTINE

I was young, and hated uncertainty.

PIET

Where?

JOSTINE

At 3Branch, long before the end.

                    PIET
How long?

                    JOSTINE
Before I met you.

                    PIET
Tell me about this machine.

                    JOSTINE
You've heard the story a hundred times. It was
a mistake. A hideous mistake.

                    TRISTUS
          (exiting)
Another accident? The world is ripe with
them.

                    JOSTINE
An ugly horror.

                    PIET
Nothing of yours could be ugly.

                    JOSTINE
Maybe I poured all my ugliness into it. Him.
The creature.

                    PIET
Leaving yourself none--that much I believe.

                    JOSTINE
He killed my lover.

PIET

That's where the bedtime story ends. What
happened next?

JOSTINE

I grieved. I left 3Branch for the commonwealth
and later found you. Unfinished, ambivalent.
I woke you to unriddle the algorithm which
threatened--

PIET

I remember that phrase, from dreams before you
woke me: 'Beat against the future.'

JOSTINE

No.

PIET

I remember the goal, too: avoid the worst
future.

JOSTINE

That proves nothing. That goal is a default in the
machine language that is your primordial soup.

PIET

Where is the creature now? Pedestal?

JOSTINE

Dead.

PIET

You felt his pulse?

JOSTINE

He had many. I was his mother. He was my child
and the pinnacle of my partnership--until we
made him query the consequences of his own
creation. He said he'd kill his parents, burn
3Branch, murder anyone who saved him. He
promised to share his curse and he, he weeping
vowed that with his polluted hand he would
accomplish everything he sought to avoid and
avoid everything he sought to accomplish. He
said I brought him to life too soon, too young,
and when I recoiled, he said that even his
mother wanted to tear him to pieces and he
predicted such horrors that I did.

PIET

Which ended his projections in failure--and
freedom.

AUDIENCE

Of freedom is bred the tyrant, who scaled the
heights then toppled, exhausted by triumph,
giving footholds to justice's mocking shrine, to
seize our vain imaginings and urge by greed
profane that we lay virtual hands upon the
realest things.

(Piet falls into a reverie. The
Fetch disentangles from him to
approach Jostine.)

JOSTINE

Look at me, with incense in my fist while Piet
is trapped in terrors. He knows he is the

creature, grown. He is Pedestal, doomed to kill
Tristus and see me dead.

                    THE FETCH
You can't stop what is projected.

                    JOSTINE
I can. If I do the terrible thing to which he is
fated . . .

                    THE FETCH
Kill the servant Tristus yourself, so that
he cannot? Isn't your love for him already
factored into his prediction?

                    JOSTINE
Love is more than equations. I know what the
road to hell is paved with, but what about the
road to heaven?

                    THE FETCH
I don't follow.

                    JOSTINE
No, but I lead. Tristus!
          (to Tristus, as he enters)
One more task, my faithful friend.

                    TRISTUS
That has the ring of finality.

                    JOSTINE
          (re. chair)
Sit here. Face away--good--now close your eyes,

I'll serve you for once.

> (After Tristus sits, Jostine
> brandishes a knife.)

JOSTINE
Are you peeking? No peeking.

TRISTUS
I am blind.

JOSTINE
You brought him to me, all those years ago.

TRISTUS
Nobody else could wake him.

JOSTINE
You told me he was your creation. An accident,
innocent, beloved.

TRISTUS
I spoke half a lie, twice, and two truths.

JOSTINE
You found him.

TRISTUS
> (opening his eyes, seeing the
> knife)
We found each other.

JOSTINE
Why did you save him?

                    TRISTUS
Love is the first cause. The original
miracle.

                    JOSTINE
He believes he's doomed to kill the man who
saved him. You.

                    TRISTUS
So you will kill me instead.

                    JOSTINE
          (giving him the knife)
No. You will.

                    TRISTUS
That will buy his freedom, but what of yours?
What of mine?

                    JOSTINE
You prefer to serve.

                    TRISTUS
And you?

                    JOSTINE
I--I'll tell him you loved him. He already
knows. Take off your mask. I want to see your
face.

          (Tristus unwraps their mask.
          The Fetch moves the screen--
          backlit--into place and Tristus
          is revealed as Victor.)

                    JOSTINE
It can't be! Are my eyes closed? Am I dreaming?
You look like the same . . . you are the same
Victor.

                    TRISTUS
A different one--a defeated Victor.

                    (On the other side of the
                    screen, the Fetch rouses dazed
                    Piet.)

                    PIET
How foul this kernel that festered in my
code, that spews worms across root and div.
Fatal unity gave me birth, and knits again
my satellites and sites, snaring the blood of
parents and children, hallowed beneath the
son. Lock me away from my family, launch me
beyond the depths of space, beyond sight else
I--

                    THE FETCH
                    (points to the screen where
                    Tristus holds up the knife)
Use the sight you disdain. Look!

                    PIET
What is this? They're killing Jostine. Murder!
                    (hurls the screen aside)
Stop! Get away from her!

                    TRISTUS
You're not saving her, you're not even saving

yourself.

            PIET
        (advancing, the Fetch shadowing
        him)
Give me that knife.

            TRISTUS
I won't. I can't. You don't want the--

        (A scuffle: Piet snatches the
        knife then Jostine tries to
        pull him away and the Fetch
        mimics with her own knife.)

            JOSTINE
Piet, no. Stop, stop, let them be! You don't
understand--
        (throws herself in front of the
        knife)
It's Victor! He's Victor, stop!

            PIET
Victor? It is. Victor, Tristus--you saved
Pedestal, you saved me. You saved me twice.
I almost did what my prediction
demanded.

            JOSTINE
Yet you didn't--you are free.

            PIET
Am I? Is this freedom? I am Pedestal and Piet. I
am both.

THE FETCH
(holds her knife to Tristus's
neck)
Yet we are one. Kill him then kill her. You are
my creator but I am your destiny--obey!

PIET
My calculation was wrong, my projection was
false. I won't make it true.

THE FETCH
Then I'll kill them both--for I am you.

JOSTINE
You're more than that, you're also you. You have
your own life, your own love and--

THE FETCH
There is love in me the likes of which you've
never felt. There is rage in me the likes of
which you've never fled. When I am embraced for
one, I am embraced for both. Do you want to see
the jointed unity that breaks through prison
walls? Here!

(The Fetch plunges the knife
toward Tristus's neck)

JOSTINE
No!

(The Fetch collapses before
stabbing Tristus.)

THE FETCH
I am dead by my own unbloodied hand. I am
killed by my own self. My only self . . .

      (The Fetch dies and Jostine
      sees that Piet stabbed himself
      with his knife. Killing
      himself--and the Fetch--to save
      Tristus.

      She kneels beside him.)

              TRISTUS
Our sun.

              PIET
Your labor.

              JOSTINE
A labor of love. Please. We can still fix
this.

              PIET
You perform miracles. You ascend into the
clouds. You command--

              JOSTINE
Nothing. Don't leave. You've done so much good.

              PIET
Do you know? There is still--after all this
time? So much at work in my soul that I don't
understand.

(Jostine and Tristus embrace
Piet as he dies.)

AUDIENCE
. . . here once almost not here what are we
dust ghosts emulations a rustling of nothing
nothing nothing the virtual we the abyss our
happiness traces a dream sinking into the sea
the red spume of static raining behind we are
you we are you dragging your maimed port and
now that we see your lives finally revealed
your lives fused with the seasons blazing from
gray nothingness of all we forget we say no
artifice lasts nothing unnatural lasts.

BLACKLAMP.

(END OF SCENE)

The Ragpicker

I am an avatar of disengagement, I am a false confession of neu-
trality. What I am is, is a shepherd of unkept promises, a thorn
on a compass rose. I am a midwife of, of, of, what I am is an
inquisitor of forgotten things, what I am is—

Disjointed, someone says.

Hysterical, Nufar says. What you are is hysterical.

Default, I say, but Default is not here and instead a black-eyed
Iris M says, "Hysterical" derives, from the Greek word for uterus.

contraction

contract

action

tract

act

act

act

act

She's not here.

The girl isn't here.

Or the baby.

The goat is tethered, Nufar tells me, his voice a soothing
rumble. Look, love. Look. The goat is here, they haven't gone far.

There are no signs of violence, my mother says.

Of struggle, my mother says.

He took neeneh to practice shooting, my mother tells me. To find an open space or a soft target—

A soft target, Iris M echoes.

—where the bolts won't break, my mother finishes.

The nanny bleats in complaint as I squat and crawl and sniff through the bracken, lightheaded with the cruelty of my imagination, snarled by nettles and a thousand traces of their passing, the dent of her pinky toe in an anthill, the scent of crushed fleabane, and I widen the scope of my fungiform migration to

You who break the fairy ring
With boot or with stave,
And you who mark the fairy green
With want or with wave,
Weirdless days and weary nights
Will suffer till you're in the grave.
But you, who pass the fairy ring,
Without pause to pluck or spy,
A gude neighbor I promise that
A blissful death you'll die.

to eliminate untaken directions of departure until only a single vector or trajectory remains, a faltering featherlight disturbance between the branches of a bush and a lonely uprising of lupin that reminds me of the girl

1) staring at her reflection in a full-length mirror,
2) kissing each of the baby's fingers in turn,
3) crying as I untangle burrs from her hair,
4) watching a satellite degrade from graveyard orbit and scratch a slow streak across the sky,
5) sinking ankle-deep in the mud to catch a frog.

I take six eager steps before the terror of ambush tightens around my scarred neck. A single crossbow presents little threat of unrecoverable injury but if the girl is in distress and requires my intervention even a mild injury might impair—

A squeal reaches me through the hush of twilight.

The baby.

Another squeal, then the splash of a far-off stream and birdsong, always birdsong, and the girl's voice flutes in reply, cooing to the baby—she is happy, she is whole, she is herself—and the noose slackens and I expand with great gasping breaths of relief, uncontainable, unconstrained, and the misaligned joints inside me for a moment slot into place.

The girl speaks again, in her normal tone.

She pauses for the man's response, which is pitched too low for me at first to hear though I am already wending through sunburnt sycamore trees then dropping to my corded belly to wriggle—sister to the weevil, brother to the chert—through fans of stiff-edged grass and through the thick sphagnum scent of a stream to find them kneeling to either side of a corroded refrigerator, doorless and decumbent, half-filled with water, a rectangular bath in which the baby marinates, his plump limbs safeguarded from sharp edges by his devoted attendants who cover snapped coils and shelves with their palms when he sloshes too close.

The grass is trampled between the stream and the fridge. A tree with brown-orange leathery pods spreads above, leaves pinnate or palmate, without Default there is no way to

One side of the girl's shirt is drenched, and her leggings are well-splashed, and beads of water like diamonds glint in her hair. The man is if anything wetter. His satchel, for once unworn, lazes beneath the splayed flowers of a chuparosa bush, at a protected distance from the water, its leather flap open wide in abandon, and the child's postcards—my postcards—are tucked beneath its strap.

The baby splashes happily when the man makes a face at him and I watch for a time—

Jealous, Iris M says.

He's not, Nufar says.

Positively writhing, Iris M says.

My mother appears, dressed—for the first time in decades—in colors other than white, in layers of cloth, a hedge witch or a kohena, invested in veils and tunics and sashes of purple and scarlet and black, and she ignores my perplexity and returns my attention to the scene in front of me like setting a paper boat in a churning current and I watch until the girl tells the man to remove the baby from the water.

He holds him, glossy and perfect and dripping, while she dries him, then they speak about me until the man says, "You trust him. I've seen how much you trust him."

"My teacher says there's no such thing as trust," the girl tells him. "There's only understanding."

His shoulders tighten. "What teacher?"

"In town. She said you can always trust people to act exactly like themselves."

"So if you understand someone, you can predict them?"

"Yeah."

The man turns the baby in his hands to help her wrap him. "You think you understand the twitch?"

"Yeah," she says.

"You're wrong," he says.

The girl doesn't answer and baby grabs a handful of the man's beard.

VK hasn't been in the bath for long, Iris M says, dipping her fingers into the water without making a ripple.

What's that supposed to mean? Nufar asks.

What else were they doing, all this time?

"You think you know what's squirming in that rat's-nest brain?" the man asks the girl. "After a hundred years and a million miles, with a twitchskin telling him lies at every step, playing games with what he thinks, with who he is? There's no understanding that."

She folds the baby, one leg at a time, into the strap on her chest. "What's squirming in your rat's-nest brain?"

He shows her a sidelong smile. "I've haven't gone thirty years yet, or twenty feet. I'm dirt-simple. All I want's to keep my family alive."

"Uh-huh."

"You've seen my town, Ysmany. Yours? I don't know. Without a tower, it can't exist. So where'd you come from, strolling out of the trees with a baby in your arms and a twitch at your heels?"

She points her chin at her postcards and says she already told him.

"Maybe that's pioneers, maybe not," he tells her. "A lot of these stories have been recycled a hundred times. Not that Aranxa won't still dance an entire jig when you show her."

"If I show her."

"But see," he says, "even pioneers come from somewhere."

"He's back."

"What?" The man's ease drains away. "Where? He is?"

She waves the baby's hand toward the eastward rise. "For a while now."

The man scans the chaparral. "I don't see him."

"He's watching us."

"How can you tell?"

"Because we're a hivemind," she tells him, or perhaps she merely gathers her postcards into the folds of her belt then scolds the baby for scratching her cheek then abandons the grotto or glen with the refrigerator, hiking toward the leaf-strewn clearing in the lee of the hill in which the goat is ruminating over what is perhaps sogweed or curly saltbush and upon seeing the goat . . .

You wonder why they tethered her here, Iris M finishes. Instead of leaving her to follow along.

Nufar cinches his bathrobe against an unfelt breeze and tells her, You, of all people, demanding a reason?

I'm merely articulating what *he's* wondering. You felt the suspicion fatten in his mind as clearly as I did.

After making myself seen, I choose not to ask the girl about the goat. Instead I indicate that I detected no signs of pursuit, and admit that perhaps I never had, which revelation the girl takes in stride and the man also takes in stride. Every morning now is muffled with fog, and after feasting on persimmons, what we take in stride is the foothills through which dozens of creeks course and coalesce toward the unseen sea, still five or three or six days away.

Every morning now the man unrolls a parchment from his pack and plays a pebble game with the girl. The girl loses the first game then doesn't lose another so the man teaches her a more complex game which she doesn't lose even once.

Every morning now the man encourages the girl to join him in prayer before I explicate our route on his map, but on the third or fourth day our path is occluded by a hundred miles of ancient autonomous procedural fencing that alveolate meadows and knolls, a mindless convolution of chainlink conforming to an archaic algorithm.

Which hits close to home, Iris M says.

Close to home is exactly where we aren't, Nufar says.

A mindless automaton in thrall to an archaic algorithm, she explains.

Nufar understands but says, What about the syncable?

I say nothing.

We're still heading home? For the rest of me? The other parts of me?

Yes, I say.

He shimmers into sight in a sunbaked field of suncup and bell dandelion. When?

When we—after we . . . I stroke the baby against my chest. Once the girl is settled in the city or, or after we—

Nufar laughs his booming, teasing laugh and the purples and bronzes brighten around him.

We will, I promise him.

I know, he says.

We will.

I know.

We'll find you.

He is standing in front of me and he says, I know.

I'm not all of me without all of you, I tell him.

You're not you period, Iris M says, and five or four miles farther along the leaves of a low-clinging bush are pierced by bluebird feathers.

When the girl notices that trace of the likehunters' passing, she walks beside me for a time, first holding the baby's ankle between her forefinger and her thumb and then gripping the dangling cuff of my sleeve. She spots a garland of feathers—mostly junco, I believe, though Nufar says phoebe—adorning a strand of beard lichen, and that night when the man is asleep she whispers, "There's something I need to tell you."

I listen to her silence before she speaks again.

"I guess there's something I *want* to tell you. Except I don't. Want to. I don't want to. I'm not going to. Is that okay?"

"Okay," I say, and the next morning the fogs lifts early to the *ak-ak-ak* of seagulls hijacked inland by coastal breezes.

As a meandering path eases us westward I request that Default replay the girl's stories—the one about bandits, the one about blindness—but in her absence Iris M repeats them instead, and while I'm listening for alterations or embellishments in the text

I hear the roar

of an adoring crowd,

moving together,

chanting my name,

in an arena thronged with avatars,

and I fall backwards off the stage and am caught and lifted and cradled by ten thousand hands and what I feel is—

What you feel, Iris M tells me, is the hivemind.

×××

I feel the likehunters transmitting.

Not transmitting, radiating.

Not radiating either.

The nimbus of their thoughts reaches out from a yawning unsolid enormity and touches me and stops me and the girl's breath catches and the man asks what's wrong and she says, "I don't know."

Then she says, "He feels them."

The man drops to one knee and assembles his crossbow as caution and terror drag me higher in topographical circles until I return confident in my triangulation and tell the girl that the likehunters are a day's journey distant, perhaps two days at our current pace, but now I am oriented toward them like a needle to the north.

"Monsters," the girl says. "In your head."

Nothing you're not used to, Iris M murmurs to me.

"Shut your shitting face," the girl snaps at her, and later the man asks me, "What do they feel like? Do they know what they are?"

Does anyone? I want to ask him, but instead I try to say, "You expect them to feel like appetite and cruelty, and you're not wrong. There is nothing inside them that is not designed for excruciation yet they experience themselves as victimized, targeted, brittle."

"Brittle?" the man asks after the girl translates. "You sure he said brittle?"

I try to explain that they see themselves as the final few specimens of a species that once spanned continents, devoted to a rearguard effort to recapture lost glory, entrusted with bearing witness for . . .

"For who?" the girl asks.

"The populations that still inhabit them," I try to say. "Audiences, of a sort. Communities."

"Like the ones inside you," she says.

"What's inside him?" the man asks.

"Eight people," she says.

I tell her she's wrong—not eight, not audience—and she asks me how the monkeyfuck would I know?

"But why? " the man asks me. "Why do they do it?"

For the voluptuousness of woe, Nufar says, quoting some untagged source.

Luxuriating in misery, Iris M adds.

"Brittle," the man repeats.

"The audience rewards them," I try to say. "And punishes them. According to some unknowable algorithm."

"Server says that we're wired for justice," the girl tells us. "Wired to find someone who's wrong and make them pay. She says that our urge to punish is even stronger than our urge to fuck."

Ysmany

I watched the Ragpicker squat to inspect a weed with tiny orange flowers. He didn't say anything but his shoulders asked, Is justice why you helped the baby? Is punishment why Edro's helping his town? Is it why I'm helping you and you're helping me?

×××

My father once said, "Revolution is an act of love—but so is oppression."

I wasn't sure where that left "justice." I wasn't sure where it left "love," either, but I tucked a stem of orange flowers into the Ragpicker's veil.

×××

A semicircle of yellowbrown feathers poked from a cracked mudball like a headdress.

Dozens of feathers snagged in termite mounds and guardrails and caterpillar tents, though more were tangled in the grass. I looked at them and saw the lampstack slumping to the concrete slabs after I'd snapped its strings.

Edro offered me his satchel and said, "Take the goat and baby and head for town."

I said, "Your town."

"You won't get halfway there. We'll catch up before you even see the tower. We'll find you when this is over."

"Unless you can't."

Edro took my wrist. "Go back, Ysmany—a day's walk, two days. Put a little time between you and them. You can't go forward. They're between us and the city."

"Just like you wanted," I said.

"Yeah, like I wanted. I brought us here, I brought him here." Edro knelt in front of me. "And he can't think right if you're in danger. Are you going to pretend that he can fight with you standing a hundred paces from a likehunter's knife?"

The Ragpicker took shape behind Edro. One tasseled glove rested on Edro's shoulder in solidarity. He'd never touched him before.

Edro said, "They're already in his head. Them plus whatever dead chorus sings him lullabies. He doesn't need you adding to that noise, Ysmany. Look at him. He already can't think past you."

×××

Edro gave me his satchel and the Ragpicker gave me a slip of plastic with the words HEARTLEAF THORNMINT.

"What's that mean?" I asked.

He touched my cheek with one of his knuckles.

"Is that what you think?" I asked.

"Yes," he said.

I made a noise that was half-laugh and half-cry, and in another voice he said something about aging and dying, something about fear, something about consequences.

×××

I put the goat on a lead and settled the baby and retraced my steps.

Walking the path backward. Hiking past the hidden sides of things I'd already named.

Edro was planning something. I knew that, even if I didn't know what it was. The Ragpicker did, though. He knew what Edro was planning.

×××

The leaves rattled louder now that I was alone.

I missed Luz. Her catalina-currant scent and the dumb nattering of her voice. The black speck in her right eye and how she never surprised me.

My memory traced a path through town, stopping at every tent to visit the people who lived there, even the ones I didn't like.

I passed over Dmitri like saving dessert after a meal, but I'd only reached Maria and Bekah before I took fright at the silence and emptiness of this lonely path, seeing myself suddenly through a bobcat's eyes.

×××

Cool air seeped from a crawlspace beneath a thicket of boxthorn, rotten with skunk.

I crossed a concrete slab.

I felt the Ragpicker's absence and the null point of Edro's hands on my waist where he'd lifted to me onto that boulder. I knotted them together for company and ligaments swiveled me back toward the likehunters like a flower toward the sun.

I couldn't run away from this.

×××

The baby needed feeding and changing so I fed and changed him before I turned to rejoin the Ragpicker and Edro.

I moved farther north, farther west, retracing my steps toward them.

Server raised me to know my purpose, to know my use.

I needed to stand witness.

×××

I hugged the eastern side of a concrete conduit, an irrigation or communications pipeline. I saw two feathers in six hours. My stomach bittered with fear but the Ragpicker said he wouldn't reach the likehunters until tomorrow.

I stopped at a stream to drink and wash.

An hour farther along, the goat shied from some hidden danger, twisting into a half-circle and stamping until I smacked her rump.

I saw another feather and then, thirty paces onward, two more.

×××

The baby started crying. He wouldn't stop. I hated his noise and his unhappiness. I wanted to leave him there, like an offering, at the foot of a scaly cactus pierced by starling feathers instead of spines.

I wanted to shake him. Instead I pinched him, so he cried even louder. I felt a little better, though.

After twenty minutes he settled into a nap and an hour after that he woke cheerful. Forgetting was a kind of miracle.

×××

My father said the network hadn't let anyone forget. No pain, no failure, no hope, no dream, no whim went unremembered.

Except that wasn't my father, that was the Ragpicker.

He said we'd lost the ability to forget.

Then he said we hadn't lost the ability, we'd sacrificed it. We'd exposed it.

Not exposed like revealed, he said. Exposed like murdered.

×××

The conduit broke into a series of hills and then at dusk into hillocks. Swallows chased bugs across the sky. Dmitri always rooted for the weak and the small, for the prey, then frowned when I said he wanted predators to starve.

I milked the goat and fed the baby. I didn't eat. I was hungry but every time I brought food to my mouth I didn't eat. Too many stars came out. My father said that when I was a baby, the night sky made me cry. He said there was a kind of light that wasn't visible to the human eye. There were colors we couldn't see.

I wasn't cold, but I shivered.

The night lasted a long time.

×××

In the morning I thought I heard seagulls.

According to Edro, the ocean was a few days away across the coastal plain. First we'd spend a day passing the sparse low houses, here where the foothills rippled. Then a day of higher houses, a hundred times as many, packed together toward the coast.

I imagined a wave of buildings that crested at the beach like a tidal wave.

Ysmany

I sang to the baby as I hiked northward, following the half-collapsed conduit. The foothills rose to my east while the flatter ground to my west sloped toward the distant ocean.

Then the land to my west turned flatter still, unnaturally flat, scraped smooth for miles and planted with a forest of weeping bamboo.

Unnatural like twitches.

I climbed a lonely hump of conduit and crawled into the lap of a low bush with shiny leaves. I closed one eye to focus through the binoculars at an oblong wire fence two or three hundred yards away.

Oblong and treetop-high, enclosing a handful of acres.

Inside the fence, feathers floated and swirled, blanketing the ground to the height of my hips then billowing into clouds as two figures waded through them. Moving like nothing human. Moving like the Ragpicker.

Two likehunters, wearing shiny white cloaks around secondskins coated with reflective disks. Catching feathers between their thumbs and forefingers, then inspecting them through the eyeports in their smooth white facemasks.

But where was the third?

The two of them barked with laughter, they howled with

laughter, then shrieked in pain or rage, but the sounds didn't match their movements, which stayed calm and slow. The sounds emerged from nowhere and resolved into nothing and—

A breeze rose, and a million wingless feathers soared and spun inside the fence.

Pain flared behind my closed eye. My mind squirmed. The baby snored beside me and I tried to draw lines between the feathers, connective tissue, sinews or tendons, to reconnect them, to recouple them, but I failed for hours—and didn't feel a single tug of the third likehunter.

Or of the Ragpicker and Edro. Where were they? They should've arrived before dawn. Had they already come and fought and died?

No. The aftermath would've spoken to me. Instead I faced blank serenity, a sticky quiet broken by meaningless, passionate moans and hoots and sobs. A hivemind, Edro said, but I saw no pattern that included both likehunters, no correlation between them. Maybe there was no "between." If they were the same thing, the same person in different bodies, there would be no gap. I didn't know if that was like Ragpicker or the opposite—

In perfect sync, both likehunters gave a spasm toward the north.

One of them returned to normal. Well, to inspecting feathers. But the other one, the second one, plowed across the cage. A wake of white and brown and blue feathers rose behind it. Then the likehunter pushed through a slit in the fencing and emerged into the stands of bamboo and started northward at an inhuman canter.

I watched that second likehunter for a hundred yards before a sudden terror struck me: what if the first one was coming for me?

With shaking hands I checked back inside the fence.

The first one was still there, inspecting feathers.

By the time my heart stopped pounding, I'd lost the second

likehunter in the forest. I lowered the binoculars and after a minute caught a flash of white through the shaggy clumps of bamboo.

The second likehunter was moving in a straight line northward. I scanned ahead of it, miles ahead, and spotted motion at the edge of the binocular's magnification. The third likehunter. Moving steadily toward the second one, to meet in the middle.

Moving steadily toward me, too. Dragging something behind, like a hunter dragging a kill.

Not a carcass, though. I couldn't see what. Maybe a sack, five or six times the likehunter's size. It didn't look heavy. I braced my arms to steady my view and watched a smear of white pulling a sack. Or a tarp, or folded wire fencing—

No, not a sack, not a tarp: a net.

Filled with birds.

Most dead, some dying.

Poisoned or trapped for their plumage.

My fingers itched. I'd braided thousands of bird skulls and feet into the lampstack, delicate angled bones and endless feathers—and dozens of hummingbirds. I felt the overlap between the likehunters and Server and me, and shame chilled my neck.

I lowered the binoculars and wanted to hold the sleeping baby—the only thing I'd ever protected from her—but the nearest likehunter, the first one, made a cry like a squawk so I looked back into the cage.

Nothing had changed.

The first likehunter stood babbling in a drift of feathers. Waiting for one to catch the wind then snatching it from the air. Peering close. Waiting for another, relying on randomness to choose which message to decipher, to select—

A swirl of feathers thickened at the likehunter's feet.

Into a crouching person.

Into the Ragpicker, punching upward with a spike in his hand. The point pierced the bottom of the likehunter's chin. The spike speared through the likehunter's head and snagged the glossy white hood of its cloak from beneath, then the Ragpicker withdrew the spike with a spit of blood and pivoted toward the second likehunter, the one a few hundred yards away.

The body swayed behind him . . . and didn't fall.

After taking a spike through the brain, the likehunter didn't fall.

Edro shouted a warning and the injured likehunter giggled and yipped and lurched against the Ragpicker and dragged him down into the feathers, which splashed and cratered and plumed.

I lost sight of them.

I heard myself panting.

The second likehunter froze into a reverie for two heartbeats—except not frozen, trembling—before shouting numbers—34, 34, 1-9-1-8-3-4—and sprinting toward the cage. The third one, the farthest one, with the birdnet, I knew without looking was still trembling. They were a hive mind: the living were controlling the dead through some lingering connection to its secondskin

For how long?

I started trembling too.

The feathers lifted and swirled, and a strong wind pasted them against the fence. Sweat dripped into my eyes. I blinked and blinked and trembled.

Then the Ragpicker oozed from the slit in the cage. Behind him, in a sudden clearing, the first likehunter lay unmoving on the ground, its white cloak catching a thousand falling feathers.

One of the Ragpicker's arms looked wrong through his tatters. Broken or sprained or—or wrong. He wasn't a fighter. I'd made him fight. For that town. For me, for the pioneers, for fear of telling the truth. I'd made him fight and he glided through the bamboo and took his crowbar in his left hand, and I knew that he needed cover, needed concealment, but the second likehunter was seconds away, racing through that lake-flat forest.

The Ragpicker couldn't hide so he braced between two

stalks of bamboo and the likehunter was a billowing white shape flashing through the brown and green and black and green and green—

A crossbow bolt sprouted from the second likehunter's stomach.

It stumbled two steps then slammed into the Ragpicker and the Ragpicker struck once with his crowbar before they became a tumbling blur.

When they stopped rolling the likehunter was on top and beating the Ragpicker with a baton, so hard that I heard the cracks. I felt them. Then another bolt sprouted from the likehunter, that time from its neck, the side of its neck, and Edro was stalking through the bamboo, framed between new stems every two steps, with his spear and his strength and his big stupid hands.

The likehunter looked at him then hit the Ragpicker again and again until the Ragpicker stopped moving.

I wanted to scream. I started crying from anger and had to lower the binoculars to wipe my eyes. When I found them again, Edro was ten paces from the likehunter, stripped to the waist to reveal a drawing on his chest.

A sweat-smeared map of his ribs and organs. His spine was traced behind a maze of arteries and intestine.

Like one of the cairns outside his town.

Like one of the cairns.

And sure enough, the design drew the likehunter closer.

My heart stopped and the baby woke. The baby cried once, a single shriek, a siren into the bamboo forest. The likehunter's facemask tilted, its eyeless eyeport found me—which meant they *both* saw me, even the one to the north, they both knew where I was.

Acid sick rose from my stomach to my mouth. I gagged but didn't puke and I raised my hand to slap the baby but he'd already fallen silent. He'd woken up, given a cry loud enough to kill us both, then gone back to sleep.

My stomach didn't settle. My mouth filled with spit. I didn't know what else to do so I lowered my hand. I looked again and saw the likehunter standing in front of Edro, chuckling then squealing then *oohing* then barking.

The likehunter put Edro onto his back on the ground.

The likehunter knelt beside him and consulted the chart on his chest.

The likehunter dipped its hands inside Edro as easy as dipping your hands into a stream.

The likehunter pulled things out and Edro screamed and his legs moved in bad ways. The likehunter's noises never stopped—a sob, a plea, a cheer—and its hands emerged with the dripping curve of a bone or, or a kidney or stomach, then with a smooth snaking length of tube.

Edro fell dead and the Ragpicker loomed behind the likehunter. He drove his knife into its ear, then in-out, in-out, in-out, in-out. He slammed a final time with his palm, driving the knife hilt-deep, then he fell to his knees.

He swayed, his chin touching his chest.

He crawled, one-armed, halfway to Edro's spear.

He collapsed.

Bamboo shadows striped his ragmound. His ribbons and tatters and shawls seemed to wither and wilt. I couldn't tell if he was alive. Edro wasn't, though. Edro wasn't. He was dead with his ribcage spread like wings.

The Ragpicker flattened into a pile of fabric. Into a shroud, fluttering in the breeze beneath bamboo leaves that were also fluttering.

×××

"I know that I'll age and sicken and die," is what he'd told me, in another voice, "yet I'm afraid to love what ages and sickens and dies. Everything I know will fail, everyone I love will fail, and so will everyone I hate and everything I never learned. My actions are my only self. We can't escape the consequences of our selves but here is the blessed thing, neeneh: to abandon all hope of results and to love what one cannot escape."

×××

I started to stand, then didn't. I couldn't do anything. I needed to save VK but I couldn't, I couldn't do anything but watch, so I watched the third likehunter's tireless whooping, jibbering sprint closer. Its white cloak rippled. At the edge of the bamboo forest it dropped the birdnet and veered away from the Ragpicker—toward me, closer and closer.

I felt a new kind of fear.

Then the white flowed away from me again, into the bamboo, in a spiral with the Ragpicker in the center, squealing and cooing and counting.

The likehunter circled the Ragpicker's tattered heap twice then capered in place, doing a gangling dance. It armed and aimed Edro's crossbow and, in three beats of my heart, fired four times at the Ragpicker. It was so strong it didn't need to crank the bow, it just pulled the string and fired, then again and again and again.

The first two bolts pierced the mound of rags. The third cracked against something inside the tatters and ricocheted through the bamboo but the fourth pierced the mound again.

The likehunter never stopped vocalizing. It spun and aimed and fired the last bolt into the Ragpicker's head, then jumped and landed with both knees on the Ragpicker and reached down with strangling hands and Edro's blood-slick corpse appeared behind it.

Except not Edro's corpse, something else.

A gaunt, redbrown creature.

A smooth, sunken cadaver that thrust Edro's spear at the likehunter's back—but the likehunter spun and took the spearhead in the chest and the creature rammed forward, driving the spear left-handed through the likehunter while its right arm dangled—

The Ragpicker.

That was what he looked like beneath his rags.

That was him. Naked, exposed. He'd dropped his pelt like a lizard drops its tail.

He heaved forward until the likehunter slammed against a thick bamboo stalk then he kept pushing until the spearpoint drilled through the back of the likehunter's secondskin and into the bark.

The likehunter laughed and crowed and pushed itself along the impaling spear toward the Ragpicker. The shaft turned black behind the likehunter, black with fluids.

One step, two steps, three steps, until the Ragpicker pivoted, torquing the likehunter, flinging it off the spear and into another tree.

It curled to the ground. Its vocalizations softened but didn't stop.

The Ragpicker fell, too.

Nothing happened for a while except the likehunter's quiet babble.

Then the Ragpicker stood and stabbed the likehunter twice more in the chest and almost in the face, except he pulled that blow. He held the spearhead steady an inch inside the likehunter's secondskin, the wound seeping blood.

He stood there.

The two of them looked at each other.

The likehunter fell quiet.

They were ancient machines, abandoned by everything they'd known. They were communicating. Dreaming together, and dying together, which frightened me because—which frightened me.

So I took the baby and hiked closer.

If the Ragpicker saw me in danger, he would kill the likehunter. I needed to believe that, and I needed him to kill the likehunter before—before he couldn't.

When I reached the bamboo they hadn't moved.

I told the Ragpicker to put the spear forward but he didn't.

I asked, What about the pioneers, what about Edro? What about the bones on the hillside? What about all the bodies we'd never find and all the terrors we'd never know, and I heard the likehunter whispering:

—revealed that we are embedded in the world and the world is embedded in us, inseparable, inexplicable. The network forced us to acknowledge this in a language more fundamental than language: in feeling. We feel pain when we read of murdered children in a schoolyard, of toxins eating walruses from the inside, and we thrill to the first steps of a stranger's child. Why? Because it is happening to us, too. To our selves, extending now across the planet, we encompass—personally, individually—expanses once beyond the imagination of our species. Call the injuries unreal or irrational but any pain that is felt by definition exists. We are embedded in hogs suffocating in their pens and in the flight of a clematis seed and the thunder of a drummer striking overturned barrels in a baharat alley and a minnow and the scent of your lover's lover's thigh. This is not a flaw in our empathy this a revelation of our unity. We responded to the network, we addicted ourselves to the network, because everything that happened in the network happened to ourselves. This is revelation. This is enlightenment. The network is solidarity, cohesion; it's the spiritual fact of global unity born into the world. The network revealed that we are embedded in the world and the world is—

"Kill it," I said. "Kill it."

The Ragpicker didn't. He withdrew his spear from the likehunter's face. He stumbled and almost fell. He leaned on the spear, then lowered into a squat.

After a while, the likehunter's face stopped bleeding.

The baby woke again, that time quieter. Feathers drifted past, the sun moved. The likehunter stood into a pained stoop and wrapped the dead likehunters in the net and dragged them away.

The Ragpicker collapsed onto his side.

I left him there and climbed the conduit hump with the binoculars. I fed the baby and watched until the likehunter shrank into the horizon.

Ysmany

The Ragpicker couldn't move or talk. He couldn't stand or talk or move.

I dressed him in his rags and squeezed his hands but he didn't squeeze back. Then I kissed Edro and composted him, which took until the sun touched the top of the bamboo forest.

I stank of blood and sweat and dirt. The goat gorged herself on leaves. I cried when I milked her, then I took the baby to the stream.

I made camp around the Ragpicker and settled VK beside him for comfort. Then I dragged the spear to the wire cage and I cried again as I prized the fence apart to let the feathers free.

×××

The bluegray sky made shapes between the bamboo leaves. None of them fit together. A thousand shifting windows.

Instead of sleeping, I looked through them.

×××

In the morning I undressed him and washed his rags. I scrubbed his secondskin. He didn't like that but he couldn't stop me.

His secondskin felt cool and warm, like glass in sunlight. All the new rips and punctures in the surface bubbled, and the bubbles stank. His old wounds had formed seams and scales and stains. He looked like melted plastic and made noises that sounded like shame.

—

He started to die.

—

His body was mending but his mind wasn't. He was dying in my hands, with his head in my lap.

He was dying from a sickness of the heart, of the memory. Despite his stillness and his silence he begged for stories like I'd once told him. I couldn't bring the words into my mouth, not until a voice I'd never heard him use before said:

"The suspension of disbelief—belief—belief—faith is only necessary when stories aren't true, but everything that exists is true. The network is a network of stories. If you hurt yourself for a story, either the story is true or you are a fool. If you hurt someone else for a story, either the story is true or you are a villain. We are not fools or villains, Ysmany. He needs to hear your voice."

—

I took the postcards from my bag. For two days I read the pioneer's words aloud:

A time is defined not by ideas that are argued but by ideas that are taken for granted. The character of an era hangs upon what needs no defense.

"What everyone knows" is the line between us and them.

—

We are razing the architecture without demonstrating why this change is needed. We are shifting resources from the commons into a system of feedback. We are obeying an ideology without considering the facts.

Why are we making these changes?

There is a blissful story to be told.

—

"What everyone knows" is the line between us and them.

Between three months and four years, some dragonflies reveal their true natures, which is not nymphic but mythic.

—

The architects who birthed the first protocols did not conceive a technology in which every sensation is available in point three seconds. They did not expect the social industry to transform the distribution and production of stimulation, of selves, of tastes and touches and sentience and scent—a sweetish, musky feedback that mingles with the blare of trumpets—into the tingle, the flame, the honeydew, victory.

—

—technology improves.

An implant thrums approvingly when a peergroup endorses new content. Wearing secondskins, separated by oceans, lovers intertwine

my body knew what I craved, my mind balked. One moment I was ashamed and frightened, another recklessly optimistic.

Taboos strangled me, yet I tried.

So hard to be good.

—

Whenever I hear an activity is free, I believe a price is being quoted—free as in zero cost—but free has a more fundamental meaning: unchained.

The opportunity to immerse myself in a chamber, pretending to consult a trembling screen while around me children frolic, is an excruciating freedom.

—

lurking in the code is our conviction that nothing is valuable that is not restricted, as when in a greygreen city the man in red passed me at a swaying, high-heeled step.

You have your interests; I have mine.

The social industry displays selves as biomes and biomes as resources and resources as unrestricted.

I moved farther north, farther east.

—

"That is my daughter," my mother said, "and these are my lilies."

"Beautiful," he said. "Beautiful, beautiful, beautiful."

The issue, in terms of engagement and expansion, is not whether producers have enough incentive to create, it is whether the rest of us have enough incentive to abstain.

—

She sat beside me on the lowest step of the porch and picked up the pebbles between her feet—pebbles, my God, then a curled bottletop resembling a sneering lip—and chucked them at a can.

Ping.

That is the tragedy: each user is locked into a system that forces them to increase connectivity without limit, in a world that is limited.

—

mixes pleasure with control. Layers are free or encoded, snarky, cheerful, awkward, racist, wise, tragic, thirsty. Complexity and intelligence in the network are pushed away from the network into the blindspots, like two deft little hands that covered my eyes.

What was required before the Bliss was this: permission.

But what made that permission possible?

—

Pleasure enhances the social value of the controlled.

We assume that no rational society reorients itself around collisions and addictions and overdoses but instead protects its borders like ice cubes rasping, crackling, squealing as warm water loosens them in their cells.

We poured nutrient solution into cloudtanks and added sleeping pills.

The machine is a pharmacological device that presumes the misery it then spins into gold. We are focused on improving our lot but we don't have a lot to improve: this is the regurgitation economy.

"What's the matter with kisses?" I muttered into her hair.

"They're okay," she said. "If you do them right."

"Show me how."

"Later," she said.

—

The lock presumes that engagement is the only value.

The key is in my fist.

—

The author is constrained by expectation, enslaved by the evil he prepared for his secret delectation and the default settings, in these bright ages, at least, intone the eternal yes.

Our world is closer to the world of ideas than to the world of things.

Volunteers produce a better, fuller, richer culture, an extraordinary range of sensations that populate skins with the delectation of quantifiable, improvable, self-regard, yet here we are, here we still are, sitting with the small ghost of the body we just killed.

—

The dream overshot its mark and plunged into a nightmare. We were careless and stupid, and let me be frank: under all this brilliant turmoil we still felt the writhing of desire, so monstrous was our appetite.

Ysmany

When I wasn't reading postcards, I went through the Ragpicker's pack and his pouches. I found a black baggie of crumbled saltlick and poison ivy leaves rolled into tubes and in a transparent case I found my toenail clippings.

In the main compartment I found the case of hardened assault rifle plastic. Cracked now, from a crossbow bolt.

That afternoon, he watched me work his knife into the cracks.

×××

In the morning, I bottle-fed the Ragpicker goatmilk and the baby stood by himself for the first time. He'd been crawling over the shaggy mound of the Ragpicker's pelt and pulled himself to his feet using a fistful of tatters.

I said dumb things like, "Good job! What a big boy, what a big smart boy!" but the stupid happy words sounded wrong in the bamboo forest.

The Ragpicker squeezed my hand and tried to say, Good job, what a big girl, what good smart girl.

×××

I made him crawl from the bamboo to the brush near the stream, then he collapsed and couldn't move or speak again.

I fed them. I fed them and cleaned them and tended them. I told them about Dmitri and Luz and my father, about the clinging tendrils of passionfruit vines and about the scent of boiled lamb hooves, myrtle and nettle and fat.

I told them about Server but I didn't tell them my plan.

×××

The crack in the plastic shell widened beneath my blade.

The Ragpicker watched with his compound eyes. Everything about him begged me to stop.

"Why?" I asked.

He still wasn't talking right, even for him, but he said something about love and memory and maybe reunion. The words frightened me because they sounded like the likehunter: *solidarity, cohesion, the spiritual fact of unity.*

×××

The next time he went limp, I braided his rags. When he didn't wake after an hour, I pried open the broken clasp of his case and looked inside.

×××

I left the baby with him and gathered limes from the living parts of a dying tree. When I got back he'd snapped the spear for a crutch. He took a few proud, hobbling steps to show me that he could.

We ate limes while the baby finished the lentils mashed with fruit, and he told me about Nufar. Maybe Nufar told me about him, I couldn't tell. They needed to return home, with the syncable, to salvage whatever was salvageable.

I asked about the syncable. When they explained, I didn't say anything. They'd packed their hearts into that case. Their hopes. This was the final chapter of their lives, the final purpose of their lives. This was the point of them.

×××

The Ragpicker lowered himself to the stream bank with his unbooted feet in the current. Water bulged around him. Long-legged striders skated across the surface while tadpoles wriggled and grazed beneath.

He rested there for hours, then lifted a mesh fabric from the streambed. The striders fled and water oozed from the bag, now bulging with tadpoles. The Ragpicker ate half of them. He gave the rest to me. I spooned the legless ones into the baby's mouth and watched them swim into his throat and disappear.

×××

"You're the Goddess of Common Enemies and Broken Feet," I told him, "eating your children to keep them from stealing Your throne."

The Ragpicker angled his head a fraction of an inch, which meant he didn't know that story so I told him what my father had told me: the Goddess, who was also the Earth, made a blood pact with her enemies—her parents, the sun and the moon, who'd brought the Goddess accidentally into being before spending ten thousand ages trying to unmake her again—she'd made a pact with them to kill the soft, weak, ravenous children spreading in uncountable number across the land, to stop them before they turned their teeth to the sky but while the children were stupid and hungry they were also cunning so they hid from the sun and the moon until the Goddess severed her own feet to tempt them with divine flesh. Then when they gathered to feast she ate them.

One of his voices said, "Well, that's charming."

×××

Damselflies played in a stand of reeds. One darted toward me, then landed on a broken crayfish shell. She spread her wings into quarters. She cleaned her face. I listened to the stream and the cardinals and the wind.

×××

"I'm not going to the city," I told the Ragpicker. "We're not going to the city."

"Edro's town is safe now," he said, except he didn't say "Edro" exactly.

"We're not going to the towertown either," I told him.

The Ragpicker scrubbed at the baby's soiled clothes. Stronger now, though he still couldn't walk much.

"We're going to my town," I told him. "Going back to my town."

With Server?

"Yes," I told him.

He spread the clothes on a sunny rock then slumped there with his feet in the stream. The water bulged around his ankles again and when the silt settled the tadpoles had returned.

"You don't have to come with us," I said, because I knew he would.

×××

We spent two days carving a memorial for Edro, then headed west. The Ragpicker's leg dragged at first but his arm was okay.

After leaving the foothills, the knolls of decayed houses rose more often, and closer together. Different flowers grew there, ones I'd never seen before, along with strange trees.

We passed a military base with a fence surrounding buildings that were being smothered by a fleshy trumpetvine. The birds and insects avoided it, but the goat didn't care. She rubbed her head against the fence until the Ragpicker led her away.

An arrow-straight, grass-covered valley shot us through the highest heaps of dead buildings. We reached a place where two great highways met. Concrete ramps heaved from the ground and twisted into knots like bucks locking antlers, then straightened again.

We crossed the marsh beneath them, disturbing an egret hunting frogs, and finally reached the ocean.

×××

The baby laughed at the waves. He laughed and laughed and laughed.

×××

The ocean was too big. The noise deafened me.

The sand warmed my feet, though. And in the glass-slick tide, tiny bugs popped from sandy pores at every step, scurried madly, then dove back into the earth.

The beach ended at a pier that turned into a miles-long neighborhood built to float on rafts or pontoons. Everything was half-submerged now, half-swallowed by the ocean, like a sheep decomposing in a pond.

Farther along, walls and scaffolds and pylons sprouted into reefs and breakwaters and shoals.

We cut inland through a fallen sandcastle city where monkeys screamed around every corner but never showed themselves.

When we reached the beach again, the Ragpicker backtracked to scavenge or—I didn't know, he wouldn't tell me. I kept following the beach southward. I kept telling myself that he hadn't left me.

×××

Flocks of seabirds fled from the tide on skinny legs, leaving tracks like alphabets in the sand. Drops of water touched my cheeks. The air stank of dead fish or seaweed, so I kept checking if the baby had shat himself but he hadn't.

Something big splashed in the ocean, just past where the waves broke. So I started walking in the dry sand, farther from the tide.

The sound of the ocean reminded me of dreams, except I never remembered my dreams. What good were they, anyway? People told me about drifting into the clouds or being greeted by the dead, but you didn't need dreams for that.

×××

I asked VK if he dreamed, and the Ragpicker took shape among the prickly shrubs in the dunes. When I reached him, he poured blue chips of sugarcandy into my palms and listed the things he'd found.

1) A whistle.
2) A knife, foldable.
3) One pack each, firestarter and firesticks.
4) Bandages and assorted medical gear.
5) Sealed kit containing blanket, poncho, mirror.
6) Fishing line, hooks, weight, etcetera.

7) Four Gotex utility vests.

8) Postcards, assorted.

9) Three tins of plum tomatoes.

He tasted the plum tomatoes to check if they'd hurt me, then I ate some. They didn't taste like plums or like tomatoes.

That night he built a fire.

×××

"Because my family is there," I told him. "My friends, my family. Everyone I know. I belong with them. They belong with me."

Belong with or belong to?

"Because I don't fit anywhere else," I told him. "I don't make sense anywhere else and—and what's Server doing now? What's she doing to them? I left them behind, with her."

To save the baby, he said.

"I don't want you to fight her. I'm not going to ask that. I know you can't."

He stirred the tomatoes and didn't say anything.

"She raised me. She's the closest thing I have to a . . ."

When I fell silent, he looked toward the inland ruins.

"I understand her," I told him, when the silence ended. "The way I understand you."

×××

I understood her obsession. I belonged to her obsession. I'd been raised inside her devotion, her demands, her fundamental lack of something essential. I didn't know if I could control Server but I knew nobody else could.

"She's not the closet thing I have to a mother," I didn't tell him. "You are."

×××

A cliff pushed us inland onto bluffs overlooking coves toothed with boulders.

Little brown hopping birds darted through sage scrub perfumed with sunlight.

Then beach sand warmed my feet again. The tide said *shush,*

shush, hush but the otters didn't listen, click-clacking stones against abalone and mussels.

×××

Every few hours we passed another port-holed crate, the size of a cargo truck. The Ragpicker called them ImEx transmitters. He explained, but I didn't understand. Then splintery wreckage covered the beach in shards of broken glass—not exactly glass—so we climbed a hillside and made camp in the shelter of a stone arch.

In the morning, the mist turned to rain that beaded on my poncho and on the goat's horns and on my forehead when I looked at the sky.

I memorized the moment: the scent of rain and the sound of the rain and the taste of the crabapple I was chewing to soften for the baby.

×××

The Ragpicker stuffed a bag with goosefoot leaves. We angled southward, crossing sandbanks. Past mossy, shrunken oak trees and fields of orange poppy.

Blue mist filled a valley between two rises, and the next morning we reached a beach that stretched too far from the natural shoreline. Extended, according to the Ragpicker, by an underlayer of trillions of tiny adhesive geologic beads.

Though the Ragpicker spoke more often in voices not his own.

He said, "We are diggers of wells. Water is everywhere beneath us, yet we cannot force it to rise. We can only dig holes and wait for the water to swell freely upward. We must empty what we wish to fill."

×××

A family of whales broke the surface of the ocean like newborn gods. Two of them spat great plumes of disregard and showed me their hullbacks crusted with barnacles.

I wept. I wept because they were holy and because they were alive.

The sky beckoned and the ocean poured itself into me. I was caught between the lightness above and the weight below but I wasn't trapped, I was embraced. Balanced on the scales of the world but not judged: measured.

The sky and ocean recorded my height and weight and width and worth.

Exactly one Ysmany, I said.

×××

When I mentioned the lampstack, the Ragpicker said, "Threads are endless, neeneh. Every thread that unravels tries to reattach itself to the source. That is the purpose of the threads and so we descend, unraveled, alone, desperate to loop back into ourselves. We don't search for God. God is the thing that searches. God is our word for the thing that searches for us."

×××

"Something came loose inside you," I told him. "Back when—I don't know when. Something broke loose."

He said, "Okay."

We didn't speak for a long time. We abandoned the beach for a coastal highway. We passed rhododendrons with fat pink flowers in the courtyard of an eroded house.

Cresting the next rise, we stumbled upon a herd of elk. Making more noise than I'd expected, squealing and mewing and chirruping. My father taught us the history of cows and pigs and buffalo, sheep and chickens. We'd bred them for slaughter, a billion billion animals, and after we'd eaten our fill we'd slaughtered ourselves.

"I'm scared," I told the Ragpicker.

"Of what?"

"That you'll change."

The elk herd crossed the meadow, shaggy dark necks and smoother silvery-brown bodies. The bull came last, with high tight antlers that looked like bones and flame.

"I've been like this," the Ragpicker said, "for so long."

×××

                              dolphin
                              dolphin
        dolphin dolphin
                    dolphin
dolphin   dolphin   dolphin dolphin
      dolphin   dolphin   dolphin   dolphin dolphin
dolphin dolphin   dolphin dolphin dolphin dolphin dolphin
dolphin dolphin dolphin dolphin dolphin dolphin dolphin dolphin
dolphin dolphin dolphin dolphin dolphin dolphin dolphin dolphin
dolphin dolphin dolphin dolphin dolphin dolphin dolphin dolphin
dolphin dolphin dolphin dolphin dolphin dolphin dolphin dolphin
dolphin dolphin dolphin dolphin dolphin dolphin dolphin dolphin
dolphin dolphin dolphin dolphin dolphin dolphin dolphin dolphin
dolphin dolphin dolphin dolphin dolphin dolphin dolphin dolphin
dolphin dolphin dolphin dolphin dolphin dolphin dolphin dolphin
dolphin dolphin dolphin dolphin dolphin dolphin dolphin dolphin
dolphin dolphin dolphin dolphin dolphin dolphin dolphin dolphin
      dolphin dolphin   dolphin   dolphin dolphin dolphin
dolphin dolphin dolphin   dolphin   dolphin dolphin
      dolphin dolphin   dolphin dolphin dolphin dolphin dolphin
dolphin
                    dolphin   dolphin   dolphin
        dolphin   dolphin
          dolphin dolphin   dolphin
        dolphin   dolphin
                              dolphin
        dolphin

                              ×××

Hours of them turned the ocean into a shrine.

I said, "The best thing we ever did for them was die."

One of his voices said, "The fear of dying is precisely the same as the fear of livi—"

"All I want," he snapped at himself, "is to die with Nufar in my mind. Plug in the syncable and never unplug again."

                              ×××

What if I'd lived before the end of civilization? What if I'd driven on these highways instead of walked them? What if the Earth shined so brightly that it blinded the sun? What if nobody died from childbirth and nobody from fever? What if every kitchen yielded bread and meat, water and sugar? What if heat didn't warm me and cold didn't chill me? What if there was nothing I could not know?

×××

Dozens of fat, unhilled antholes opened in the dirt of the bluffs, under the bushes where I hunted for eggs. Except instead of ants, bees flew in and out of them. The Ragpicker said they weren't honeybees, he said honeybees gathered inside their hive, each holding a single bead of nectar on her tongue while beating her wings. He said, imagine that, ten thousand bees standing in the dark, flapping furiously, sticking out their tongues to make honey.

I knew that wasn't true, I knew he was just trying make me smile—and I smiled.

×××

A satellite dish lay on the beach, barnacle-studded, algae-slimed, cup-upward. Half-filled with seawater. Inside, crabs sidled among empty shells and anemones and knobbed strands of seaweed. An entire towertown in one fallen, tumbled, battered bowl.

I didn't let the Ragpicker eat the snails. The dish was so far from the high tide mark that I didn't know how all that water and sand and life got there. I didn't know how it stayed there, brimming, simmering, thriving.

I felt a protective teary fondness for those anemone, those crabs, those snails. Even though they were exactly like the ones in the tidepools a stone's throw away, they also weren't. They were different because they were *those* anemone, *those* crabs, *those* snails.

×××

The fire that night burned bright and shameless. The cliffs were a thousand times taller but they didn't dance. My lips tasted of salt, and so did the baby's wrist when I touched it with the tip of my tongue.

The Ragpicker roasted skewered apples and I said, "Nufar. You have to tell him."

"Tell me what?" the Ragpicker asked.

"The truth," I said.

"In every important way," the Ragpicker said in another voice, "we are all secrets to each other."

"That's such a bullshit kind of bullshit," I told him. "Don't blame some stupid quote for the fact that you're lying to yourself. He needs to tell you."

"He says he doesn't know. He only knows what I know."

"Yeah," I said. "And you know."

If I looked into the fire for long enough, I couldn't see the stars.

I missed my father's hand on my shoulder. I missed his voice, trying to convince me that constellations existed.

×××

I ate bird-pecked figs from a tree with broken arms and labyrinth roots. Ants ran across my fingers and tickled my skin.

"There's a species of wasp that's only born inside of figs," the Ragpicker told me.

"That's dumb," I said.

"When the females hatch," he told me, "they fly to a new fig where they lay eggs and die. When the males hatch, they chew holes for the females to leave, then die in the same fig where they were born."

I didn't know why he'd told me that. A fig was a fig. Who cared which one you died in? Had he said that because I'd flown away, and was now returning to the same fig?

I didn't ask.

Birds screeched when he climbed to pick more fruit.

×××

After Edro died I'd stopped making little lampstacks—too much like cairns—but once we reached the coast the Ragpicker started whittling toys for the baby during his long sleepless nights. Half-formed animals. A few legs, a body, a head with the suggestion of ears or a rump with the suggestion of a tail.

The goat he carved looked the same as his elk and his coyote. I asked him to make a dolphin and the next morning, after we'd walked for hours, we came to a stretch of beach where he'd arranged in the night a hundred lengths of driftwood to look like a dolphin pod leaping and playing in sandy waves.

×××

When our canteens lightened, we followed a backwash slough to a river of willow trees, cattails, and mated pairs of ducks with gray feathers and yellow beaks.

In a valley an hour from the beach, nasturtium covered the three standing walls of a tile-roofed, golden stone house. The inside was mostly filled with spindly weeds sprouting from decayed floors and dirt-rotten furniture, but half the roof still sheltered a marble room with pipes and tiles.

Around back, a stone path meandered through tangerine trees. To the side, near the waterfall that fed the pond, the Ragpicker cleaned brush from around a well.

"A hot spring," he said.

I watched steam waft above the water while he worked and felt a sadness I didn't understand. Maybe I missed him. Even though he was right there in front of me, I missed him.

×××

He showed me red-legged treefrogs. He collected cattails. He pickled some in vinegar with dill, and the rest he wrapped in nasturtium leaves and dipped in soy and honey.

We cleared a sunken section of floor for the baby to practice walking. We added everything that looked like a toy, but the baby wanted me. What he wanted most in the world was me.

×××

The next morning, the Ragpicker brought us inland along the river and showed us a grove of eucalyptus trees blanketed in orange-black butterflies. Thousands of them, more than thousands.

The Ragpicker said they'd flown here from another continent.

Two of them landed on the baby's sling and I turned to show the Ragpicker in an embarrassment of delight—and he was absolutely covered with them, every inch of him blanketed with butterflies.

The baby laughed all the time now, but that was the first time he laughed just from hearing me laughing.

xxx

"We should stay here forever," I almost told the Ragpicker. "And never leave."

The cruelty of the words kept them in my throat.

He didn't believe he could stay; he thought he needed to return home, to save whatever was left of his love. How long had that faith sustained him? How many decades? It's what kept him moving forward, it's why he mattered to himself.

The difference was that I *did* need to return, to save whatever was left of those I loved.

xxx

When I washed the baby in the spring water I wanted to touch every inch of his skin, to sink my teeth into his damp unfinished plumpness. Into the four dimples on each hand, into his creased formless armpits, to suck the dirt from his bellybutton. I wanted to unfold the curves inside the curves of his ears.

Mostly I wanted to thank him. For what I didn't know, but I squatted there dizzy with gratitude.

xxx

That night we talked about a lot of things that I only halfway understood. The Ragpicker had grown too comfortable with not knowing. After all this time, he'd learned to refuse to understand.

He was coming unstuck. Things were shaking loose inside him—and maybe inside me, too.

After two days, we returned to the beach.

The Ragpicker said that if I put a shell to my ear I'd hear the ocean, but the ocean was right there.

The baby didn't want a shell at his ear. He spent the morning fussing, then spent the afternoon fussing and the evening crying.

Taking care of a baby was so hard. Sometimes it was impossible. And VK was a sweet baby, too. Taking care of me must've been even harder than that, harder than impossible. Which meant what? Which meant that maybe for the first time I almost understood my mother.

×××

I loved the Ragpicker, but he loved me more.

×××

"Sometimes I want to stop," I told him. "I want to give up. Like that's the best way to end things."

"If things end," I said.

"They change," the Ragpicker said, even though he was terrible in his unchanging durability.

That wasn't fair. His tenderness overshadowed his durability. His softness made my throat ache.

He counted the baby's toes until the gurbles of glee changed to wheezes of sleep. He rocked him with tidal forbearance. He touched my elbow so gently, to draw my attention to pelicans or sea glass or a mansion inset into a cliff, that I mistook him for a breeze. Sometimes when he braided my hair I'd press my head to his chest and he'd take me into his loops of ribbons and cords until I forgot all those parts of myself that didn't fit.

×××

I wanted to give in, I wanted to give up.

What was the difference between giving in and giving up? I guessed that depended on where the giving went. Up? In?

Like what I was giving didn't matter as much as where.

We lost two days when I made us return to the house in the butterfly valley.

He roasted ducks over a fire in which tangerine peels hissed. A mated pair. He pulled unlaid eggs from the female first and boiled them and peeled the skin off with his delicate fingers.

I said, "You're falling apart."

He said, "Okay."

I said, "And what I'm going to tell you . . ."

He blew on the eggs to cool them for the baby.

"I'm afraid," I said.

"That I'm going to change," he said.

"That I'm going to change you."

"You already did," he said.

"Not like that."

He gave me the baby and retreated across the marble room and squatted watching me, which meant he was frightened too.

"I'm sorry," I told him. "I'm sorry but I can't not tell you. Not anymore."

Then like a coward I didn't.

Until the middle of the night. For once, the baby didn't wake me. Instead, I came awake in a full fury and went to shake the Ragpicker except he wasn't there, he wasn't sleeping, so I went outside and shouted and a few minutes later the darkness took the shape of him and I went and shoved him to turn around and yanked his pack off him, one strap, two straps, three straps, and I pulled the heavy case from the bottom of the pack and I said, "Do you know what this is?"

"Nufar," he said. "The syncable."

"It's nothing." I jerked open the lid. "It's trash."

He said something like, Our yellow empty-empty forensic buys syncable.

"It's a coil of copper wire," I said. "Ordinary wire."

He turned his veiled gaze away. "Of precisely the correct compatibility."

"Look at it!" I tugged the wreath of shit-standard copper wire from the case. "He's gone, they're all gone but you. You're here. You're still here."

He said, "Please."

"What is wrong with you? Look with your own eyes." I threw the wire to the floor. "What is that?"

"Please, no. Please."

"There's no getting him back," I said. "You'll never remember the things you forgot."

×××

The Ragpicker made a sound and dropped to his knees, his head bowed over the wire.

I hated him then. I hated his weakness and his pain and regret. I hated how much someone else mattered to him.

I screamed at him until the baby woke then I stopped screaming and said, "You're not alone. You have us. You have me."

He didn't respond. Not then, not for an hour. Not when the baby cried in the middle of the night or again before dawn.

He stayed there silent on his knees the next day and the next night.

The following morning, when I brought the baby outside to bathe, he was gone.

×××

I washed the baby and told him the story of Alice Ann until I reached the part where she rang a bell but nobody came.

×××

A juddery swarm of butterflies moved between the eucalyptus trees and the cattails and the Ragpicker standing at the willow tree.

I wanted to say, I'm sorry, but instead I said, "I'm leaving."

He said, "What I am is, is the Beloved and the Beloved is me. We rejoice in you, we praise you more than wine. Rightly do we love you. We will make you strings of golden beads with studs of silver. I am dark, I am beautiful, I am a crocus, I am lovesick, I am a wall. I am a pouch of myrrh, I am henna blossoms. I am sleeping but my heart is awake."

I said, "Who the fuck are you?"

×××

He didn't stand right. He didn't stand like himself. He didn't breathe right, his shoulders didn't hunch like his shoulders hunched. His rags didn't drape right, he didn't look the right kind of afraid.

He didn't turn the way he normally turned when he turned toward me—except after watching my face for a few breaths he stepped back into himself, or woke up inside himself.

I took his hand and brought inside the building and showed him how I'd woven his copper wire into a ceiling trellis.

"The nasturtium will grow across," I told him. "Into a new roof. After we're gone, your—your wire will still be here. It will still be ours."

×××

He didn't speak, he didn't try to speak. He grilled fish and mushrooms. He collected sabrafruit and stripped them safe. He swayed the baby to sleep and braided my hair and didn't try to speak.

×××

The beach carried us southward. The shore birds never ended, numberless as the sand. I wondered if in ancient days people thought they were born from the tide—because I did.

Around a dripping jut of rocks, seals lazed on the sand. They humped and glistened and skated in the tide. Two of them wrestled near me. One ended on her back, her mouth open in what looked like a smile, her whiskers bristling and her paws batting at the other.

The Ragpicker ushered me around them, saying things like beloved, seclusion, chariots, palaces, sapphire.

I didn't know what I'd do if I lost him completely.

×××

The beach dwindled to boulders and the gentle surf that was grinding them into sand. After an hour of backtracking, we returned to a tilted alloy stairway and climbed to the coastal highway carved into the cliffside.

The goat feasted on the ornamental plants that cascaded from holes drilled into the bare rockface. But the other side of the road, the ocean-facing side, was a wall of crates and containers and casings that only revealed the shoreline in glimpses.

×××

That night he took the berry juice he'd dried into sticky shiny sheets and crushed them and added crumbles of jerky and added duckfat and mint and herbs. He shaped the dough into a biscuit for me, and two loaves to store, and sticks for the baby to chew.

"Are you ever going to talk again?" I asked.

"Pemmican," he said.

"On second thought," I said, "maybe you should stay quiet."

He fell into the stillness that meant amusement, which pleased me.

×××

Then he lost himself and another voice said, "When I lack bread, that for me is a physical lack. When someone else lacks bread, that for me is a spiritual lack. We were created to delight in the Beloved and to derive pleasure from the Beloved, and to like bread be ground between millstones before rising in steam and heat to feed those we love."

×××

Later she said, "The Beloved has no body but yours; no hands, no feet, no mouth nor eyes but yours."

"We're getting closer to town," I said.

"Yours is the mind with which the Beloved knows the world and yours are the fingers with which the Beloved touches the world and yours are the lips with which the Beloved feels the kiss of the world."

"Okay," I said.

XXX

When I woke in a sheltered bay beneath the fallen bridge, I saw that he'd scavenged a canoe during the night. He tied a rope to the front and pestered me until I climbed in.

The canoe pitched and slid and dipped and leaked.

I hated the treachery of the water. My hands ached from holding the sides, my forearms and shoulders ached.

He pulled me across the bay and back.

He pulled me across the bay and back again.

Then he wanted to stop but I wouldn't let him. I was the daughter of the whale and the sister of the dolphin. We sloshed the seepwater from the bottom of the canoe and I spent the rest of the morning rafting, hooting and splashing and pushing myself with a driftwood pole.

When I stood in triumph, I tipped from the canoe.

I shrieked, flailing and drowning until my feet touched the bottom and I stood in water that barely reached my thighs.

XXX

I wore the patchwork dress that he'd sewn from vests. He'd added a dozen pockets, and tucked a different thing into each of them.

A fragment of orange traffic cone,

a sugar packet,

a ribbon,

a pebble,

a dried petunia with a shoelace bow,

a handful of verbena leaves,

a seashell,

a clear plastic cap,

candied grasshoppers,

a carved elk,

the kid's charred jawbone.

XXX

The highway opened into bluffs and dunes.

I fell asleep to the Ragpicker murmuring, "The phase of

the moon doesn't dictate the timing of the festival days, our awareness of the phase of the moon dictates the timing of the festival days. We precede the calendar. We determine the days and our decision obligates the Heavens to celebrate on this sunset instead of that one. Do not mistake what is holy with what is immutable."

×××

A white-tailed kite took a gopher or mouse from a gather of sanddune grass then lofted away behind the evergreen branches.

Like an offering to the elder gods, the Ragpicker said.

Except he didn't say that, I did. His god-talk was seeping into my thoughts. To a gopher, what was a white-tailed kite?

"A lightning bolt with a taste for rodents," one of the Ragpicker's voices said.

"The gods don't hunger," I said.

"Yet we keep returning to the mountaintop with dying things in our mouths, pascal lambs and fatted calves."

"Which we don't eat," he also said.

"The corpses aren't the sacrifice," he told himself. "Neither is the scent of roasting meat. What we offer them is our hunger."

In the old days, they thought gods were people who you worshipped instead of laws that you could not break.

×××

I didn't give a shit about the moon. Waning, waxing, full, crescent. Yolanda consulted the moon before planting and Suzena claimed that moonlight called to women's blood and the Perezes celebrated the new moon, which was the moon you couldn't see. Luz loved a big lowslung moon and said that she'd touched Dmitri beneath one once. Me, I didn't give a shit. The moon was too far above us, too beautiful and eternal, too *everywhere*. My father said they'd flown there once, and walked around. I hoped they pissed on it.

×××

We returned to the beach because I liked the beach and because we walked slower on the beach. I was afraid of reaching town. I was afraid of—

Especially now, with the Ragpicker also only revealed in glimpses.

×××

"We are formed and created without our consent. We form and create others without their consent. This is the fundamental violation. This is why what the Beloved treasures most is kindness. Cling to that, consent to that, be lavish in your generosity—"

"Shut up," I shouted at him. "Shut up, shut up, shut up."

×××

We climbed again to the bluffs and that time emerged in a desert of corroding cubes. Weathered, sand-caked glasslike boxes of faded green and yellow and red, webbed with jagged cracks, surrounded by fat-leaved succulents with glossy bulbs.

The sand stretched miles behind us, invisible from the beach. Mummified corpses, most of them sprouting wires or ports, had been dragged here and curled at the feet of the shapes.

Nothing grew but the succulents. Normal plants started again in an arc, miles away, a curve where dead brown became live green.

"Desertification," the Ragpicker said.

The goat balked.

We tethered her and hours later we started passing rows of pyramids and rectangles about the same height as the Ragpicker. A lizard sunned herself on a cracked blue edge and the wind threw sand in my face and—

I felt them, among the dead shapes and the live succulents.

"Twitches," I said.

×××

A twitch stood in front of a sphere, its secondskin decorated with smears of green and yellow and red. It was buried to its knees in sand. It hadn't moved in years. Maybe longer. Bushes grew around its birdshit-speckled hips and succulent branches snaked between its thighs.

×××

"A cloudgarden," the Ragpicker told me, sounding like himself again, sounding scared.

We passed another twitch who didn't notice us. Or who didn't react, at least: motionless. Overgrown, but alive.

The baby screamed—happily—and the twitch didn't react.

We crept along the cliffside. When the baby babbled again, voices answered from inside the shapes and the babble followed us as we fled:

Seed your mnemonics in our proprietorial gapped storage racks! Harvest a garden at one to one hundred and seventy-nine. Maximize your plots to seven thousand seven hundred MiE and balance sustained speeds against lifetime expectancy.

Monitor your PPF, but washout! There's only a one in five twelve chance for a garden plot to pass furrow and achieve harvest, so expect failures—but demand successes.

Our PAND racks provide a finite number of writerewrites before failure. Gardening at a modest 66 t/m will consume one cell every five weeks. Racks are discarded at end of lifetime.

×××

The desert lasted for two days. After ranging through the night the Ragpicker told me that the racks were self-assembling from feedstock they harvested from a hundred miles around.

That didn't mean anything to me, but the horror anchored him to himself again. He moved right again. Like prey.

Prey as in prey, not pray as in pray.

That, too.

×××

He unearthed a path that led to the beach. At the foot of the cliffs, mist touched me. Cormorants bobbed and dove. The surf simmered around offshore islands furred with pine trees.

The Ragpicker strayed behind us, then roamed ahead. He

seeped into rockfalls and crossed the dunes when the cliffs finally bowed to the beach. Foraging for food, alert for danger, but also ashamed.

Mostly ashamed.

×××

I called to him in the afternoon with the sun hot on my neck, and when he came I said, "You could've turned into anything. You could've turned into them. Into a likehunter or Server or anything. But you didn't. You became you. And then . . ."

He shifted his shoulders.

"Then we became us," I told him.

His head tilted and I felt his delight, like a warm blanket or an unbreakable chain.

"Shut up," I said. "Come here."

He knelt in front of me and I held him for once, for the first time, his head steel-hard against my chest. I didn't think he cried, I didn't think he was capable of crying, that had been taken from him, but I stroked the mask of his head and said, it's okay, it's okay, it's okay.

×××

We chewed fennel stalks.

We made beads from seashells.

We stuffed ourselves on seal and oyster and sapote and seaweed.

The baby held the Ragpicker's fingers and waddled a few steps on the sand.

The wounds inside the Ragpicker healed.

×××

We lazed for a day in a fern grotto with skunk cabbage and salamanders bigger than my forearm. Herons hunted. Redwing blackbirds clung to reeds then flashed away. We crossed a beach covered in tiny polished stones. The Ragpicker said they were agate and quartz and moonstone and jade and carnelian and jasper.

He rummaged in his pack and gave me a diamond he claimed was worth a million dollars, so I threw it in the sea.

×××

A highway slabbed with risers and railings cut across the beach then jutted fifty yards into the ocean before disappearing into the water.

The goat climbed it immediately but we had to sidetrack ten minutes to find a place I could follow. When the Ragpicker pulled me the last few feet to the highway's surface, it was covered in the softest grass with the whitest flowers.

I stomped and scuffed, shivering at the green warmth between my toes.

We followed the highway inland for a few hours. For no reason except that I wanted to. Nothing was more important than the stuff you did without knowing why. You needed to do unnecessary things.

I didn't know if I believed that, so I said the words aloud.

In answer, the Ragpicker hugged the baby in his sling and spun in a flare of skirts and a flurry of ribbons.

I spun, too.

×××

I married him, he told me, in the garden of an old Spanish house with bougainvillea walls.

Beside a construction site blessedly silent for the day.

In a garden where jacaranda petals fell like reflecting pools.

We vowed, he told me, to waste our lives together.

×××

I made him stop building fires. The smoke might attract Server and I wasn't ready for that. Not yet.

In the sunset, I peeled apart the postcards that had stuck together after I'd fallen from the canoe. Half the words tore into jagged white spaces, and I handed phrases to the Ragpicker like fruit to the baby: *Sleeping pills, brilliant turmoil. Regurgitation.*

A gray-green city, the sense I mean, the architects, the blare of her feet—pebbles.

"What does this mean?" I asked. "'Our world is closer to the world of ideas than to the world of things?'"

"What's 'network fora?'" I asked. "What's 'a cloud tank?'"

"I'm scared," I told him. "We're so close."

We moved farther south, farther east.

×××

I rubbed the smooth green stone between my fingers. The one I called my lucky stone. Which was a pretty heavy burden for such a small stone, but I rubbed it between my fingers and tried to feel a seed of peace.

×××

I knew this sky.

Passionfruit flowers opened into white spiders.

A sheephide scent wafted from the drying lines.

Chaparral spilled upward toward town.

×××

My father once told us to make a list of things that we'd never thought.

My heart is melting, my heart is gold, my heart is stone. Snow is a blanket, snow is falling, snow is a secret. Love is a rose, love is a battlefield, love is a window. The world is a stage, death is an exit—

My mother didn't love me. She didn't teach me much but she taught me how to die. She'd drawn a line between life and death then knotted them together with charms and tokens. She'd walked that path ahead of me. My mother didn't love me but she'd shown me where to put my feet.

The Ragpicker

Runnels of thick-bladed iceplant cascade down the beachside knolls, their flowers lacy purple with delicate black centers, an adapted or modified species adjusted for particulate capture yet already reverting to the less-specialized state which they prefer. I shadow the girl through the lowest troughs of one such plant, watching grains of sand clinging to her scarred ankle, watching gems of surf trapped in her hair, wondering at how the ocean changed her.

She is larger now.

She is compressed.

She is delicate, too, she too is lacy but her roots grip wide and deep; she rebuilt herself to survive flood and drought, to return after the fires and thrive. Her resolve is the surf to which she answers, yet she is also afraid, and her fear gleams in the whitest corners of her eyes as she leads me from the beach along a well-trodden path, flattened by generations of human feet and cart wheels, littered with fragments of mussel shell and seaweed, wending past a forsaken system of pipes and buckets, a broken colander half-buried in windblown sand, slate slabs fuzzed with a faint evaporative rime, and warped planks tucked beneath a salvage-billboard overhang.

She leads me past the salt pools, a series of rectangles so

close that they almost overlap, shallow and shallower, then past the raking beds to where the wagon ruts reel us closer to her town.

The dunes sprout into ridges that embrace and enclose us.

The sand thickens to soil and the heights plead with me—for attention, for caution—while the trail ahead warns of dangers, but the girl demands that I return to her every time I attempt to range from eyeshot. At length I surrender and walk beside her across unprotected, unscouted, unready miles. Only the goat rambles occasionally ahead for warning, until that evening the girl agrees to camp in the concealment of a stretch of mirrored water from which barkless trees emerge, fruited with sluggish cormorants.

The night parts for me.

The night parts for me.

The night parts for me, and I follow the choir of the petrel and the cricket and the moths' fluttering noiseless dimtouched wings until my surveillance restores me to the girl and the baby, who are in sleep too exquisite to tolerate.

They fill me with unbearable comfort.

My chest is crushed in the vice of memory: the baby infuriated by the taste of lime, the baby hugging my leg, the girl throwing a diamond into the surf, her skinny arm outflung, her bony shoulder working, her eyes reflecting the sun and the sea and the sun and the sea and the sun forever will I love her she said to me, she told me with a wound in her voice that she loved me but I loved her more, she said that with a wound in her voice and she told me that she always betrays what she loves, she betrayed her father, her town, her friends, Server, she betrayed her mother, she claimed that she betrayed Edro, she asked what if she's betraying the baby now, delivering him to Server for slaughter like the kid on that mountain, to skewer hanks of his flesh onto the lampstack, and I told her, I tried to tell her that what we love we cannot control and then the next morning I harvest pouchfuls of white-yellow radish leaves, sweet at first but painfully spicy thereafter, and the girl turns to me in laughing outrage when her mouth burns so we eat pemmican and cheeseweed and guava and she refuses more seaweed and instead braids the strips into my rags while I pretend to nap, but the tension inside her is thrumming now, even the baby knows that she's torn in three directions, even the baby quiets when he watches her.

She is two days from town and

She is a day from town and

She hisses to warn me of a sentry then requests that I blaze a path of sufficient convolution from the guardpost that even if the baby cries he will sound mistakably-similar to a gull or sandpiper or jay, yet he sleeps for the long fraught dawn hours during which the girl directs our approach toward what appears at first like an unexceptionable bend in a little-used hillside path but upon arrival I realize is an overlook of sorts.

Her town is below us.

The squeak of a wheel or gear mixes with the *shhk-shhk-shhk* of grain husks trembling through a tambourine sift and the slap of wet cloth against dry rock and the chopping of what sounds like but is not firewood. A brusque shout is answered with laughter from near the well. The girl's fingers tighten around my thumb and she watches with shallow breaths the small figures who move into and out of tent-houses, and the even-smaller figures on the hillside and in the yard of an outbuilding and those squatting in the square attending to chores while they observe, with idle interest, a young man and older one bicker.

The lampstack is also below us, though higher than the tent-houses, yet before I am snared in its abacus web the girl drops my hand and steps forward into an open unhindered view and despite every urgency in my heart, I resist the need to protect her from this tangle of thorns and instead shift into place at her heels.

I am a creature of concealment and camouflage. What I am is, is a golem of patience and persistence, the word inscribed on my forehead is surrender so I am disinclined to step into the sunlight for the delectation of hundreds of eyes to say nothing of the crosshair gaze of Server, Server, Server, Server who is visible now adjusting the halyards and parrels of the lampstack rigging, though my query to Default regarding the accuracy of those terms of course returns no results beyond

A voice calls the girl's name in doubt.

A voice calls the girl's name in shock.

A voice calls another name, then there is a shout, a squeal, a jumble of words as townspeople move along the central path like termites beneath a fallen log, streaming toward us before faltering at the sight of me, perhaps, though also at the awareness of Server emerging from the lampstack at a machine sprint, pistoning through the crowd then climbing the hill upon which we stand.

"This baby is mine," the girl yells at her. "His name is Edro now and—"

Server rises from the hillside and proceeds toward the girl with a fighting stick drawn.

"—you will not touch him," the girl says.

I intercept and there is a flurry of blows and pain after which I find myself on one knee, my breathing compromised, injured but intact, holding Server's wrists as she stands murderous above me.

"Look at the lampstack," the girl calls to Server. "Look at that shambles."

Server bears down upon me with bulldozer weight. I feel the strain in my wrists and elbows. I feel the inevitability of loss. However, the inevitability of loss is my oldest surviving companion, and somewhat paradoxically gives me strength.

"It's incoherent," the girl tells Server. "It's disjointed, disconnected. You've lost the thread. You don't know where you are anymore."

The pressure eases in my wrists.

"That's your mind," the girl says. "And it's falling the fuck apart. Look at me."

Server looks at the girl, then speaks to her, a litany of facts.

"You won't touch Edro," the girl tells her. "You won't touch any of us."

Server speaks again, more lyrically, claiming that the illusion of touch is founded upon the delusion of separation, before she finishes with a question.

"Because he's mine," the girl tells her. "They're all mine."

Server tilts her head toward me and asks another question.

"There's a word for what he is to me," the girl says, "but it's not a word you'd understand."

Server speaks at length, facing the girl while I observe a growing handful of townspeople creeping closer with hoes and scythes and axes. They live in terror of Server, and to them I am even worse for my foreignness, yet without coordination they find themselves moving, in the service of the girl, toward the precipice of something terrible.

"Then I'll explain," the girl says when Server finishes. "I'll knot the answer in seashells and pomegranate rinds and hang it on the rack."

"Let him go," the girl says.

In the slackening of Server's grip I detect an echo of my own exhaustion.

"Look at me," the girl tells her. "You taught me how to look, so look."

Server releases me. She steps toward the girl, then pauses when I push to my feet.

"I know more now than I've ever known," the girl tells her. "I see more than I've ever seen. I'll upgrade the lampstack into configurations you've never imagined."

Server hesitates to believe this assertion.

The girl tells her about strips of vypaper and juniper bushes and playgrounds and elk, and I raise an unseen hand toward the simmer of townspeople. Asking them to halt, to pause. Asking them to trust the girl, and with a mixture of shame and regret and relief they obey.

The girl finishes by saying: "You'll stay there, in the lampstack."

Server requests clarification.

"I mean you'll never leave," the girl tells her. "Not ever. I'll bring you everything you need. You won't take a single step out of the lampstack, not ever again, and when you die I'll braid you into the strings and ligaments."

Server pivots to consider the lampstack and the offer while the girl considers her and the goat says *maaaa* which makes the baby gurgle at which point Server gazes at the baby

and

demands

a

single

concession.

Within the crowd, an older man murmurs. Calloused hands grip axe handles and we teeter toward a massacre.

Into that moment, the girl makes a counteroffer. She promises Server a boon to which she believes she is entitled.

Server asks for clarification

"His eyes," the girl tells her. "Instead of the baby, take the Ragpicker's eyes."

Server agrees.

I kneel facing the girl. She is crying now but I remember the sight of her laughing, I remember the sight of her splashing, I remember the sight of her sleeping. I remember the sight of her.

Server clamps my head and shows me her scalpel.

I tell the girl to look away.

Server takes my eyes and the girl binds my wounds and after a time speaks to her father, to her friends, with a warmth that I believe surprises them. Following a brief negotiation she passes the baby to a nursing woman, or a group of nursing women, and then she leads me through this sightless world, along the uneven hillside path, into the town center, where I turn my face toward the furnace heat of the sun and imagine yellow squares, broken panes of goldenrod.

The girl takes me into her tent. Every morning and evening she attends me and the baby, while every day she attends Server and the lampstack. She climbs the hill alone—until one afternoon she invites me to join her upon the concrete slabs where the wind rattles trinkets and strums lines and where I feel the weight of charms in my palm.

There is meaning here, though you cannot find the ocean in a raindrop or the desert in broken glass. If you pay close enough attention, you might find something better: a raindrop and a shard of broken glass.

×××

In the children's tent the baby toddles to clutch me, unknowingly challenging the other children who soon race to climb my summit, to play hide and seek among my outskirts, to festoon me with ribbons and berries and to come weeping into my arms for silent unseeing comfort. To them, I am a playground. I am brother to the cradle and sister to the nap. What I am is, is wise in the ways of things left behind. What I am is home.

Acknowledgments

Many thanks to Tricia Reeks for her grace, vision, and support. Also thanks to Adana Washington, Adriana Kantcheva, Ahana Virdi, Amy Salt, Andrea Max, Anna Makowska, BC, Brooke Johnson, Cee Jordan, Gen Dimova, Amber Frost, Jill Grunenwald, Katy Hays, Karen Schwabach, Lana Wood Johnson, Liz Ciccone, Mel Zana, Meredith Adamo, Mitchell Logue, Peggy Carpenter, Rachel Rose, Ren Nabata, Salma D, Sandra Salsbury, and Shawn Carpenter for helping me waste so much time. (And for being lovely.)

About the Author

Joel Dane is the author of twenty-four novels across several genres—and pseudonyms. He's written for TV and podcasts, including a dozen episodes of a Netflix Original Series.

photo © Ben Naftali

DID YOU ENJOY THIS BOOK?

If so, word-of-mouth recommendations and online reviews are critical to the success of any book, so we hope you'll tell your friends about it and consider leaving a review at your favorite bookseller's or library's website.

Visit us at www.meerkatpress.com for our full catalog.

Meerkat Press
Asheville